PRAISE FOR T
GRAHAM MYSTERY SERIES

"Another fun, edge-of-your-seat mystery with a lovable cast of characters."
"Captivating and spectacular."
"Bravo! Engrossing!"
"This is her best book, so far. I literally could not put this book down."
"I'm in love with him and his colleagues."
"Phenomenal!"
"Alison Golden has done it again."
"Powerful stuff!"
"A terrific mystery."
"These books certainly have the potential to become a PBS series with the likeable character of Inspector Graham and his fellow officers."
"Delightful writing that keeps moving, never a dull moment."
"I know I have a winner of a book when I toss and turn at night worrying about how the characters are doing."
"Totally great read!!!"
"Refreshingly unique and so well written."

THE CASE OF THE
UNCOMMON WITNESS

ALSO BY ALISON GOLDEN

The Case of the Screaming Beauty

The Case of the Hidden Flame

The Case of the Fallen Hero

The Case of the Broken Doll

The Case of the Missing Letter

The Case of the Pretty Lady

The Case of the Forsaken Child

The Case of Sampson's Leap

The Case of the Uncommon Witness

COLLECTIONS

Books 1-4

The Case of the Screaming Beauty

The Case of the Hidden Flame

The Case of the Fallen Hero

The Case of the Broken Doll

Books 5-7

The Case of the Missing Letter

The Case of the Pretty Lady

The Case of the Forsaken Child

THE CASE OF THE UNCOMMON WITNESS

ALISON GOLDEN

GRACE DAGNALL

Cover Illustration: Richard Eijkenbroek

Published by Mesa Verde Publishing
P.O. Box 1002
San Carlos, CA 94070

ISBN:

"Books are engines of change, windows on the world, and lighthouses erected in the sea of time. They are companions, teachers, magicians, bankers of the treasures of the mind. Books are humanity in print."
- Barbara Tuchman -

"Your emails seem to come on days when I need to read them because they are so upbeat."
- Linda W -

For a limited time, you can get the first books in each of my series - *Chaos in Cambridge* (exclusively for subscribers - not available anywhere else), *The Case of the Screaming Beauty, Hunted, and Mardi Gras Madness* - plus updates about new releases, promotions, and other Insider exclusives, by signing up for my mailing list at:

https://www.alisongolden.com/graham

CHAPTER ONE

THE GROUP OF four women and one man stood in a loose row. Captivated by the scene before them, hands holding paintbrushes raised expectantly, they stared out over a calm, sun-washed bay. They were on a cliff top, the sky a deep sapphire-blue streaked with only the odd wispy cloud. Below, the waves of the English Channel lapped gently.

"Breathe the scene in, my friends," Peregrine Wordsworth began. He paced slowly behind the row of students, his hands behind his back like an amiable, encouraging professor dispensing wisdom and guidance. "Feel its shapes, its subtleties."

In front of each student stood an easel and a canvas on which was painted a seemingly random arrangement of colourful splodges. Almost an hour into their first session, none had yet begun to represent Crescent Bay that lay below them or the bluffs that surrounded it, on top of which a stylish, modern home was built. First, Wordsworth insisted, they would collaborate to "achieve the conceptual origin" of the painting.

"Breathe with the waves," Wordsworth continued. "Let the light of the bay *speak* to you."

"Talking light?" scoffed the lone male. "Really?"

"Mr. Barr, *everything* is talking to you," the veteran artist assured him. "It is we who fail to listen." Peregrine Wordsworth was sixty-seven but seemed almost immune to aging. He could pass for forty-five. His was a slender frame, topped with a mop of white, corkscrew curls. The loose, black shirt and charcoal jeans he wore made him seem lithe and nimble one moment and strangely statuesque the next.

"Ridiculous," Fergus Barr muttered. He was a tall and skinny Scot with wavy, brown hair. He was constantly moving, exhibiting a series of tics—twitching, scratching, jiggling, brushing his hair off his face. In contrast to the smooth, graceful movements of his mentor, he was a distracted, agitated figure.

"Talking to us, yes!" the woman next to the Scot exclaimed. "Every scene, every blade of grass." She glanced appreciatively at the sky. "Even the clouds. Like waves of energy." Dr. Hiruni Ramachandran was a pleasantly plump woman wearing a long, flowing maxi dress and sandals which showed off toes dusted with long, dark hair and un-manicured toenails. She was the very opposite of her neighbour—calm, still, softly spoken. She had big, brown eyes with long, thick eyelashes and full lips that sprung readily into a wide smile, displaying perfectly straight, white teeth. "Sound, magnetism, kinetics—they all use the same base substance."

"The very same elemental energy, Dr. Hiruni!" Wordsworth agreed, happy to find a kindred spirit. Pere-grine Wordsworth had been considered a voice in the art world for over three decades. He'd lectured all over the world, gaining as much fame from his outlandish attire that often involved wearing makeup and the odd item of women's clothing as he had from his art. He'd even hosted a reality show in which a group of non-artistic celebrities came together at a retreat. He taught them how to paint. He set them challenges. Each week, based on the strength of their work, they were voted in or out by the public.

But then, in books and interviews, Wordsworth hypothesised the existence of a world *behind* the one we see, claiming that very few people had "the gifts" to access it. He appeared rarefied and out of touch with the audience he had courted with his earlier, more accessible endeavours. Subsequently, he was pilloried in the British media, and his work dried up. After a drink or three, Wordsworth would devolve into complaints about being "cancelled." These days, his teaching engagements existed to pay the bills.

"Crescent Bay vibrates with that same energy, don't you think?" Wordsworth turned to look out at the horizon and admired the play of light on water and the stubborn jut of the cliff standing defiant against the sea. "A place of oppositions, each one crackling with something we can barely perceive. It is these contrasts," he added, "that make this place special."

Dr. Hiruni, as the group had agreed to call the Sri Lankan-born physician, opened her mouth to answer, but Fergus cut her off. "So, what you're saying," he said, visibly tiring of Wordsworth's esoteric and often verbose viewpoints, "is I should learn how to paint better by using 'the force'?"

Fergus's quip sent Belinda Dunn, a local teenager whom even Wordsworth had to admit possessed an uncommon talent, into a fit of giggles. While the usually taciturn young woman recovered, Dr. Hiruni refocused the group. "The contrasts create the character of the bay, you mean."

"We could say 'character' or 'spirit', I suppose," Wordsworth said, "but think of it as layer upon layer of wave forms. The water," he said, his gestures fluid, "is the fastest, the most obvious, but above all, is not the atmosphere obeying the same rules? Being pushed and pulled?" His hands embodied the tension, locked together but tussling for control. "Not by gravity, but by heat and moisture. And beneath," he continued, completing the metaphor which appeared in one of his books, "there are waves of geological activity, each millions of years long. Everything is *energy*, after all."

"Interesting idea." Dr. Hiruni nodded. "I don't know if I can *paint* it," she qualified with a smile, "but I think I see what you're saying."

Peregrine Wordsworth meandered around the group, peering over his students' shoulders as they attempted to represent the scene as he described it on their canvases. The beautiful weather allowed them to work outside today, but behind them stood the grounds of a private school. The artistic hub of their retreat was the former headmaster's cottage. It offered them a large sunroom to paint in when they needed it and remarkable views over the bay.

Wordsworth approached the artists one by one, delivering sage advice to each. "There can be beauty in every single brushstroke if we pay attention and bring our *unfiltered* selves to our work."

One of his students, Magda Padalka-Lyons, was a solid, affluent woman in her mid-forties, dressed today in a tight, pink velour sweatsuit and accompanied as usual by her Pomeranian, Pom-Pom, who sat by her feet asleep. Magda had made a start by sketching the outline of the cliff that stood on the other side of the bay and then shifted her focus to the house that stood on top of it. "The owner is friend of mine," Magda told Fergus in broken English. She remained indivisible from her East European accent despite twelve years of marriage to a Jerseyman and an even longer time spent on the British mainland. "Katerina Granby. She's a lovely person. Such nice parties. Dog lover."

The new, custom-built Granby residence seemed precarious atop the cliff. Perfectly private, divorced from neighbours by swathes of green, the house was surrounded by manicured lawns. A long driveway that ran from a road the artists couldn't see highlighted its isolation. The house was a modern fusion of glass and white concrete that, despite the suggestion, integrated with the landscape by appearing to emerge from it. It was one of those rare cases where the form and function of a home matched the ambition of the architect's rendering. The tasteful lawns and the occasional flowerbed were given height and interest by hard landscaping that comprised walls, walkways, and platforms of wood, rock, and more concrete. There were sun-traps, sculptures, and shady spots. At night, a constellation of low-level lights lit up the features. There was even a swimming pool. Magda would have been jealous, but her pool was bigger.

On Magda's right was a refined woman in her seventies. She'd found a stool on which to perch. Wordsworth found her first efforts—bold, geometric outlines—a little too confined. "Imagine, perhaps, that the cliffs are made not of rock, but of something alive and breathing." Mrs. Courthould-Bryant glanced between Wordsworth and her sketch a few times before saying simply, "Lovely," and carrying on precisely as before.

Fergus continued his monologue of quiet scoffing. "First, light that can talk. Now, cliffs that can breathe. What's next?" he wondered, gesturing to Magda's Pomeranian. "Dogs that can write poetry?"

"Pom-Pom *very* expressive," his owner said.

"Look, why did you even come if all you're going to do is criticise?" Belinda, the talented teenager said to Fergus. "You knew what you were in for." She jabbed the end of her brush at Wordsworth, who was quietly talking to Magda over the woman's shoulder. Belinda exhaled and shook her head as she refocused her attention on her painting.

The artists continued to apply paint to canvas, working over the pencil sketches they had started with. Wordsworth monitored his time carefully so that his attention was evenly divided between his students. He had an excellent memory for what he'd already observed, a skill honed during dozens of these small, three-day workshops. "Remember," he said, speaking quietly as he patrolled the group, "your plan reflects your intentions, but we also make second-to-second decisions *within* the plan." He stopped and posed a question. "Ultimately, can we even say which is in control: the plan, or the artist?"

"But . . . the artist makes the plan!" Fergus responded, unable to restrain himself despite Belinda's remonstrations.

"You know, I sometimes wonder if it's the other way around," Wordsworth said, his mind momentarily carried away by the idea. "I really do. I sit in my bathtub, and I ponder that *very* question." The group fell quiet for a while. There was silence except for brushstrokes and the mixing of paint.

Wordsworth resumed his patrol. His look—pale and tall, black-clad and elegant—made him at once invisible and, somehow, omnipresent. "Miss Dunn," he said quietly to Belinda, "what has Crescent Bay said to *you* today?"

Belinda spoke quickly, in anxious, truncated bursts, as though afraid of being interrupted or causing offence. "Contrasts and layers of waves. Like you said. They're everywhere." She looked up and found the edge of the cliff with her fingertip. "A precipice, but also a home." She spread her hands, trying to encapsulate the tension through her gesture as Wordsworth had earlier. "Safe, but also in peril." She turned to face the sea. "Shallows and depths, starlight and sunlight," she said, realising the possibilities. "Ancient chalk and yesterday's dust."

The group hadn't quite known what to make of Belinda, but mostly they were relieved that she seemed to be on Wordsworth's wavelength from the outset. At breaks, he had monopolised her, leaving the rest of them to relax. "Yes, the contrasts, those collisions and agreements between elements," he trilled. "Now, what *is* the house, from the cliff's point of view?" The veteran artist's workshops were full of open, intriguing questions like this.

"Impostor. Invader. Tyrant," Belinda replied.

"But never a partner?"

"There's no contrast in partnership," she pointed out.

Wordsworth smiled. "You're not married, I can tell. What about parent and child? Cliff and house? A symbiotic relationship rife with tension as one pulls away and the other clings, or maybe turns away. Do you see anything there?"

Belinda dropped her brush and stared at him. "No," she said bluntly.

"Spontaneity, within a good design, should never find itself confined," Wordsworth said to the sea air before moving on to ponder the achievements of the others.

After lunch, they would imagine the bay anew with a different affect. It was about capturing the basics and then bringing imagination to complete the details. As far as Wordsworth was concerned, the more varieties of execution on display at their final exhibition in a few days' time, the better.

CHAPTER TWO

AS COUNCILLOR ZARA Hyde had hoped, Peregrine Wordsworth's name ensured a steady stream of visitors throughout the three days of the exhibition held in the lobby of the Gorey council offices. At the opening reception on Wednesday evening, those with business there paused for a moment, joining the tourists and locals to peruse the display of workshop paintings in the lobby. Their reactions were as varied as the styles of the paintings.

"It was a *deeply* difficult selection process," Wordsworth was saying to Freddie Solomon. "Each of the artists is naturally talented, and at my workshop, they are guided to depict the view, of Crescent Bay in this case, not as they ordinarily would, but as *someone else* might. Happily, there was time enough to make several interpretations, not just one. In this way," he told Freddie, who transcribed these grade-A, highbrow quotes into his phone with flying thumbs, "we enter undiscovered territory. Our thousandth view of a place becomes our first. All it takes is a simple change of perspective."

An excited cluster of exhibition visitors lined up to take photos with Wordsworth, a task he was more than happy to undertake while adopting just the right air of resignation to communicate he was above the trappings of celebrity, more interested in answering questions and interpreting the artists' works. "You find it confusing?" Wordsworth was asking a visitor whose expression gave him away.

"Why . . . I mean, all these funny blocks and what have you," the man said, unimpressed. "What's wrong with painting it as it is?"

While Belinda joined Wordsworth in a combined explanatory offensive, Freddie took notes on the discussion. "Solid gold," he whispered to himself, finding that Wordsworth was compelling enough that even the arrival of Laura Beecham didn't distract him too much. She was flanked by Janice Harding and her fiancé, Jack Wentworth.

"I see they've tidied the place up nicely," said Janice as she entered the lobby.

As part of a renovation of the council offices, wood panelling had been painstakingly stripped away from around the lobby walls. Without their severe, almost ecclesiastical influence, the council office's lobby seemed brighter than before, and more spacious. "The whole place looks great," Laura said, tucking blonde strands behind her ear.

"*And* they approved the budget for some of the new cameras we wanted. Only six, when the DI wanted nine, but it's a start. Amazing what they can do when they try," added Janice. "A new broom on the council, apparently. Ambitious. Boss told me about her." The newly appointed Councillor Hyde was determined to adopt the constabulary's recommendations on the cameras and had hit the ground running. In his first meeting with her, Detective

Inspector Graham had been cautiously impressed. Promises were made. So far, they had mostly been kept.

Two war memorial plaques were displayed on the newly whitewashed walls, and Councillor Hyde had also installed a suite of enlarged, century-old photographs of Gorey, showing the town as it had been for so long: a quiet fishing village. But Laura, Janice, and Jack hadn't come to see them.

"Right, where's this art, then?" Janice wondered aloud. The display occupied one half of the lobby, but the cluster of people around Peregrine Wordsworth was holding up those interested in seeing it. "Might have to do some traffic duty in a minute."

"The more *avant garde* pieces are at the end. So, we'll see the students' progression," Jack told her.

Since they'd been together, Jack had introduced Janice to all sorts of new cultural phenomena. To her surprise, Janice had found she loved learning new things, and was proud of her intelligent and sophisticated fiancé, even if she didn't always appreciate what he introduced her to. She'd never been to an art exhibition before and wasn't sure it was her thing, but she was willing to give it a try.

If she was honest, despite their best intentions, both she and Jack mostly reverted to type after a period of experimentation. They'd made a decent attempt at installing a varied and eclectic tea habit similar to Graham's but had eventually given up and returned to their favourite Yorkshire brew, a type they could readily get just about anywhere. They enjoyed their experiments, even if most of the time they found they preferred what they'd been doing all along. It was a good way to learn what the other liked and to bond as a couple, which Janice deeply appreciated.

She turned to Laura. "It's becoming a habit, this is. He watches a documentary and suddenly he's an expert."

"I only said, if you remember," Jack responded innocently, "that I think I've got a more sensitive eye for artistic merit."

Janice made things crystal clear. "More sensitive *than me* is what he's saying." She winked at Laura.

"That's quite a claim," her friend replied, returning Freddie's wave from across the room. He seemed caught between wanting to say hello to her and his need not to miss any juicy quotes from Peregrine Wordsworth.

"Just making an observation," Jack said with a little shrug. "Art is everywhere if you care to look. There's artistry to the way you solve a crime, wouldn't you say? The way you work as a team, pooling intel, navigating evidence, compiling theories. It starts out as a random series of datapoints which eventually merge into a cohesive form that identifies the perpetrator of a crime. That's pretty much what's going on here." Some space opened up amidst the crowd, and Jack peered closer to take a look at one of the paintings. "Except perhaps they haven't *quite* come to a conclusive resolution."

The idea of policing as an art form struck Janice as profound. She went quiet. "Yeah, maybe. I hadn't thought of it quite like that. Hmm."

Jack wrapped an arm affectionately around her waist. The crowd was beginning to move through. They joined a loose, rightward-drifting gaggle of visitors.

About a dozen people still wanted to get a moment with Peregrine Wordsworth. They eyed him expectantly or stood patiently in short lines. This was Wordsworth's chance to drum up business for a second annual workshop in the early spring, or maybe a commission from the well-heeled, of which there were many on Jersey. He was always at his most engaging when potential customers came along.

Some of the visitors looked at the artwork and, apparently feeling nothing, moved straight through as if browsing a shelf in a bookshop. Others took more time, trying to puzzle out the artist's intent or reading the short description by each canvas. A dapper man in his fifties seemed to be comparing two or three of the paintings, peering closely at each as though judging them in some way. One or two visitors were dismissive, their criticisms muted only by the presence of the artists themselves. Laura heard one observer, a craggy curmudgeon with a West country accent, telling his wife, "Bloody rubbish." He finished up with the inevitable "I could do better than that."

Laura was drinking in the details the way David would, more interested in her surroundings than merely the art on the walls. His habit of cataloguing people had rubbed off on her. She could hold more in her mind now, her memory more accurate. Clothes, shoes, hair colours . . . She had yet to graduate on to gestures and facial expressions; that was "people *reading*," she'd told Graham, not "people watching," and for her, this habit was recreational, not professional. But David's mind never stopped, and some days, she found herself struck dumb at the sheer level of detail he was able to soak up. For Graham, casing this lobby would have been child's play.

"Don't tell me you're starstruck too?"

Caught unawares, Laura turned to find Freddie Solomon, his keys clicking in his busy hands. "Oh, hey, Freddie." Since the triumphant evening as part of the team involved in the public solving of a 200-year-old cold case, the "citizen journalist" had heeded Laura's plea to give Graham some space. He had downgraded his former habit of haranguing the local police to mild chiding. Such cooperation, quite out of character for Freddie, earned him a friendly smile.

"Not starstruck at all," she said. Like Graham, Laura was not at all affected by the common markers of celebrity. The pub she'd worked at in London had been frequented by a slew of them, and there was nothing like seeing people "off the telly" under the influence of alcohol to correct the impression that they were anything but utterly ordinary. "Just intrigued," Laura added, "at how others are reacting to the paintings."

"Did you have any idea that Gorey was harbouring a half dozen Picassos?" Freddie asked.

"Sounds like you've been impressed by the art."

Laura glanced across the room. Standing next to her paintings, Philomena Courthould-Bryant discussed her artistic choices with some visitors. A few yards away, her husband, Percival Courthould-Bryant, long-time Jersey resident and former curator of the Jersey Heritage Museum, indulged in his usual brand of unconfined snobbery, mansplaining his wife's work to a few others, and leaving Laura sympathetic toward his wife.

Freddie qualified his enthusiasm. "Some of it, sure." In a rare show of self-deprecation, he added, "I can paint with the enthusiasm of a five-year-old and with about the same level of skill. Some of us paint with brushes and colours," he said. "Others use words."

Notwithstanding Jack's contention that art was everywhere, including down at the local police station, Laura found the idea that Freddie's "scribblings," as Graham referred to them, be considered "art" a bit of a stretch. That said, she wasn't about to burst his bubble. In the last few months, whether Freddie recognised it or not, she'd found that his writing had indeed changed. Although still entitled the *Gorey Gossip* and still targeted at the prurient, Freddie had recently taken to using titillating (and often unfounded) material to draw in his target audience before socking them over the head with more complex subjects. Topics such as the local economy, social issues, and the development and future of Gorey were a move away from his earlier, exclusively crowd-pleasing efforts. He could still toss in the occasional firework, and his manner toward Graham remained judgmental, but his attitude had moderated to one of cautious and watchful deference.

"Well, then, did you get some nice, big scoop from the great man himself?" Laura nodded over to Peregrine Wordsworth.

"That man," Freddie said, "is *unbelievable*. Never interviewed anyone who—"

"Thought so much of himself? Produced so much rubbish?" Appearing out of apparently nowhere, Mrs. Taylor, proprietor of the White House Inn, was evidently unimpressed with the exhibition. She folded her arms. "My six-year-old granddaughter could do better than that."

"Not a fan, then, Mrs. Taylor?" Freddie said, hoping for a juicy, slightly controversial quote which would guarantee her an appearance in his blog.

"A fan?" A couple of minutes had been enough to persuade Mrs. Taylor that her evening would be better spent elsewhere. "Not my cup of tea. And that 'artist,' Mr. Wordsworth . . ." She tutted dramatically. "Well." She left her thoughts unsaid but effectively communicated. Regarding Wordsworth with visible scepticism, Marjorie Taylor patted her recently wavy-permed hair and strode out.

CHAPTER THREE

"THEY SHOULD HAVE skipped that house and painted the White House Inn instead," Jack said, overhearing Marjorie Taylor's words. "Mrs. Taylor would have been thrilled in that case."

"Not if they'd transformed her hotel into some impressionist monstrosity," Janice said. "Some of these are a bit . . . 'out there.'"

"They're just experimenting," Jack said. "Doing Wordsworth's 'contrasts' thing, I suppose. At least he didn't bring his loony friends with him and make Crescent Bay vibrate." It had been ten months since the incident in the Lake District. The artistic event which had been billed as "an opportunity to generate abundance, trust, and connection through a meeting of minds, hearts, and vibration" had consisted of a group of people descending on Lake Windermere who, at Wordsworth's urging, hummed without interruption for twenty-four hours. It had been innocent enough, but wilfully and hilariously misinterpreted by the media. A visitor to the local youth hostel was quoted as saying it was like "living in the middle of a beehive without the benefit of honey."

Jack, Janice, and Laura slowly walked past interpretations of the bay, some of which were comprised of unidentifiable swishes of simple, swooping lines, while others were dioramas, exquisitely detailed and precise. By the end, the artists' efforts defied description; in one of them, even the fastidious realist, grouchy Fergus Barr, had let his guard down and interpreted the scene more freely. The house atop the bluff, sheets of glass held together by columns of white pebbled concrete, became a reflective surface for clouds and sunshine, a huge mirror on the cliff top.

"Well, I think I've done my bit for the creative arts today," Janice decided, waiting for Jack to finish his viewing. "How are you doing?" she asked Laura. "Generally, I mean. I haven't seen you in a week or so."

"Oh, you know. Juggling as usual, trying not to drop anything."

"The library was jam-packed last Saturday," Janice said. "I only went in to return a book. Crossed my mind that I might need to do some crowd control."

"The Early Reading Festival," Laura said proudly. "It went better than we could ever have expected. Since we worked on the Sampson case last year, ideas for new literary and historical educational projects have piled up. Councillor Hyde has lobbied the mayor, who seems ready to support a few of our more ambitious plans. It's just been so much fun." Laura's excitement was never far from the surface. "Helping children to read, people of all ages, really, and being able to help them find what they need has never felt more gratifying."

"And didn't I hear that you're head librarian now?" Janice flicked a glance over at Jack. He seemed to have caught the celebrity bug and couldn't resist loitering within a few feet of Peregrine Wordsworth.

"*Acting* head," Laura said. "Nat is due in about three weeks, and she'll have another three months' maternity leave after that."

"Those are big shoes to fill, but you'll do great."

They stepped away from the crowd. "What about you? How are your plans for the big day coming along?" Laura observed her friend carefully. She knew Janice to be stressed.

The bride-to-be heaved a sigh. "Can I plan another police conference instead?" she joked, then made an awkward face. "Maybe *without* two really awful murders."

"Nobody's fault except the killer's, remember," Laura reminded her. It was the kind of thing she regularly said to David.

"Right now, Jack and I are just trying to successfully get married without killing *anyone*."

"Is it the choice of venue again?"

"No, that's all sorted," Janice said. "St. Andrew's on Princess Road. This is different. Family stuff."

"Ugh."

"Jack's got a crazy, belligerent aunt . . ."

Laura snapped her fingers. "We'll sit her next to David," she suggested at once.

"Wow, that doesn't seem very fair. What kind of girl-friend are you exactly?" Janice laughed.

"One who knows that a word from David will shut your aunt down and we'll all have a great time, including her." Laura winked at her friend.

"And I've got this cousin," Janice whispered, raising an eyebrow, "with an alcoholic husband." She paused, then clarified. "I'm not talking about a few drinks and some silly dancing. This man has a tendency to spontaneously give long, morose speeches."

"Maybe make it a cash bar?"

"Not the worst idea," Janice said. "There's lots of other stuff to sort out. It's getting out of hand. We wanted to keep it small but then we'd exclude the people we do want to enjoy our day with. And the church will be rather empty. Plus, it's getting expensive, especially for my family, who'll be travelling. Jack's family is being great, offering to put my side up, and we're trying a few less expensive options." Janice blew out her cheeks. "It'll work out. Jack's helping out where he can. Just listening to me blow off steam is a great help."

"A man who can provide tech support for complex police investigations," Laura marvelled, "*and* contribute helpfully to a wedding? Definitely a keeper, Janice."

Jack walked up, and Janice pulled her fiancé to her. "He's so shy about how brilliant he is sometimes. Only I know how truly incredible he is. And how helpful to Gorey police." Janice smiled. "Did you know he once thought about being a lawyer? He finished the first half of a law degree."

"Really?" Laura was surprised.

Jack gave her the short version. "Got myself recruited by a tech company in London midway and kinda fell in love with encryption and firewalls. But I still love the chase, so what I do for the police is just up my street."

"Jack, a frustrated lawyer?" Laura laughed. "Will wonders never cease? What else have you been hiding?" She let out a deep breath. "Are we done here? I think I've had my fill."

"I think so," Janice replied. Jack nodded. Janice linked arms with Laura, leaving Jack to bring up the rear. Feeling dispensed with, he good-humouredly pursed his lips. At least he wasn't facing the complete destruction of his masculinity and carrying Janice's handbag. Ahead of them, fingers still jangling his keys, Freddie Solomon pushed through the council building's wide glass doors and meandered slowly down the steps.

Janice called to him. "How did you like the exhibition, Freddie? Did Wordsworth say anything worth your readership's time?"

"Yes," Freddie said, brightening and leaning in close when they caught up with him. "But I'm debating whether or not to use the best bit. It's a little scandalous."

"Doesn't sound like you, Freddie," Laura said. "What did he say?"

"He said," Freddie confided, suppressing his own laughter, "'I'm profoundly uncomfortable watching the public consume art. It's like feeding time at the zoo, only less dignified.' Amazing," the blogger added as he absentmindedly wandered off, his thumbs still flying as he composed the first draft of his next missive.

"Wordsworth's a snob," Janice said, sniffing. "And his paintings are weird."

"Now who's the art critic?" Jack said.

"I know what I like," Janice replied.

"You know, they might just be amateurs trying out different styles, but it was kind of fascinating to . . ." Jack stumbled. A man barged past an elderly couple walking behind Jack, knocking one of them into him. Surprised, Janice and Laura both moved to steady the pensioners as the man stormed down the steps.

"Ack, sorry!" he cried without stopping.

"Hey!" Jack called, ready to reprimand him, but the

man was away, jogging across the high street and merging with a crowd of shoppers.

"An unsatisfied customer?" Laura wondered. "Or maybe he's just not a Peregrine Wordsworth fan."

"Well, all I can say is he's doesn't look very happy," Janice said. "Are you alright, Jack?" She looked at him with concern.

"Yeah, I'm fine, fine," Jack said, brushing himself down. "By the way, where's Detective Inspector Graham this evening?"

Laura pulled a face. "I'm a bit worried, actually. Jim Roach normally coaches the kids' soccer, you know, the under-twelves, under-fourteens, and such. For the older ones, he acts as referee on game nights. But with Jim away in London, he asked David to . . ."

"Oh, no," Janice muttered. "What's tonight?"

"A game night." Janice pulled a face. "Yeah," Laura said, clearing her throat. "David's refereeing the game." She checked her watch. "Started half an hour ago."

"Well, let's hope it all goes off smoothly. I'm sure it will." Janice turned around to pull a face at Jack, one Laura couldn't see.

"I hope so," Laura said. "It's like the start of a bad joke. 'What do you get if you cross a rabble of muddy teenagers, lots of competitive parents, and the single most unyielding referee in the history of football?' I'm going to make my way there now to see what's what."

Janice enjoyed the mental image. "I'd line up for days to buy tickets to *that*." She grabbed Jack's arm. "I think that's enough experimental art for one day. What do you say, oh future husband of mine? Ready to try another cake place?"

"Is this going to be the one with gluten-free almond flour?" If so, Jack's tone implied there would be rebellion.

Checking the list on her phone, one of many in a large folder labelled ~Wedding!~, Janice had good news. "No, this is the place with the mind-blowing Swiss chocolate, French buttercream, pâte à bombe icing. We have half an hour until closing. It's only a five-minute walk."

"Well, there are worse ways to end an evening. Laura, always a pleasure," said Jack, clicking his heels and giving her a slight bow. He'd daydreamed about this particular cake from the moment Janice had suggested it. He knew already that it would get his vote over the eight other cakes they'd already tried. "Say hello to David for us."

"I will," Laura chuckled, "once I've pulled him out from under a pile of squabbling parents." There was time for Janice to wish Laura luck, and with a quick wave, they were off.

"Right, then," Laura said to herself. "Time to rescue the under-fourteens."

CHAPTER FOUR

The Gorey Gossip
Saturday, April 9th

It's been another week of opposites in
Gorey. Maybe you were woken by the loudest
thunder in years last night—I certainly was
—but this morning, only a few hours later,
the sky is an outstanding springtime blue
and families will be back to sunbathing on
the beach by lunchtime. These strange
swerves in the weather help us remember to
cherish the sunniest days and not waste
them. Me, I've been growing vegetables. For
the record, it's murdering my back, but I
can see why people like it, and the sense
of teamwork at the allotment is a tonic for
any writer, normally such loners.

Last week, I was fortunate to interview
the controversial and irrepressible artist
of TV reality show *Art Lover's Island* fame,

Peregrine Wordsworth. He presided over an exhibition of his students' paintings from his most recent retreat. Peregrine and five artistic visionaries spent three days painting their impressions of Crescent Bay before their works were exhibited at the council offices. I have to say, the refurbishment has gone very well, and it was the ideal space to show off the town's talents.

Dressed in his trademark black, Wordsworth was in an affable mood, sharing with me, "I like the rhythm of returning to Gorey. Consistency is hard to find in a life like mine. Annual fixtures help keep me settled." When I spoke to him, he quickly meandered into the poetic style with which he has become synonymous. "The waves provide one rhythm, the turning of the world provides the other. It is the ideal period of rest from my other work."

Like most people, I was curious how his "other work" contributes to these more conventional workshops. "There's real permeability there," Wordsworth said, apparently in answer to my question. "It's not that one informs the other," he (sort of) clarified. "They share a stage but have different drummers." Those who understand this answer might find they enjoy one of Wordsworth's (many) books; if you get through one, you'll have done better than I.

Wordsworth must be used to an uneven

public reception by now. After all, when it comes to modern art, the occasional outburst is to be expected, particularly in Gorey, where affluence has encouraged a new wave of interest in art collecting among would-be connoisseurs. Not everyone appreciates these modern interpretations, however. Wordsworth would probably be appalled if they did. Perhaps the only real *faux pas* is to storm out angrily, refusing any debate with the artist. An open mind is necessary, but not always afforded.

CHAPTER FIVE

"CHEERS, MIKE!"

BARNWELL held the door open for the man coming toward him, who nodded as he passed the constable. Outside, a woman on a bench lifted her face to the sun. She rose as the man walked up, and hand in hand, they wandered off in the direction of town. Barnwell's eyes tracked them for a few seconds, then he bundled through the doors of the police station. His dog, Carmen, trotted by his side.

Barnwell had had Carmen for a while now. They'd got into a smooth routine of walks at the weekend with Melanie Howes, the ultra-efficient Gorey fire crew manager, and her pit bull Vixen. He'd also taken Carmen on early morning runs, sometimes with Fortytude, the group of forty-something men led by adventurer and local celebrity Bash Bingham. An animal lover, Bash encouraged doggie participation in the runs once a week on Saturdays.

During the workday, caring for Carmen had required some creativity. Barnwell had held some concerns about how he would handle her while on shift, but Detective

Inspector Graham had come through for him. Graham was partial to a good dog and had quickly recognised Carmen's community building advantages. He'd granted permission for her to come into the office, where she was cared for by the police team during Barnwell's shifts, and he had suggested that the constable take Carmen with him when he was patrolling low-risk daytime beats.

While it was helpful to Barnwell to structure his day like this, it made operational sense too. The benefits that ensued from the opportunities a beagle puppy provided when out in the community far outweighed the small risk that she hindered Barnwell's work or distracted him. Far from it; it was amazing how the barriers between the force and the public dropped away when Carmen was "on patrol."

Barnwell had also added a new duty to his role as community police officer. Carmen regularly accompanied him on school visits, a new program he'd devised. He called it "Dog and Doughnuts." Carmen was very popular. Barnwell's schedule was booked up. The doughnuts didn't hurt either.

Barnwell was Carmen's official "puppy walker." Under the police dog training scheme, she would stay with him until she was a year old. After that, if she passed her assessment, she'd leave to move onto formal training. And a new handler. Carmen was coming up on twelve months, and Barnwell had ringed her assessment date on his calendar. A small knot of dread was making a permanent home in his stomach.

"Morning, sir."

Graham's eyes flicked up. He stood at the reception desk sifting through some post. "Morning, Barnwell. Good weekend?"

"Not bad. You?"

"Pretty good." Barnwell cocked his head in the direction of the station's doors. "Who was that?" he asked.

"Hmm? Oh, an inspector from Truro. Came in to file a report. He's on his honeymoon and needed to wrap up some unfinished business to do with a case. I had a chat with him, let him use our computers. Good guy."

Barnwell unclipped Carmen's lead from her collar before walking into the break room. "Tea?" he called out as he flicked the kettle on and prepared to finish getting dressed. He pulled his tie and uniform jacket from his locker and looked at himself in the mirror.

"No thanks," Graham called back. The inspector, while not averse to a cup of generic tea prepared by someone else, vastly preferred his own, brewed in his own teapot, to his own specifications. Could he be a tea snob? Probably.

Barnwell returned, steaming mug in hand. He sat at his desk and prepared to review his to-do list. He'd started to make one ever since he'd taken an online course suggested to him by Melanie Howes. Carmen, as was her habit, sniffed around the office, proceeding to check into all the nooks and crannies that the tables, chairs, filing cabinets, and masses of cables offered her. Satisfied, she curled up at Barnwell's feet for a snooze.

Graham eyed his constable from the reception desk. There was churn in the lives of his officers. Janice's wedding date was getting closer, and Roach was off in London with the Met on a week's assessment. In the last few months, Barnwell had lost both his parents, and while he seemed to cope admirably, Graham had observed the constable getting noticeably gruffer as the days to Carmen's first birthday drew close. He wondered where the team would be in a year. Still together—a tight-knit bunch, an effective operational unit in touch with the hard and soft policing needs of the island? Or would they face change, fresh blood, a new team for him to forge in the burning fires of the Gorey community?

"Your brother's in town, isn't that right?" Graham said.

"End of the week he arrives, sir."

"Will it be his first time?"

"Yeah, it'll be good for him to get away after the events of the past few months. I've promised him a different pub each night. But my guess is he'll settle in on the Foc's'le as his favourite. He's something of a whisky connoisseur, and they have the best range."

"Are you the eldest?"

"By a few years, but we're quite different. He's a bit of a scally, unlike me." Barnwell grinned. "Likes the ladies, bit of a drinker, although he keeps it in check. Works in marketing. I looked out for him a lot when we were younger, but he seems to be managing on his own now."

"What's he going to do while you're working?"

"Ah, he'll go for walks, visit the beach, see the sights I expect."

"He might like the war tunnels. I went there this weekend. Not sure why it took me so long. Fascinating insight into life during the Nazi occupation. What do you have on your plan today?"

"I'm taking Carmen to Brickhill Primary for a Dog and Doughnuts lesson, Year Ones. Carmen's a great help breaking the ice between the kids and the uniform. I want to teach them that, you know, we're friendly faces, you can trust us. Get 'em early kind of thing. I'm trying something new today. I've thought up some tales about Carmen, about road and stranger safety and such. I typed them up, and today I'll try one of them out. Miss Edwards, she's one of the teachers, says she's going to develop a curriculum around them, whatever that means."

"I think it means that you are doing a very impressive job, Constable. Is that what's in the box?" A cube of blue cardboard wrapped with a white ribbon, the words "Ethel's" in a flowery script written across the top, lay next to Barnwell's to-do list. "Doughnuts?"

"Yeah. I got all glazed today. I've learned a box of mixed doughnuts and twenty five-year-olds don't go well together. Last time, everyone wanted the iced ones with sprinkles on top and I only had two. There were tears."

Graham laughed. "Never get between a five-year-old and an iced doughnut with sprinkles, I always say."

Barnwell smiled. These easy morning conversations were a welcome change from the awkward "all-business" ones he and Graham used to have. The detective inspector was never going to be an open book, but he was smiling more these days and even joined them for a drink on the regular. That could only be a good thing for a station as small as theirs. Strained relationships, a bad mood, or even just a hangover had a disproportionately greater impact when the team comprised only four people, five if you included Dr. Tomlinson.

"Can you put the careers open day at Gorey Grammar in your calendar for the eighteenth? I need a wingman. St. Helier told me it's time I showed my face at a few more community events."

"No problem, sir. I can bring Carmen along if you like. She's always a hit. Takes me ages just to get to the shops when she's with me."

"You know, I wasn't sure when I saw you come in with her that first day, but she's been a great addition to the team.

Good for the community. I'm excited to see what she does next."

At Graham's words, ice crept across Barnwell's heart. When he'd signed up, he'd considered the finite puppy walking period a plus. Full-on commitment wasn't his style. But now, he found himself getting more and more anxious. He wanted Carmen to pass her assessment, to move onto the next stage of her training as a police sniffer dog. She'd be used at the ports and airport to search for drugs and explosives. It was what she deserved. She'd been the best dog. But he would be very sad to see her go. Very sad.

"Roach is back in today, isn't he?" Graham said.

"He is, sir. Do you reckon he'll have some news for us?"

"You mean about transferring to the Met? I don't know. Maybe. Depends on how he found it. It's a big change from Gorey, the biggest. Might be overwhelming for him. But he's a big lad; I'm sure he'll know if it's right for him. We'll see. I suspect we'll be able to tell the moment he comes through the door."

Roach had been away for a week on a "Meet the Met" trial. Ostensibly it was to introduce officers from other forces to the work and practices of the Metropolitan Police in London, but in reality, it was an opportunity for the Met to identify high potential recruits and for those officers to see if life in the Met was for them. Graham had suggested Roach attend. It was an efficient way for Roach, a local boy, to test the waters of police life beyond those of the Channel Islands. Like a father duck guiding his young, Graham had unselfishly prodded Roach into rougher waters, hoping he'd take to it despite the unavoidable chore of replacing him if he swam away.

"Where's Janice? She should be here by now," Graham said, checking his watch.

"Hmm, not sure," Barnwell responded. "She hasn't left a message. Not like her to be late." Barnwell's phone rang. "Speak of the devil." He accepted the call. "Hey, Jan, whassup? . . . Uh-huh. Is it bad? . . . Uh-huh. Need back up? . . . Okay, on my way." He hung up, gathering his papers. "RTA, sir. On the corner of Park and Bolton. Elderly woman hit while crossing the road. Janice was on her way in when it happened. She needs help directing traffic. Paramedics are en route."

"Okay, I'll hold the fort here. Off you go. Car's two spots down. When's your appointment with the children?"

"Eleven forty. I'm sure I'll be back before then." Barnwell slapped on his cap, Graham threw him the car keys, and the constable rushed out the door.

CHAPTER SIX

"**W**HAT SHALL I do with you?" Graham gazed into Carmen's big, brown eyes. The dog looked up at him expectantly now that her master had gone. "Want to join me for a cup of tea?" Graham went into his office and turned on the kettle, Carmen padding after him. As the water spluttered and bubbled, Graham stared out the window at the long grass that led down to the beach and the sea in the distance. Carmen curled up under his desk. Graham's thoughts turned to a holiday. He was due a break.

He thought back to a recent visit he and Laura had made to her parents, his first. As they had prepared to leave, Graham peered at a picture on the wall in their hallway. It was a pen and ink drawing of women racing around a track, long skirts flying. It was labelled *Women Racing Aquarium, London. 1896*. "Six-day racing, eh?" he'd said.

"Yes!" both Sandy and Meryl Beecham cried together.

"Have you heard of it?" Laura's mum asked, quickly coming over to stand next to him and showing a level of gumption Graham hadn't thus far credited her with. Her husband was the dominant one of the pair.

"Started in 1878, endurance cyclists would race for as long as possible each day for six days. I've read the use of amphetamines was rife, but those Victorians did love their extreme sports.

"That's right," Meryl said, astonished.

"It faded in popularity, in Britain at least, around the turn of the last century. European cyclists went to America where the sport was taking off and offering more prize money."

"Gosh, I . . . I've almost never met anyone who knew anything about it, let alone the history. My great-great-great grandfather was one of the first ever six-day cyclists," Laura's mum said. "I've always had a fascination for it. In fact, it was at a meet-up for a few enthusiasts in Ghent that Sandy and I first met."

"Really?" Graham looked between them, trying hard to imagine this conventional couple's interest in a sport most people had never heard of. The big events had been hugely popular. In the Victorian era, six-day cycle racing had been accompanied by dancing elephants, acrobats, and carnival games.

"Next time you come, we'll get out our photo albums," Sandy said, rubbing his hands at the prospect.

"Just for a few minutes," Meryl said, wrinkling her nose. She reached up to kiss Graham's cheek, a gesture he found surprisingly touching.

"Look after my girl there," Sandy called over Meryl's shoulder as she ushered Laura and David to the front door.

"Speak to you on Tuesday as usual, Mum," Laura said.

"Yes, dear. Drive carefully. Text me when you get home, so I know you've arrived safely."

Laura and Graham walked to their car and got in. They banged their doors shut and Graham turned on the engine. He smiled at Mr. and Mrs. Beecham through the windscreen. They waved at him.

"Well?"

"Well, what?"

"Did I pass?"

"I think you did." Laura reached behind her to pull on her seat belt. She looked out of the window and waved back at her parents standing on the steps of their home. "They're going to show you their photo albums. *Next time.*"

A clunk from reception jolted Graham from his reverie and Carmen from her snooze. "Anybody home?" Graham heard Roach's voice call out, followed by another bang and more voices. Barnwell and Janice had returned. Carmen's ears pricked up and she raised her head, alert to the sound of her owner's voice. The dog scurried into the main office and ran over to Barnwell, who knelt down to give her a good scrub with his knuckles, owner and dog equally delighted to see each other.

"How was the RTA?"

"All sorted, sir," Janice responded. The phone rang. She picked it up.

"Nothing serious?" Graham asked Barnwell.

"No, victim was taken to hospital, but she'll be fine. Driver was a bit shaken. Both were elderly. Combined age of one hundred seventy-eight. Six of one and half a dozen of the other it seems. She was slow to cross, he panicked in the middle of a junction. It'll all be in our report."

Roach had gone to change out of his motorbike leathers and now came back in his good weather uniform—open-necked white shirt, black trousers, and boots. He straightened the epaulettes on his shoulders that indicated his rank.

The transformation from leather-clad biker to uniformed officer took only moments, but it was stunning.

"Morning, Jim. Good to have you back."

"Thank you, sir. Good to be here." Graham and Barnwell eyed the younger officer carefully. Seeing nothing that would clue them into the sergeant's state of mind, Graham turned to his other sergeant.

Janice was still on the phone. She gave Graham a patient glance as if to say, "Want to trade?" when suddenly, the call was over. She gratefully put down the receiver.

"Do you think we can solve a computer problem for the ever-patient DI Graham?" he asked her. "I'm in a bare-knuckle fight with my laptop. Can Jack do it ASAP?"

"I'll make sure of it, sir." Janice promptly called her fiancé, who fixed the problem over the phone in five minutes flat.

"Magnificent," Graham said, putting down the receiver. "He's one of a kind, your Jack. I thought we could rely on the coastguard to protect us from illegal fishing, but apparently Jack's got responsibility for that too."

Genuinely unsure as to whether her boss was being funny or shockingly behind the times, Janice felt it best to say carefully, "That's 'fish' with a *ph*, sir. Not an *f*."

Graham's eyebrows shot up. "Crikey, these cyber-criminals are terrible at spelling, aren't they?" He gave Janice a reassuring look and a wink. "Anyway, according to Jack, I'm now *slightly* less likely to get hacked by Freddie Solomon. Or the Russians." He reflected on his words, eyebrows still aloft. "Hard to say which would be worse." His eyes roamed the office and settled on Roach. "So, good week was it, Sergeant?"

"Er, yeah, sir. Great, thanks."

"Right. Good." Graham paused. Roach looked back at

him evenly. "Well, I've got some phone calls to make," the inspector said.

Graham returned to his office. After what sounded to the others like a sequence of platitudes, some mild-mannered defence, and finally some laughter, he emerged looking as though he'd been bamboozled by a prank. "One parent tells me off, then another gives me a pat on the back." He shrugged. "I don't know which way's up."

Harding had heard some rumours about Graham's brand of "proactive refereeing" but chose to play it safe. "Still refereeing, sir?"

"Yeah, I quite like it, actually. Thinking of making it a regular thing." Behind him, Janice saw Roach frantically shake his head and draw his finger back and forth across his throat. "Parents can be a bit of a trial though. It was all I could do to keep my temper with them. If they think refere-eeing's that easy, they should get off their backsides and try running around for an hour with their eyes in the backs of their heads."

"Parents these days . . ." Janice sympathised.

Behind Graham's back, Roach rolled his eyes. "Was that Mr. Allsop on the phone? He called me too. Said something about his grandson being given a red card."

Graham began to explain just as Barnwell appeared from the break room. "Wait, wait, I don't want to miss any of this," the constable said with a grin. "Alan Allsop's red card, yes? Quite the controversy. Even been grumbling about it down the pub, his father has."

"The *red* card doesn't seem to have been the problem," Graham explained. "Mr. Allsop accepted that jumping into a tackle with both feet constitutes dangerous play. He'll be speaking to Alan."

"From what I heard," Roach said, "you had words with Alan before sending him off. What did you call him?"

"I called him a *troglodyte*," Graham announced. "It only means 'cave dweller.'"

Roach scratched his neck and winced. "What happened with Vinny Weston, then? I got two calls from his mother, one more upset than the other."

"Ah, you see, Master Weston was genuinely caught by Master Allsop's challenge, but his injury wasn't nearly as serious as he made out. Surprisingly," Graham deadpanned, "young Weston was able to continue. And so I gave him a yellow card for simulation, as the rules insist."

This was perhaps unorthodox, but at this level, not the strangest choice. "So, alright, that's one," Roach said. "Where did the second yellow card come from?"

"Once Mr. Weston learned that Mr. Allsop had received the red card," Graham explained as though in court before a jury, "he started laughing hysterically, and then did a *backflip*. So, I gave him a second yellow for excessive celebration."

"You sent off one player for a bad foul," Roach said, piecing things together, "then you *also* sent off the player he fouled?"

"Unsportsmanlike conduct," Graham confirmed. "Two separate incidents. Two yellows still make a red, don't they? I was well within my rights."

Sergeant Harding cleared her throat. "If I may quote the great Mrs. Hetherington, 'It's tasteless to gloat when others are punished. And they'll laugh all the harder when your turn comes.' I hope both boys learned their lessons."

Roach would have applied the rulebook a little less stringently in support of community relations, but he had to concede Graham's correct interpretation. Even if his decisions had been overly fastidious, he wasn't short of a strong rationale for each one. A bit like his investigations.

"How did your week at the Met go, Jim?" Janice asked. She, at least, wouldn't beat around the bush.

Roach scanned his emails. He didn't raise his eyes. Distractedly, he said. "Wha—? Yeah, yeah, good. Learned lots, you know. London was a bit overwhelming. Phew."

Janice, Barnwell, and Graham stared at him. Roach picked up a pen and wrote a note on a pad.

"So did you meet anyone interesting?" Barnwell asked. Roach leant his elbows on his desk and looked at him squarely. "Yeah, loads. Good lads."

"And what did you think? About the Met, I mean?" Graham added.

"I thought it was very interesting. Big. They do important work." Roach's phone pinged. He glanced down. The other three stood like statues, waiting for more. "It's Dr. Tomlinson. He wants me down at the lab. Okay if I go, sir?"

"Erm, yes. That's fine." Graham, Harding, and Barnwell watched Roach disappear into the break room and come out again in his leathers. He'd threaded his arm through his helmet. "Right, I'll see you lovelies in a bit, no doubt. Ciao!" Roach stuck his helmet over his head and pushed through the doors.

"Ciao?" Barnwell repeated.

"Do you think he was evading our questions?" Janice added.

"If he was, based on that performance, we all need an interview techniques refresher. That was pathetic," Graham said.

CHAPTER SEVEN

THE TWO MEN dashed through the rain—one large and muscular, the other shorter, slighter, and leaner. They headed toward the big awning of the Foc's'le and Ferret, side by side, close enough to touch. With its lights on and laughter just audible from outside, the old pub was a welcome sight on such a stormy evening.

"Where d'ya think this little lot came from?" the younger, smaller one asked, breathing hard while shaking rain from his dark hair. It had been unseasonably warm, and the pair had decided against bringing jackets. Inevitably, they were caught out by a "low pressure area" which was yielding short, sudden squalls. Steve Barnwell's jeans had taken a soaking, but he laughed it off. "I suppose I've come far enough south," he said, "that I've found a place where the rain's nearly warm! I mean, it's like taking a shower."

His brother, on the other hand, had begun to rue his wardrobe decisions. "The people who invented 'summer' shirts," he said, pulling navy fabric away from his body, "have yet to encounter *British* weather."

"Don't you worry, mate! Nice, warm pub like this, you'll

dry off in no time." Steve grabbed the door handle with an expectant flourish and flashed him a winning smile. "Besides, you never know who we'll meet. No harm showing the girls how you've tightened things up, eh?" He patted his brother's stomach—a gesture that Barnwell silently prayed Steve wouldn't repeat in public ever again. He gave his brother a steady push in the back. "Go on, it's your round."

Striding in, they walked up to the bar. Steve set a black satchel down by his feet. The pair waited for Lewis Hurd to finish pouring pints for a large group who'd pushed together some tables on the far side of the pub lounge. "Kids," Steve noted. "It's never just two or three, is it? Always ten or twelve. Clogging up the place."

"They might look like kids to you, Stevie, lad. But they're customers to people like Lewis here. And later tonight, they might end up mine and all. An important boost to the local economy," Barnwell said. "Or so the boss says."

"Are we, you know, sure they're all legal?"

Barnwell's inner policeman was never far from the surface, but there was no need to intervene. "Lewis is scrupulous about proof of age. Speak of the devil . . ."

"Evening, gents." Lewis looked a bit harried. "Scrupulous is, in fact, my middle name," he said, wiping his hands on a towel.

"Especially when it comes to underage drinking, am I right, Lewis?" Barnwell added.

"Very important responsibility," the barman said gravely. "One of the most important. Now, what can I get you?"

Steve was extremely interested in Lewis's top shelf. "I count sixteen whisky bottles up there in a long and glorious row. They aren't there just for decoration, so I'll have one of those, please."

"All ready to pour. Which'll it be?"

"One can't be hasty about a decision like this," Steve said, stroking his chin.

"You'd get along well with Dr. Tomlinson," Barnwell said as his brother hemmed and hawed. Steve was very particular about his libations.

"Oh?" Steve's eyes never left the row of scotches; each was equally tempting. "Is he also a cultured, well-educated man of the world with a refined nose and sophisticated tastes who enjoys the company of attractive, stylish women?"

"Yes, he is, actually."

After contemplating the matter for as long as Lewis could stand, Steve decided on his perfect tipple, a peaty Highland malt. He then insisted on opening the bottle and taking a dramatic whiff of the whisky's long-restrained aroma.

"Ah, lovely," Steve said, closing his eyes briefly.

Barnwell wasn't impressed. "Smells like a can of paint thinner, if you ask me."

Steve perused the bottle's label, paying it his gleeful respects. "It's enough to keep my nose happy for a week." The distillery boasted an agreeably Scottish, and therefore wholly unpronounceable, name.

"Steve, mate, are you sure, like?" Barnwell said, his brow creasing. "The hard stuff?"

"Just one. I've transformed, you see."

"Ah." In the thirty-odd years of Steve's ups and downs, he'd promised Barnwell a good number of "transformations." Many of them hadn't led to much. But after spending his twenties building a reputation as a "jack-the-lad," getting drunk on stag-dos and pub crawls, going from job to job so often that it made his work history as jumpy as a jack-in-the-box, Steve Barnwell had settled down. A bit. He'd been working for the same company for two years now, a record, and the pub crawls were only once a week nowadays.

"It used to be about quantity, didn't it, lad?" Steve went to tap his brother's flat stomach again, but Barnwell was on to him this time and dodged out the way. "Bit too much, on occasion, back in the day. Eh, Bazz?"

Pulling himself up to his full height, Barnwell found his patience stretching thin. "You *are* aware that I have powers of arrest?"

"Alright, alright," Steve replied, backing up theatrically, palms up. "Just striking a contrast, one Barry Barnwell with the other. You're barely recognisable." Steve swept his wet hair back. Soaked, slightly crumpled, and sporting a two-day beard, he looked part budget traveller, part unconventional lothario. What he lacked in height, he made up for in chat, especially with women. "It's like night and day," Steve was saying. "Like a before-and-after picture. You could be on one of those dieting adverts on TV."

"Same person underneath, though," his brother said.

"I know! That's why I'm trying to congratulate you, big fella. No need to douse me with tear gas." Despite how it might appear to a casual observer, Steve was tremendously proud and fond of his older brother. He tutted and rolled his eyes. "Come on, let's sit down. Nice talking to you, Lewis." Steve would have been more than happy to chin-wag with the staff and other customers, but he steered Barnwell away from the bar, toward the largest empty table. "I've got something to show you," he said.

"Why didn't you show me at the restaurant?" Barnwell sat down on an upholstered bench against the wall. Steve pulled a heavy volume from his bag and slapped it on the table.

"Maybe I thought," Steve said, "we'd both be better off with a drink in hand, you know?" Barnwell eyed the thick, padded photo album carefully. The gold lettering on the front was ornate, almost funereal. "Reckon this was the fashion in 1996 or whenever it was."

"Likely as not," Barnwell guessed, "these were on special offer, two for one. You know what Mum and Dad were like, always up for a bargain." He recognised the album that chronicled their parents' married lives, and the first years of their new arrivals—Barnwell first, and then Steve four years later. "Blimey, you could have warned me you were bringing out the baby pictures. Making fun of my physique not enough for you?"

"Well, if your unbuttoned shirt and your new physique don't do the trick with the ladies . . ."

"It's for *work*," Barnwell reminded him.

"'For work,' sure. That's why your biceps are yelling 'Hey, girls! Get a load of *this*!'" Steve laughed loudly at his own joke. "But that's not all," he said as if advertising heavy discounts. "Just wait until Jersey's fine womenfolk see what a cute baby you were!"

"Pipe down, will you?" Barnwell shrunk a little. The photos had come out of nowhere, a complete surprise, leaving him more than a little off-balance. "Do we *have* to do this in public?"

"Well, there's a reason for that."

"Hmm?"

"This way," Steve confessed, "I could be sure you'd not be losing your temper."

Steve opened the photo album to the first page. It was filled with pictures of Barnwell as a baby. He'd been a rosy-cheeked, chubby cherub, smiley with a shock of dark hair. "Takes you back, doesn't it?" Neither Steve nor Barnwell had looked at these pictures in years. The selection of photos carried a weight, and not just literally. "In our school uniforms, you remember?" The two were pictured, grinning excitedly, getting ready to walk to school through the streets and alleyways of the East End. By Steve's side was Mopsy, their long-lived and faithful greyhound/pointer mix. "Feels like a thousand years ago. A different planet, even."

"Lot of water's gone under the bridge since then," Barnwell agreed. He was skipping through the pages, uncomfortable and still unsure as to his brother's intent. It had been eight months since their father's funeral, and only three since their mother's. It was a lot to lose both parents inside a year. Each photo dredged up strong memories, some welcome, others not. "They went through some tough times together," he said admiringly. "And they worked so *very* hard."

In the Barnwell household of the 1980s and 90s, the greatest sin had been indolence. Leslie Barnwell hated inefficiency, waste, and what he considered laziness. A Tory voter who had come to fatherhood later in life, Barnwell senior had no patience with the "something for nothing" crowd he termed scroungers. And relaxation, fun even, was strictly rationed to holidays and Christmas. His sons knew to knuckle down when he was around and to get their kicks when they were out of his sight. He was fond of saying that a reluctance to get up early, an untidy bedroom, or watching too much TV were certain and direct routes to "the criminal lifestyle." The Barnwell boys certainly knew, or found out quickly enough, how to behave in public and what to keep hidden from his view.

The photos brought back memories. Barnwell's teenage

arguments with his father had gone badly, never really resolved, leading to their distant relationship as adults. "Crime isn't like a choice of haircut, Dad. And it doesn't define the person either," he'd said during one of their hot debates, a rather enlightened, philosophical thought for a sixteen-year-old who rarely read a newspaper beyond the sports pages and never a book if he could help it. After that, for a long time, Barnwell had refused to refer to people as "criminals." "Most crimes sort of happen *to* the people who commit them," he remembered saying, a thought his father called "muddled." Twenty or so years later, Barnwell found it harder to disagree with him.

"'Restraint and discipline,'" Steve remembered. "Those were his words for life. And did he walk the talk. Guess I didn't inherit either of those genes. He got most of his personality from the army, Mum used to say."

One of the last photos in the album was of a family gathering to celebrate their parents' wedding anniversary. Even sitting among his family, raising a glass to the camera, Mr. Barnwell had a steely, stubborn air. He had a wide moustache and a full head of dark hair, hair that both sons had inherited. In the photograph, Leslie Barnwell (he insisted on being called by his full name rather than the more common "Les") wore his button-down shirt, sleeves rolled up to his elbows, his tie tucked in between his third and fourth buttons. He looked every inch the factory floor foreman he was. He was no union man though, something that gained him approval from his superiors and suspicion from the shop floor workers during the union weakened nineties.

"Given the chance, Dad would have run our family like a platoon," Barnwell said. "Glad he stopped short of that —just."

"Amazing how Mum and he stayed together when you think about it."

"Yeah, she was more alive when he wasn't around."

"Don't think I got that gene either. Can you imagine me in a forty-year marriage?" Steve said with a wink.

"Nope," Barnwell confirmed. "Wait, is that what this is about?"

"Eh?"

"Are you getting married? Or have you met someone?" Steve laughed uproariously, taking just enough care not to spill the scotch that had been halfway to his lips.

"Alright, alright, then what is it?" Barnwell said, feeling a little played by his brother. "Some other kind of announcement? Are you going off the booze again? Got some woman up the duff? Turning vegetarian?"

Steve took a lengthy, theatrical pull on his whisky before answering. "I'll go off the booze," he said, "when the booze goes off me. And no, and no."

Barnwell didn't particularly love secrets or being kept in the dark. It felt too much like work. "Then what's going on, mate?"

"Like I said, I wanted to show you the photo album. Notice anything odd about it while you were flicking through?"

Barnwell sighed. "Are we playing detective now? I get quizzed enough at the station, thanks. Some days, it feels as though I'm being groomed to infiltrate MENSA. The boss's got this game where you put a dozen objects under a blanket, and then—"

Steve interrupted him. "Did you notice anything *missing*, I mean?" When his brother remained nonplussed, Steve turned to a page halfway through the album.

Staring, Barnwell's mind raced to figure out what Steve meant. "I don't get it, mate. What are you on ab—?"

Shouts travelled from the other side of the pub. A woman screamed. His senses on high alert, Barnwell was on his tiptoes even before the bloodcurdling sound ended.

"Just kids mucking around, isn't it?" Steve said.

"That wasn't kids just mucking around, bro," Barnwell said. Like a mother interpreting her infant's cries, he began to move toward the source of the noise.

CHAPTER EIGHT

"HELP!"

BARNWELL RAN, pushing people out of his way. A man leant against the wall near the pub's back door. He was bleeding heavily, his neck and shirt bright red. The back of his head was matted with blood, the wound feeding rivers of red that trickled down his face like tributaries of the Amazon.

Barnwell tried to hold the man upright, but he was slipping sideways, his eyeballs rolling upward. "Lewis, nine-nine-nine!" The barman was on it.

"Sir, can you hear me?" Pub patrons cleared a space, and two other men helped Barnwell bring the man safely to the floor. "Bar towels," Barnwell ordered the men. He pressed his hands to the injured man's head to stem the bleeding. Immediately, trails of blood appeared between Barnwell's fingers and ran down the backs of his hands. The guy was barely conscious. He gasped for breath. Blood dribbled from both ears.

"Stay with me, mate," Barnwell urged. The man's eyes focused for a second, then drifted upward again. Barnwell was losing the battle. He quickly grabbed the bar towels that were waved in his face and placed one around the man's head. Within seconds, he added another. And then another.

Steve jostled his way through the small crowd that had assembled. He held his arms out to keep the onlookers at a distance. He watched his brother work, as amazed by how fast he'd moved as by his calm, competent first aid.

"Ambulance on its way." Lewis Hurd appeared at Barnwell's elbow. "How bad is it?"

"Very bad. He's out," Barnwell said. "Unconscious but breathing. We've got to stop the bleeding, but the injury's gushing like a geyser." Barnwell's navy shirt, just about dried out from the rain, was drenched again. He doubled up two fresh bar towels and added them to the sodden ones that covered the man's wound.

His phone in one hand, Lewis described the man's injuries to the emergency services dispatcher. "Yes, from the back of his head. It looks serious. He's pouring blood."

"Make sure the ambulance team can get through this lot, will ya?" Barnwell told Steve. Steve switched places with another pub customer, a big, beefy man whose exposed skin was covered with thick hair and tattoos. Barnwell's brother went outside to await the paramedics. Barnwell looked down at the stricken man. His breathing was becoming laboured. "Come on, man, *come on*! Ergghh!" The man vomited.

As news of the incident and its gravity spread, two-thirds of the Foc's'le's customers left. "What's the status, Lewis?" Barnwell said, trying to ignore all the reasons why his soaking clothes stuck to him.

"Police on the way," Lewis reported. "I can hear the sirens."

Barnwell nodded. "Janice is on duty." He frowned again. "Can you check his pockets?"

Lewis Hurd gingerly felt around the man's clothing and pulled out a weathered, black leather wallet. "Flip it open, see if you can get a name. I can't move." Barnwell added another towel to the wad he was pressing against the man's head. "He's very pale." He felt the man's neck. "His pulse is weak. That ambulance better get here quickly."

He gazed into the faces of the surrounding crowd, almost all of them teenagers, their heads tilted down as they furiously worked their phones. "Did anyone hear him say anything? See where he came from?"

The young people who heard Barnwell shook their heads. Those who didn't ignored him. They continued to film or text. No matter, Janice would make more rigorous enquiries. Speak of the devil; the wooden doors to the pub opened, and Sergeants Harding and Roach strolled in. They immediately got to work pushing back the crowd. Arms outstretched, Janice shouted, "Okay, back please! *Back!*" The room around Barnwell cleared out.

Six minutes after they were called, the ambulance team made their way through the crowd. They were brisk and efficient, making their initial assessment mostly by sight. There seemed little need for anything else. "He needs the trauma centre," senior paramedic Sue Armitage said. "More options in St. Helier. And he's going to *need* some options," she added in a low voice. Sue was no-nonsense. She'd seen a lot, even on an island the size of Jersey. With the help of her partner, Alan, they quickly loaded the injured man into the ambulance.

With a medley of lights rhythmically pulsing but no siren, the ambulance carefully drove off, watched by the Barnwell brothers as it headed for St Helier and the island's largest medical facility. The rain had started again, although mercifully, not as heavy as before.

Janice walked up, her nose wrinkling. "How are you doing?" She carefully avoided mentioning the meaty, acrid stench coming off her fellow officer.

"He's in bad shape," Barnwell replied. "Not sure he's going to make it." He roused himself. "But no point standing here doing nothing."

"Give yourself a cleanup and go home," Janice advised. "Jim 'n' me'll take it from here."

"You sure? You don't want me to question anyone? Give you a statement?"

"Nah, I know where to find you. Lewis said he just staggered in, all bleeding like."

"Yeah, I heard the shouts and went over to see what was what. Did Lewis give you his wallet?"

"Yeah, his name's James Reeves. Ever heard of him? I haven't."

"I think I've seen him a few times in here. Never spoke to him, though."

They walked back inside, and Barnwell spent a few minutes in the pub's bathroom attending to his appearance. Wetting paper towels, he fruitlessly tried to clean away the blood and vomit that had soaked into his trousers and down the front of his shirt. Lewis Hurd and Steve joined him. The barman wordlessly handed Barnwell a fresh T-shirt and a pair of jeans.

"Thanks, mate. That's more like it." Barnwell's hands were bright red. When he stripped off his shirt, so was his chest.

"Abs!" Steve hissed.

"What?"

"Abs! You've got a six pack. If I squint a bit."

"Barely."

"But still—"

"Look, shut it, mate, alright? I've had enough. This isn't the time."

Steve sobered. "Yeah, fair enough. I just can't get over the change in you, though. Out there . . . you were the dogs—"

"Yeah, yeah, alright," Barnwell cut in, always uncomfortable with compliments. "Rubbish thing to happen while you're visiting, though. I'm sorry, mate."

Steve saw it differently. "Not a bit of it. I'm sorry I missed your escapade in the speedboat with the Royal Marines. And that other crazy thing with the helicopter in the middle of the night? No wonder they gave you a couple of medals."

Barnwell texted Janice. She was methodically taking statements from the pub goers still left in the bar. She texted back to say that Roach had left for the hospital to follow up there.

"Tonight," Steve said, proud of his brother as never before, "I got to see you in action. Doing what you do."

"Doing what anyone would."

"Don't sell yourself short. Helping others," Steve insisted, "is our highest calling."

"*Trying* to help. That chap was in grim shape when they took him away."

"You did your best. No one else even stepped forward. You notice that?"

"Well, I mean, it's quite a challenging situation. And I did take over. Someone else would have stepped in if I hadn't."

"I'm not so sure. All those kids were interested in was

content for their social media. You were out of your seat and around the bar like a rocket, Bazz!"

"Of course, yeah, of course," Barnwell said vaguely. He'd lost his enthusiasm for light-hearted banter. The evening was over for him.

Steve caught his mood. "Look, I'm here for two whole weeks, so let's say this. I'll take myself back to the Black Horse Hotel or whatever it's called . . ."

"The White House Inn," Barnwell said, finding he could still laugh. He wondered if Steve's mistake was deliberate to lighten things up.

"Yeah, yeah. You go home, rest up, have a shower, and get those bloodstains out so you're not mistaken for a serial killer. Toss your clothes in the rubbish too. You stink."

"Definitely."

"And tomorrow we'll have breakfast at . . . what's that place called?

"Ethel's."

"Right. At what, eight thirty?"

"Seven," Barnwell said. "I'll have to go into work if they don't catch who did this tonight." He felt self-conscious now in his borrowed clothes, with his bloodstained hands. His chest felt a little crispy. Blood residue. "Yeah, I'd best be off."

"Okay, chief," Steve said, a little pale at the idea of such an early start but keen to appear supportive. "See you at Ethel's at seven."

Half an hour later, Barnwell's hands finally stopped shaking. Five times a minute, he felt the impulse to call St. Helier General and get a read on the injured man, but the hospital staff would have their hands full, and Roach had promised to text him if there was anything to report. If the man remained unconscious but stable, there wouldn't be any news until tomorrow.

Bazza paced around his flat. He showered, letting steaming water drain the evening's tensions from his system just a little. When he flicked on the kettle to make himself a hot drink, Carmen, sensing his mood, whined and looked up at him. She tilted her head, her big, brown eyes pleading. Padding over to the bench by the door where Barnwell kept her lead, the young beagle took it between her teeth and padded back to him, dropping it at his feet.

"Good girl. You know what's best for me even more than I do, don't 'cha?" Barnwell bent down and scratched between her ears. "Hang on."

He had an idea, one which sounded better the more he thought about it, and better still when he saw the rain had stopped. "Time for a breather after a complicated night." He pulled on a football jersey and his trainers. He attached Carmen's lead to her collar. Opening the front door, he saw the sky was black, starless. The air, silent and cool. Barnwell opened the wrought iron gate on to the street. It creaked noisily. He tugged on Carmen's lead, and with a little skip to push off, they went for a run.

CHAPTER NINE

The Gorey Gossip
Saturday, April 16th

It is my sad duty to report that Gorey has been the scene of another explosion of violence and grief. Some of my readers were in the Foc's'le and Ferret last night when local man, Jamie Reeves, stumbled in, blood gushing from the back of his head. He attempted to ask for help before collapsing.

Our grateful thanks—yet again—to Constable Barnwell from our local police force for administering first aid, keeping poor Mr. Reeves alive until the paramedics arrived, and to the staff at St. Helier General, where Jamie currently lies in critical condition. In true Gorey style, well-wishers have reached out to Jamie's family.

But what has Gorey come to when someone can't be sure of making it back home without being viciously attacked after a night out? According to local sources, there was no sign of robbery, so what are we to assume? That it was a simple mugging that went wrong? Or something more darkly sinister? Time for our boys (and one girl) in blue to step up! I'm talking to you, Detective Inspector Graham.

As a sudden storm consigns the beauty of a sunny day to a memory in the blink of an eye, last night's barbaric violence reminds us to be vigilant. In Gorey, we are grateful for our small and capable police force. Their recent performance continues an upward trajectory. I'm certain DI Graham's team remains committed to our safety and their own improvement, and sources have promised plenty of old-fashioned "knocking-on-doors" policing to bring the attacker to justice.

I encourage you to tell the police everything you can, even if it's background or peripheral information. And please keep Jamie in your thoughts as doctors work to restore him to rude health.

CHAPTER TEN

"**M**ORNING, JIM," GRAHAM said. "Nice and cool in there, is it?"

Roach gratefully swept off his helmet in a smooth move and quickly shook out his hair, not unlike a dog that had just climbed out of a river. "Not really," he said. The sergeant was uncomfortably hot. He flattened his matted hair with one hand, spiked it up with the other, then used both to give it some semblance of formality. "Great ride, mind. Day after a big rainstorm," he said, taking an exaggerated deep breath. "Fresh as a daisy. Like the place has just been hosed down."

The phone rang. Janice answered. She soon hung up. "That was Barnwell, sir. He's going to pop in for the meeting."

"On his day off?" Roach said. He considered the constable's efforts the previous evening. "Yeah, I suppose he would. Asked me to text him if anything happened. Must've really shook him up. One minute you're having a lazy end-of-the-week drink, the next you're covered in blood, trying to keep some poor bloke alive."

"We've got no evidence," Harding said. "Not a thing. Nobody saw or heard anything outside or inside the pub, no forensics. And the lad's probably going to—"

"Medical science is capable of wonders beyond our imagining, Sergeant," interrupted Graham. "Let's not write him off yet." Privately, he was surprised Jamie Reeves was still alive given his injuries, and it gave their investigation a sliver of hope. What Graham wanted most was a phone call from the hospital to say Reeves was awake and ready to talk.

There was a clatter from the back. Barnwell came through into the reception area. He must have come in the rear door. "Morning, Barnwell. Thanks for coming in on your day off," Graham greeted him. "Get yourselves some tea and meet in my office in five."

"Yes, sir," the trio said in unison.

Five minutes later, they crowded into Graham's office, Janice at the rear so she could keep an eye on reception and an ear listening for the desk phone. "The other stuff can wait," Graham began. "This case is our priority. Right, we've got a twenty-eight-year-old male, a James Reeves, in St. Helier General with serious head injuries. He was attacked just a few yards from his home. His life is hanging by a thread, so I'm told, and this case could turn into a murder investigation at any minute."

"Terrible," Roach said. "I played five-a-side against him a couple of times. Marcus said he hired him to do some gardening for him."

"I've seen him in the Foc's'le," Barnwell added.

"Jack told me he fixed his computer once," Janice said.

"Sounds like he was well ensconced in the community. Tell me everything we've got," Graham said.

Roach took the lead. "Right, sir. Well, he's lucky to be alive. Someone gave him a *ferocious* whack over the head."

"He didn't say anything? Identify his attacker?"

"All he could do was ask for help when he came into the pub," Barnwell said. "Nothing else. Someone really did a number on him. By the time he got to the Fo'c'sle, he'd lost a good deal of blood."

Roach spoke up. "The attacker inflicted a single wound. Dr. Tomlinson says that the margins weren't uniform as you would expect with a tool, but not as irregular as something natural. While we can't run a formal examination, analysis of the bar towels Barnwell used in the pub and bandaging at the hospital didn't reveal any residue. With the rain and everything, we haven't got much, but if it had been a brick or a rock, we'd have found red brick dust or particles of organic matter on them."

Harding reflexively cradled the back of her neck. "Ouch."

"So, he was subject to the classic anonymous 'frenzied' attack, as no doubt Mr. Freddie Solomon will tell everyone when he finds out." Graham was making notes. "Who is this chap? Local lad?"

"Yeah, he's Gorey, born and raised," Roach confirmed. "Works for Sanderson Landscaping. Started out doing what they call 'hardscaping'—putting in driveways, patios, pools, that kind of thing. Plus, a bit of planting too. But now he does some of the design work."

"Okay, what else do we have? No one saw anything, Sergeant Harding? I mean nothing?"

"No, sir. We interviewed the people in the pub and neighbouring houses. They don't report hearing or seeing anything. There was a trail of blood, which suggests he was attacked just a few feet from the pub, so he must have been hit over the head and dragged himself there to get help. He lives alone in a flat close by, but it isn't clear where he'd been beforehand or where he was going. It's all a bit of mystery, really."

"Well, that's our speciality. Mysteries." Graham made a face. "Any sign of the weapon?"

None of them spoke. "No, sir," Roach finally said.

"We haven't been able to do a thorough search of the area yet, but if I can have some help from St. Helier, I can arrange one," Janice offered.

"Not sure I'll get that today, Sergeant. The Bulls are playing the Green Lions this afternoon. Everyone will be drafted to that." Rivals Jersey and Guernsey football clubs were playing a local derby. They were always fiercely contested and well attended. The streets of St. Helier were likely to be quiet, but the football ground would be heaving. "We'll have to do it ourselves. I'll leave organisation of the search to you."

"Yes, sir."

Barnwell was keen to get his boss's first impression. "What do you reckon, sir?"

"Not much to go on, is there? Unusual for the area." Gorey was not known for random, nasty crimes like this. There were incidents of violent conduct when the acutely boisterous met the overly intoxicated, often in the same physical body, but they were extremely rare. "A street mugging gone wrong, maybe?"

"My first thought too. But he had his wallet on him," Barnwell reported.

"And his phone, sir. Jack worked on it last night. Nothing," Janice said.

"There's been no activity on his cards," Roach piped up. "No useful camera footage either."

Graham sighed. He finished his notes and laid out his

plan for the day. "Alright, Roach, I want you to go to St. Helier. Check on the victim, then get with Tomlinson. Butter him up a bit. Get him talking about wine and California again. Whatever it takes, I want him to give us something more." Graham looked back at his notes, which were depressingly scant.

"But the victim's not dead, sir. It's not his case."

"He can liaise with the treating doctors, talk their language, leverage the relationships, and perhaps get us some more info. If we can't talk to Jamie Reeves, *anything* will help, Jim, seriously."

"Righto, boss."

"Barnwell," Graham continued, "well done again with providing prompt and professional first aid at the Foc's'le last night. Mr. Reeves certainly owes the fact he has a fighting chance to you . . ."

Barnwell attempted to deflect the compliment. "I was only there for a quiet drink with my brother. I never know what kind of trouble he's going to get me into."

"Nevertheless, you're a credit to us, Barnwell," Graham said. It was perhaps his highest praise, and this time there was no deflecting.

"Thank you, sir," Barnwell said humbly. "Lewis Hurd, the barman at the Foc's'le, texted me about a trio of young lads he calls DKN . . ."

It took only two seconds. "Drunken, kleptomaniac, and nefarious?" Graham tried.

Eyebrows bunched, Roach whispered to Harding, "Remind me never to play Scrabble with him."

"I don't think you're being complimentary, sir, and as character assessments go, I'd say you're on the money. Names are Duncan, Kevin, and Neil."

"Neil Lightfoot?" Roach said.

"The very same," Barnwell confirmed.

"Your very first collar, wasn't he, Jim?" Harding recalled.

"Nah, my first one was that fence-line dispute up on the Longueville Road near Banbury Meadow. Remember? That drunken idiot of a homeowner who brought out his chainsaw and started waving it around, terrorising his neighbours? That was a satisfying nick." Roach laughed. "Neil Lightfoot was my *second* arrest. I found him trying his hand at a new profession. In fact, during his first spell of on-the-job training, he was kind enough . . ."

"Dim-witted enough," Barnwell tossed in.

". . . to let me watch for three whole minutes while he completely failed to break into a new Audi four-by-four on Lyme Avenue."

"It does make things easier," Graham agreed, "when our would-be criminals prove to be gratuitously stupid."

"Anyhow, Lewis thought they might be worth a chat," Barnwell summed up. "I thought I'd go and see them.

"Alright, track these three lads down. If they don't know anything, they might know someone who does. But it's just a chat, mind. Make sure they know that. Janice, you hold the fort down here. Work your magic with the databases. Find out what you can about our Mr. Reeves and his associates."

"Yes, sir."

"I'll go to Sanderson's to speak to his colleagues. Let me know what you get when you get it. Okay, off you go."

The officers, their tasks allotted, smartly walked out of Graham's office. He watched them go, but after they left, he turned to gaze out of the window. They had nothing to go on. But they'd had nothing before and had turned things around with hard graft, teamwork . . . and tea. Graham strode over to his filing cabinet and flipped the switch on the kettle. He'd make himself a pot of Assam before he did anything else.

CHAPTER ELEVEN

"**T**HEY TOOK HIM into surgery in the early hours." Tomlinson led Roach from the hospital's covered entrance and down a long hallway with countless doors leading off to departments of every type. "There was evidence that things were getting worse. He has a brain bleed. They'll decide whether to airlift him to the mainland in a few hours. Tricky decision though; he might not survive the journey."

They washed their hands and walked into the blue-floored, medical quiet of the intensive care unit. Jamie had his own small room, though someone was constantly monitoring him from a nurses' station that looked more like NASA mission control than Roach remembered. Two computer monitors displayed real-time information from eight rooms, including Jamie's.

"Have a seat for a minute," Tomlinson said. "He's got visitors. Besides, all the interesting stuff is here," he added, pointing to the screen. There were a range of scans available, and with a moment's help from one of the ICU nurses, Tomlinson found a CT scan of Jamie Reeves's skull.

"There's intracranial bleeding." He called up another high-resolution picture. "It's not looking good, Jim."

"Oh."

"But even depressing, avoidable tragedies can be moments for learning," Tomlinson told his protégé. "Why don't you tell me everything you know about"—he turned from the screen and gave the request a little theatre, performing a quiet drum roll on the desktop before cuing the sergeant with a director's finger—"brain stem herniation!"

Jim collected his thoughts and attempted to sound confident. "When someone takes a traumatic hit to the head . . ."

"Not unlike the one you're in for if you've skipped your anatomy reading," warned Tomlinson with a wink.

". . . a bleed can begin. The buildup of blood puts pressure on the brain stem, resulting in unconsciousness." Roach thought back to his textbook reading. "Then, there's cessation of the breathing reflexes, which leads to asphyxia. Oh, and finally, death."

"Even in the ICU," Tomlinson lamented, "we struggle to successfully treat *that*."

"So, what happened during his surgery?" asked Roach.

"They drilled a hole in his skull to relieve the pressure. He held on," Marcus said, sounding grim. "But barely. I wasn't there, but from what I heard, it was complicated."

Roach frowned. "So . . . what can I tell the boss?"

Tomlinson closed his eyes for a second. "In the first place, Sergeant," he said, irritation creeping into his voice, "you can tell him the patient is stable, gravely ill, and the next few hours will be critical. And second, I can't rightly give you an post-mortem report because he's not actually dead, you see."

"Got it."

"I've said all along that the assailant hit Jamie with a weight of some kind, but I'm going to add a detail. They hit him like they *really* meant it. Caused the kind of damage you might see from a hammer blow."

"No wonder his brain decided to call it quits for a while," Roach said. "How long do coma patients stay asleep for?"

"It's not *sleep*, for heaven's sake, boy," Tomlinson wailed, throwing up his hands. "It's . . ."

"Just a slip, Doc. No need to go ballistic. I know it's not technically sleep. It's like, well, the brain's emergency mode. His brain has shut down."

Placated, Tomlinson said, "About two weeks, typically. By that point, the coma tends to resolve, one way or the other."

"As in, he will either . . ."

"Yes, young man."

"Do *they* know that?" Roach wondered, nodding at the window of Jamie's room through which they could see a small, slight woman sitting anxiously by his bed, her hands clasped in front of her. The woman's face was fixed on Jamie's figure lying quite still in the bed, his arms by his sides. Next to him, machines beeped, administered, and monitored. A man stood behind her, his arms tightly crossed. Every aspect of the woman's body language spoke of concern for the stricken patient, while her companion seemed defensive, even angry. Him being a foot taller and a hundred pounds heavier than the young woman boosted this impression.

"Not sure. The nurse told me they got here an hour or so ago, and the girl was in a terrible state, bawling when she saw him." Tomlinson hadn't taken his eyes off the screens and clicked to another view, a cross section that showed Jamie's brain in remarkable detail. "Just *extraordinary* what we can do these days."

"I'm going to say hello to them," Roach said.

Marcus Tomlinson checked his watch and closed the folder of images. "I'll stay here. They'll only pester me for news, and I don't have any. He's not even my responsibility. Yet."

"Cheery thought. Thanks, Dr. T." Roach left the nurses' station and crossed the corridor. He knocked on the door and went in. The room was a place of intense, worried quiet, except for a susurrus of background hums and clicks and hisses. Aware of the effect his uniform would have—it communicated there was trouble—Roach spoke immediately. "Just a courtesy visit from the Gorey police. We're investigating the attack on Mr. Reeves," he began. He glanced at the patient.

A respiratory tube had been fitted in case Jamie's ability to breathe became compromised. A cluster of IV attachments at each wrist led to two drips. Pads adhered to his skin fed data to a rack of medical machines. The skin around his closed eyes was bruised, his lips parched and swollen.

"He's just . . ." said the woman, her knuckles whitening as she spoke, "so . . . *absent.*" She glanced at Roach and her companion, as though hoping for a more positive interpretation, her teary, blue eyes sheltered by bleached-blonde hair.

"He'll be back in no time," said the man who accompanied her. He seemed in his early thirties and possibly the woman's boyfriend. He had curly, brown hair and the generous frame of a heavyweight boxer but with none of the grace. He wore a stern, uncomfortable expression like he would prefer to be anywhere but at Jamie Reeves's bedside.

"They can do miracles these days, love," he said, trying to sound reassuring. "Absolute miracles."

"Are you members of the family?" Roach asked. He was confused by this couple. Was she a sister? A girlfriend? An ex-wife?

"Old friends," the young woman said. "From Les Quennier school in St. Helier. We were," she stumbled to add, not sure what word to use, "well, we were *together* until a year ago. I'm Paula Lascelles. This is my new boyfriend, Matthew Walker," she said, nodding at the big man.

"Missed his chance," Matthew added tactlessly.

"I left Jersey," explained Paula a little more sensitively, "but Jamie absolutely loved it here. Refused to move. That's why we broke up. I'm just taking over for a bit while his mum and dad go for something to eat. That was kind of them, wasn't it? To let me in. I'm sure I'm not their favourite person." Paula looked up at Roach forlornly, her eyes wide with anxiety.

Roach made quiet notes on his tablet, angling it into his chest. "Can you tell me anything about who might have done this? Anyone who might have held a grudge against him?" Paula shook her head. "Any other ex-girlfriends?"

"No," Paula shot back angrily. "Only me. There was *only* me."

"Take it easy, babe," Matthew told her. "The sergeant 'ere is just askin' questions."

Paula closed her eyes and took a deep breath. "Yes, yes, sorry."

"Nobody saw anyfin', right?" said Matthew. "So, how're you gonna arrest the person who did it?"

"Examination of the evidence, investigation, and deduction," replied Roach crisply. He had taken an instinctive dislike to this brittle couple. "Honed techniques aided by some of the most amazing technology you've never heard of." He thought he sounded like Graham as he listened to himself and wondered if that was a good thing.

Matthew seemed entirely nonplussed. "And maybe someone just whacked him, random-like. I mean, it 'appens."

"It's possible. But even if they weren't seen doing it, we have ways to discover who it was."

"Some people . . ." Matthew began, but Paula had apparently had enough. She pulled him to her side, and they turned away from Roach, returning to their morose, silent vigil over the motionless Jamie. Roach got the hint and left, but not without leaving them both his card with a reminder to stay in touch. "My detective inspector," he muttered to himself on the way out, "is *definitely* going to want to talk to you two weirdos."

CHAPTER TWELVE

ROACH WANDERED DOWN to the hospital canteen. His eyes roved over the diners, searching for a couple who might be Jamie Reeves's parents. In the corner next to the windows, he spied a pair—mid-fifties, weary. The man had ordered a full English. He chewed thoughtfully. The woman next to him ignored her toast and was sipping tea. She stared ahead, her hands wrapped around her mug, clasping it tightly as though its warmth was life-sustaining.

"Mr. and Mrs. Reeves?" The couple looked up. "I'm Sergeant Roach, Gorey Police. I'm investigating your son's case. May I ask you a few questions?"

Phil Reeves nodded at the empty chair at their table. "We were expecting you last night. Isn't this a bit late? Whoever did this could be miles away by now. Off the island, even."

"I tried to speak to you, but you were in distress and the doctors advised that we wait." Roach's voice was gentle, courteous, respectful.

"Hmph, okay then. What do you want to know?"

Reeves senior put his knife and fork down and sat back in his chair. Mrs. Reeves's knuckles whitened as she gripped her mug even tighter.

"Could you give me your full names, please?"

"Phil, Philip Reeves, and this is my wife, Christine."

"May I say that I'm very sorry for your situation, and we're doing everything we can to find Jamie's attacker. Can you tell me when you last saw him?"

"Last night. He was walking back to his flat from our house when that person hit him. He left us around ten p.m. He'd come for dinner and a beer, a bit of a chat."

"He often did that," Christine Reeves said in a whisper. She peeled a hand from her mug and rubbed it across her face. Like her voice, her hand shook.

"Was there anything about his visit that concerned you? Did he seem agitated or worried?" Phil Reeves shook his head. Roach looked at his wife for confirmation.

"No, nothing. Everything seemed perfectly normal," she said.

"We had a couple of beers like we normally do, got fish and chips, watched a bit of TV. Then he left to walk home. Just like many other Friday nights we've had over the years."

"Are you aware of any disputes he's involved in, anything that might get him the attention of someone who might have done this?"

Phil Reeves sat forward now. He glared at Roach. "What are you trying to say? That Jamie was involved in something criminal? Like this was some kind of payback or warning or something?"

"I'm just trying to ascertain the facts, Mr. Reeves. I'm not suggesting that Jamie had anything to do with anything illegal. This might end up being a random street mugging, but I have to ask the questions so we can do our best to see that justice is served on Jamie's behalf."

Mrs. Reeves let go of her mug long enough to put her hand on her husband's arm to placate him. Phil Reeves sat back at his wife's behest. "It's alright, Sergeant. Ask away," she said. "But please be quick. I want to get back to his bedside. I am not aware of anything that might have led to this attack. Jamie is a good boy, not in debt, no troubling friends. He was well-liked, enjoyed his beer like they all do at his age, but nothing to excess, had a few girlfriends, but no one serious at the moment."

"What about Ms"—Roach checked his notes—"Lascelles? I met her in Jamie's room. And her friend."

Christine Reeves and her husband exchanged glances. Mrs. Reeves let go of her mug. "Paula is Jamie's ex-girl-friend. They went to the same school but got together after-wards. They went out for nearly a decade—"

"On and off," Phil Reeves interrupted. "Mostly off."

"Until about a year ago, when she went to the mainland."

"Best day of my life," her husband said. He folded his arms again. Now he pursed his lips. "I wasn't a fan."

"Paula's a very attractive girl, but she had Jamie wrapped around her little finger. He'd do anything she asked, and then she'd tell him to get lost. Just like that. Always picking him up and dropping him again, she was," Christine Reeves said.

"You should have seen the fights they had. Embarrass-ing. Slamming doors, screaming at each other. Did my head in. I kept telling him to dump her, but she'd call and off he'd trot like he was her dog or something." Phil Reeves tutted and shook his head.

"Eventually she went a step too far. She wanted to leave the island, and Jamie loves it here. He wouldn't leave."

"Oh, she tried to get him to. Wheedling, crying, threatening. But this time he called her bluff. She'd have left him the moment she found someone better anyhow. Someone with more money, status. Girls like her are always like that." Jamie's father stabbed a bite of sausage and munched on it aggressively.

"We were relieved to see her go, to be honest. So much drama." Mrs. Reeves gave Roach a wan smile.

"And we weren't happy to see her turn up this morning when she heard the news," her husband added.

"Apparently, she's visiting her family for a few days. Brought her new boyfriend with her. She offered to give us a break, which is why we're down here . . ." Mrs. Reeves trailed off. "Anyhow, is there anything else you need to know?"

Roach's mind worked furiously. "Wha— er, no. I think that will be all for now. Do you have a photo of Jamie that we can circulate? It will help us with our enquiries."

Christine Reeves seemed grateful for something to do. She rapidly swiped through the photos on her phone, finally settling on one that showed Jamie, bottle of beer in his hand, smiling broadly. "I like that one. It was his birthday. We had a good time. He was happy." Her voice broke, and she handed her phone to Roach so that he could send the image to his email address, the process beyond her.

"Thank you. I'll leave you in peace. We'll be in touch if there are any developments." Roach left his card on the table. Neither of them paid it any attention, and Christine Reeves picked up her mug again, unaware or not caring that her tea was now stone cold.

Alone at the station, Janice banged away at her keyboard with her fingertips. She was the station's police database expert. Training her had been one of DI Graham's first directives, and it was a role for which she was grateful. It had afforded her a small increase in pay, status, and possibilities for advancement should she seek them. But today as she searched, cross-referenced, and categorised, she felt resentful, restless, sidelined.

She wasn't sure why. She didn't normally feel like this. Maybe the wedding was getting to her. She punched another query into the search bar. Nothing. Jamie was as clean as her kitchen at home. Carmen sniffed at Janice's feet and gave a little whine.

"Yeah, me too, doggie." Janice let out a sigh. "I know we shouldn't, but . . ." She punched some numbers into the reception phone. Taking Carmen's lead off a hook in the breakroom, the sergeant clipped it onto her collar. "Come on, let's get out of here. Let's give you some sniffing practice."

CHAPTER THIRTEEN

LOOKING DECIDEDLY HARASSED, his thick, grey-flecked hair in disarray, Lewis Hurd finally stood up and stretched just as Barnwell appeared in the pub's doorway. "We don't open until eleven thirty," Lewis said, tossing down a sodden rag. "Oh, it's you, Bazza. Provided you're not here for a pint, come on in."

It was strange to see the place empty, so orderly, clean, and neat instead of packed with diners and drinkers laughing and talking. Chairs and barstools were stacked neatly upside down on the tabletops. The bar gleamed. Most importantly, though, Lewis had finished soaking and cleaning a patch of carpet near the bar, exactly where Jamie Reeves had come to a bloodied halt.

"Just saying hello, Lewis," Barnwell said. "Seeing if there's anything new. The place scrubs up nicely, doesn't it?" he added, looking around.

"Rumours spread quickly," the experienced barman told him. Hurd walked over to the heavy wooden door and locked it. "I've had a hell of a time trying to persuade people a fight didn't happen *inside* the pub. If we don't clear that story up sharpish, the Foc's'le will get a reputation. And no one wants to come in to the sight and smell of blood, do they? Best if we look shipshape." This had been his morning message to his two junior staff, teenagers who had laboured all morning to give the pub a thorough clean. "We had to get the carpet seen to, in any case. Figured we might as well tidy the place up a bit while we were at it." Lewis cleared his throat. "Got to say, the presence of a uniformed constable won't be a welcome sight once we open."

"I won't harm your bottom line or your reputation, I promise," Barnwell said, keeping an eye on the time. "Your staff did well."

"Thanks, mate," Lewis managed. "Well, like I say, it's busy around here, so if there's nothing else . . ." He said it not impolitely but with genuine enthusiasm to get the Foc's'le back on its feet with a positive Saturday lunchtime crowd. It was one of the busiest times of the week. "I've got a big screen out back so people can watch the game." He raised his eyebrows. "Can I help you with anything?"

Barnwell brought out his tablet and found his notes on the Jamie Reeves case. "Obviously, I'm checking if you've heard anything more about the attack."

"Not a sausage," Lewis replied. His ever-busy hands slid from glass to glass, polishing them quickly with a new, white cloth. "People are shocked; they want to know what happened. But nobody's paraded around the pub claiming responsibility if that's what you mean. And if they do know something, no one's talking." A loud series of thumps on the outside door made both men jump. "We're not open yet!" Lewis bellowed. "That'll be DKN. They always try to get me to open up early. And I always say no. Don't know why they bother, but they're not the smartest."

"I'd like to talk to them actually, but I can do that

outside, leave you in peace," Barnwell said, making for the door.

"Hang on," Lewis said. "That would look bad. And I don't want that after all our efforts. I'll let them in. Your presence should keep them from hassling me to open the bar out of hours." Lewis checked his watch, set down a glass, and marched to the pub door. He slid back the bolt. "Come on in, lads. There's someone here to see you."

"'Bout time, Lewis!" said one of the three young men dressed in track suits who had been standing outside.

"We're not open for drinking. Constable Barnwell wants to talk to you. Though Lord knows why he wants to look at your ugly mushes any more than he has to. I certainly don't." This apparently insulting invective from Lewis passed for banter between the barman and the three men that passed through the doors. None of them batted an eyelid.

"What's all this, then?" Kevin Croft, twenty-three, a bit full of himself, and usually affable enough until he'd had a skinful—after that, all bets were off—strode confidently into the pub. He pulled at the crotch of his low-slung trackie while loudly chewing gum. Barnwell considered it extraordinary that he managed to achieve both tasks at the same time, a feat that, had he not seen it for himself, he would have considered Croft to be incapable of.

The tallest of the three copped an eyeful of Barnwell. "What's he doin' 'ere?" Duncan Rayner appeared to be their leader, after a fashion. He hitched up the tracksuit bottoms that hung off his nonexistent backside. His features were sharp and unattractive, like a rodent's, a comparison not aided by hair that was suffering from a clearly recent and ill-advised shaving incident.

"Me?" Barnwell asked. "Oh, I'm just here to gaze into

the crystal ball." He hovered around the skinny lad's oddly shaved head. "You know, the Victorians put a lot of store by phrenology." The three men held Barnwell with a steady gaze but said nothing.

"Reading the bumps on your head," Barnwell explained.

"'Ow the bleedin' 'ell did you know that?" Duncan, the leader-after-a-fashion, exclaimed. He squinted.

Barnwell shrugged. "Monday is trivia night down at the Pig and Whistle. I learn all sorts. In olden times, they reckoned they could tell if you were a criminal or not just from looking at your bonce. Absolute codswallop, of course," he scoffed. "But that's what they believed. Interesting people, the Victorians. Really into body snatching . . ." Barnwell trailed off, staring into space. The lads were now gawping at him like he was an alien. "Anyhow," Barnwell said suddenly, snapping back into character, "I've learned to be open-minded about where leads might come from."

"Funny that," Kevin said, poking a thumb at his mate. "Because Duncan here comes from Leeds!"

"Ah, you're the comedian of the group, are you?" Barnwell said. "Listen, why don't we sit down for a chat? We can work on your material, maybe get you a slot at the London Palladium."

The last of the trio was Neil Lightfoot—the twenty-two-year-old whose car-thieving skills had so disappointed Sergeant Roach a few years prior. "Wotcha wanna talk to us for?" Neil asked. He had the most reason to resent Barnwell's uniform, being unique in the group for having served a custodial sentence. He was also chewing gum, and he looked Barnwell up and down while masticating forcefully. He leered, the gum clenched between his top and bottom teeth. Barnwell felt the urge to prize them open and grab

Lightfoot's tonsils. Neil called out to Lewis, "Three pints of your best, mate. Chop, chop."

"I already said we're not open," Lewis called back. "Sit down and answer the officer's questions or you'll find yourself outside again looking at the pub sign."

"Why don't we have a quick chat over there, eh?" Barnwell said, guiding the three men to the table by the window. It was the brightest part of the pub. The lads were a little nervous as they sat down, eyeing Barnwell as though he might slap cuffs on them at any moment.

"I'm making enquiries about Jamie Reeves, the lad who was beaten up around the corner last night. About ten thirty."

"Yeah, so what? Did he die or something?" Duncan wondered as if he were asking the time.

"Your concern for Mr. Reeves's well-being is moving, Mr. Raynor," Barnwell said. He made a creditable attempt to focus on the young man's face rather than his odd haircut. "But no, he's still hanging on in intensive care."

"No list of suspects, then?" Kevin said.

"Probably just a mugging," Neil, the inept car thief, added. "Things go wrong, someone gets hit with a brick, and here we are."

"I don't know why I'm bothering!" Barnwell said. "Detective Chief Inspector Lightfoot seems to have solved this one all by himself!"

"Just saying, like," Neil said.

"First things first, lads. Where were you all last night?"

"Playing X-Box at mine," Kevin replied. "*Ring of Fire.*"

"*Awesome* game," Neil said.

"Imagine kung fu, but with magic," said Kevin.

"And swords," Duncan added.

"Fantastic, I'm sure. Did you go out at all?"

"Nah," Kevin said, "what with the rain. We were gonnu, but it was coming down straight."

Barnwell remembered his brother's rain-soaked laughter, his willingness to find fun in difficult circumstances. "And did anyone else join you at home playing *Ring of Fire*? Anyone who can vouch for you?"

Three different facial expressions communicated belligerence, indifference, and intransigence. "Nah, it was just us," Neil said.

"So, no one else? You realise that's what we call an 'alibi,' right?" said Barnwell. "Someone who can prove you were where you said you were."

"But we was all together, the three of us," Duncan complained. "I can alibi Kevin, then he can alibi Neil, then Neil can –"

"Sorry, DCI Raynor, it doesn't work like that. You can't alibi each other."

Ratty-looking Kevin sat up straight. "Look, are you dobbing us for this? We had nuthin' to do wiv it." He thrust out his chin.

Barnwell put his hands up. "Just routine, getting that bit out of the way. Keep your shirts on."

Kevin was incensed. "This is police harassment, this is!"

"Stick to comedy, Mr. Croft," Barnwell said. "Alright, look. Tell me what's been going on lately? On the streets, like."

"Oh, so now you want us to grass, is that it? Do your dirty work for you?"

"Not at all. I'm investigating the brutal attack on an innocent victim not much older than you. His attacker is at large. No one wants that. You lot keep your ear to the ground; you know what's going on. This is your chance to do your bit for the Gorey community." The lads stared back at Barnwell, mute.

"Look, did you hear anything, any news on the streets? You're well-connected lads. You see things, hear things. Did you see or hear anything about this beating?"

Apparently Duncan couldn't think of anything pithy to say, so he said, "I never, ever hit anyone. Scout's honour."

Kevin picked at his tracksuit top. He had the air of someone who'd seen the inside of too many pubs during long days without work. "If we do hear or see anyfin', I'm sure we can make an arrangement where it falls into yours, pronto-like, if ya know wha' I mean?"

Neil agreed. "We'll do anything for the filth." He grinned sarcastically.

Barnwell glared at him. "You can start by never calling us that again." He stood and left each of them his card. "Don't be strangers. And stay out of bleedin' trouble, the three of you." He headed back to the bar, leaving the three men in a morose, seething huddle around their table. "Lewis, a word if you don't mind."

"Yes, Bazza," Lewis said.

Barnwell leant over the bar. "Any drug business going on? Anyone dealing in the toilets out the back that you know of?"

Lewis rolled his eyes. "Not that I know about. If I did, I'd have told you. That kind of thing's not going on in my pub. We're the most popular in Gorey because we're clean, we're family-friendly, and we've got great local beers. The tourists love us, you know that. They're spilling out onto the pavement in the summer. That doesn't happen if there's a drug problem."

Drugs being the motive for the attack on Jamie Reeves would make more sense than anything else they had, but

Barnwell had to admit that Lewis was right. This was his beat, and the Fo'c'sle was not in the middle of a turf war or anything remotely like it. Gorey was remarkably drug-free, just a little bit here and there. Teenagers mostly, making a day trip to St. Helier to source a stash for the weekend. Confiscation and a chat with the parents was as much action as he'd ever had to take. But this case was unusual enough for Gorey that Barnwell was prepared to entertain the idea that the situation might have changed. "You'll let me know if you hear anything?"

"The very second," Lewis said. He dropped a shoulder and whispered, "Now skedaddle, would you?" It was past opening time, and the pub was filling up fast now with couples and families rushing to grab an early lunch.

As he left, Barnwell noticed that the three young men were sitting not in dejected silence but had begun an animated discussion. Duncan, in particular, seemed angry and frustrated. "Are you teed off about the state of the world, Duncan?" Barnwell asked the afternoon air as he walked back to the police station. "Or are you afraid I'm onto you?"

While Barnwell had been inside the pub, unbeknownst to him, Janice had peered into the front gardens of the houses on the street that led to it. Bloodstains on the pavement signposted where Jamie Reeves had met his attacker. At intervals, she pulled Carmen back to her. The young dog was finding all kinds of enticing smells but hadn't found anything that interested the sergeant.

Calling the few square feet of ground in front of the terraced houses "gardens" was a bit of an exaggeration.

They were more like small, walled flower beds, many left to nature or the less desirable habits of man. On windy and wet nights like the one they'd had previously, these small, boxed areas transformed into traps for leaves and discarded takeaway boxes.

Janice poked around, looking for something that might prove to be the weapon that had assailed Jamie Reeves. She did find a pile of house bricks, but Tomlinson had rejected those. Another house seemed to be storing the contents of a repair shop outside their front window, but none of the items were of sufficient weight to inflict deadly force.

With a sigh, and mindful of the time, Janice turned back. She didn't want to be caught deserting her post.

CHAPTER FOURTEEN

THE DAY WAS becoming warmer and more pleasant, so Graham chose to walk into town, carrying his jacket as he went. It would be healthier, he told himself, and a chance to get some sunshine. He followed some of the smaller roads, preferring residential streets to the main route into Gorey. The last of these, a street where the driveways with hybrid cars parked in them outnumbered those without, boasted a former residential property that had been converted into business premises.

The frontage was now all glass, through which could be seen two sleek, pale wooden desks topped with large screens and laptops. Chairs, presumably for clients, sat on one side of the desks, and set against the wall was a white leather sofa. A purple van sat outside on what had formerly been the front lawn and was now a tarmacked forecourt, the van's purple doors emblazoned with a big, yellow *S* intertwined with a similarly coloured *L*: the logo of Sanderson Landscaping.

Graham opened the door and walked inside to find himself immediately greeted by a disembodied but cheery

"Good morning!" The voice came from the back of the room. Graham turned in its direction to see a petite, attractive woman with auburn hair walking toward him. Her hair was pulled back into a ponytail which swished from side to side as she walked. She looked in her mid-twenties. A sprinkle of freckles dusted her nose and cheeks.

"Sorry to keep you waiting. We're digitising our records, and all the machines are in the back." The woman stuck out her hand. "Molly Duckworth, how can I help?" Molly struck Graham as bright and confident, if a little tired. There were dark circles under her red-rimmed eyes. He brought out his identification and explained the reason for his visit.

Molly's face dropped. "Oh!" Her open, welcoming expression turned to one of fear. "Is there any news?" Graham saw trepidation in her eyes.

"No change, I'm afraid. I'm here to ask you some questions."

Molly's face fell. "No change isn't bad news, I suppose, but it isn't good either."

"Jamie's being looked after by the best," Graham assured her. "One of my officers is there now, liaising with the medical staff and his family."

"Oh, okay," she said, relieved but obviously hoping for better news. "Should I call Mr. Sanderson?" she asked, still nervous. "He's with a client in St. Helier, but I don't think he'll be long."

"I'll wait. It's fine," Graham said. "We can talk for a bit, if that's alright." There was something about her demeanour, the way Molly's face had shown sudden pain when Graham mentioned Jamie's name. Perhaps it was concern for a friend or a much-valued colleague, though Graham sensed there was more to it. "You see, I don't know

Jamie, and the more we know, the more it helps to get to the bottom of things," he said, keeping things simple. "Maybe you could help me?"

Molly pondered for a moment, then made a decision and went to lock the front door. Using a remote control, she activated blinds which quietly sank to cover the windows. "Let's sit down," she said, gesturing to the white leather sofa. "Can I get you some tea? Some water?"

"Some water would be nice, thank you." Graham was warm from his walk. As Molly left to get his drink, he found his trusty notebook and pen and looked around the room. It was tidy and neat. The desks were cleared of papers. A few brochures were displayed in a wall rack. It was unnaturally free of signs of human activity. Graham wondered if anyone actually worked there.

"You don't ever expect that something like this will happen to someone you know. It's just terrible. I've been so upset," Molly said as she returned with Graham's water. She seemed relieved to be unburdening herself to someone, *anyone*. "I mean, one minute he's just walking along, showing up at work with a smile on his face, and the next . . ." Molly handed Graham his water. She caught his eye and her poised exterior suddenly crumpled into tears of anguish.

Embarrassed, she tugged a tissue from a box on a nearby desk and, composing herself again, sat on the sofa. Graham reminded himself that Molly was a *colleague* of Jamie's, and not a sister or girlfriend. But there seemed to be more to the situation, and he gave Molly time to collect herself. "Why didn't this happen to one of those awful people out there? Why did it have to be Jamie?" she cried, getting herself a new tissue and flapping it in front of her face.

His years in the force had never afforded David Graham a satisfactory answer to questions like this. Why did it rain one day and not another? Why did *this* plane hit a mountain and not *that* one? Weren't these events just random? Well, perhaps. Or perhaps not. And it was his job to find out which.

"Molly, what is it that you do here?" he began kindly.

"We're a landscaping business, specialising in hardscaping and native planting. The size of our projects can be quite large, and we work across all the islands, mostly with clients at the wealthier end of the spectrum. We also have corporate clients. About sixty percent of our revenue comes from projects, the other forty percent from ongoing maintenance contracts."

"And what do you do here?"

"I manage the office, making appointments, liaising with suppliers, that kind of thing. Mr. Sanderson does the designing and project management work, but Jamie . . ." Mollie's voice cracked. After a short pause, she recovered. "Jamie was starting to take some of that off him, lighten his load."

"I see," Graham said. "So, a trusted member of the team." Molly nodded. "How long had Jamie worked here?"

"He started as a labourer about ten years ago but worked his way up from there and was learning the software, doing classes online. He wanted to take over the business or start his own."

"Can you tell me when you last saw him? We're trying to understand his movements before the attack."

"He came in to get his things yesterday around three p.m. He'd wrapped his job for the week, but we didn't talk much. Just 'have a good weekend' as he left"—Molly's voice broke again—"and I suppose he walked home. He lives in a flat near the high street, near the Foc's'le and Ferret."

"And after Jamie finished work yesterday, what then? Did he say anything about his evening plans?"

Molly shook her head. "I asked him, as you do, but he just said he was planning to hang out at home, perhaps pop round to his parents—they're close—nothing special. He wasn't—isn't—a wild lad, not much of a drinker. The girls like him, though. They often do—landscape gardener, good shape, tanned, good-looking." Molly's voice hardened. "Once that old girlfriend of his was off the scene, they started buzzing around. But he was pretty easy come, easy go. No one in particular. Hard worker. When he took a break, he often simply sat and read seed catalogues."

"Does he own a car?" Graham knew that Jamie did not, but it often amazed him what information was shared following a seemingly innocuous question.

"No, he has a licence so he can drive the firm's vehicles, but no car of his own."

"So, his job would bring him into direct contact with your clients and he'd travel all over the islands, is that right?"

"Oh, yes," Molly said. "He was well-liked; our clients would request him specifically. That's partly why Mr. Sanderson gave him more responsibility."

"And what had he been working on most recently?"

Molly straightened her green skirt and took a deep breath. "He finished the job up at the Granby place recently . . . That's the modern, custom-architected home up on the bluff. Do you know it? Above Crescent Bay?" Graham nodded. "They've recently renovated it, practically rebuilding it from scratch. The landscaping was the final part of the project. The place was worth millions *before*, but Mr. Sanderson designed them a fantastic garden and pool. Who knows how much it's worth now. Jamie was proud of the work they'd done. But once it was finished, he was straight onto another job just outside St. Helier. We're very busy right now. With the weather as it is, we have to make hay while the sun shines."

Graham's pen never stopped. "Now, I know this is difficult, but can you think of anyone who might have . . ."

Molly stopped him. "I haven't thought about anything else, not since I got the news. I was up all night thinking about it. I figured, maybe the same as you . . . that it could have been an old client who was unhappy with our work, or someone who'd felt Mr. Sanderson had ripped them off. I even called up five or six recent clients when I got in this morning just to hear their reaction to the news, to see if I could hear guilt in their voice."

"That's fine detective work," Graham said warmly, although he didn't approve. "Did anything come of it?"

"No, and I decided not to continue down the list I'd made."

"Why?"

Folded in her lap, apparently peacefully, Molly's hands suddenly clenched. They turned white. "I popped into the hospital. Shut up here and took off. Couldn't help myself, even if I couldn't get in to see him, which I knew I probably wouldn't. I mean, why would I? I'm not family." Graham raised his eyebrows, prompting Molly to get back on track. "But then neither was she." Molly closed her eyes and breathed in through her nose, pressing her lips together so fiercely they also turned white. "Anyhow, I didn't get any further than the ICU reception because I saw her . . . *She* was there. With that man of hers."

"Wh—" Graham heard a key in the front door. They both rose to meet Adrian Sanderson, proprietor of Sanderson Landscaping.

CHAPTER FIFTEEN

ADRIAN SANDERSON WAS a powerful man with a heavy build. Bulging forearms, the result of years wielding a shovel, protruded from his purple polo shirt emblazoned with the business's logo stitched neatly in gold.

"Adrian, this is . . ." Molly paused, having forgotten Graham's name.

"Detective Inspector Graham, Gorey Constabulary."

"Adrian Sanderson," the man said gruffly. He shook Graham's hand. The inspector suppressed a wince. Sanderson pulled up a chair and sat, his feet apart, elbows resting on his thighs, ready to hear what Graham had to say.

"Do they think Jamie'll . . . you know . . . wake up?" he asked, his brow knotted with concern. "We're all worried. My wife's in tears."

"I would be guessing, I'm afraid," Graham said. "And that's no use to anyone. I wish I had better news. They're doing everything they can," he added. "I'm down here making a few enquiries. We don't have any witnesses or motive as yet."

Sanderson nodded. "Fire away. Happy to do anything that might help."

"Can you tell me how you found Jamie as an employee? Miss Duckworth here has told me he was taking on more responsibility."

"He was a great guy, well liked. Never late, did everything he was asked to a high standard. He's been with us for ten years, practically since he left school. He was like family really. The business has thrived, in good part thanks to his hard work, so it only seemed fair to involve him more in the running of the business. He was a young, fit, strong man who wanted to go places. He was even studying for his landscaping exams. Terrible he should end up like this."

"Have there been any arguments with clients? Any complaints?" Sanderson shook his head. "He's been leading the team on the Granby place most recently, but they were overjoyed with his work. Mrs. Granby couldn't stop going on about it."

"Anyone been enquiring after him?" Graham tried. Another shake. "And you've never had a need to reprimand him or drug test him?"

"Not at all. He was always as fresh as a daisy when he arrived for work. Can't say that for everyone in our business. It's one reason why we don't work Saturdays as a rule. Too many hangovers from the night before. But Jamie was never any trouble. A model employee." Sanderson sat back in his chair. He glanced at his watch and jumped. "Look, if that's all, I'm late for a meeting with a fella at the lumber yard."

"One more thing, Mr. Sanderson. Can you tell me what you were doing last night?"

"Sure, I was at home with my wife. We watched the *MasterChef* semifinal. She likes that."

"Thank you." Graham made no move to leave. He

offered his card to Sanderson who, with a jangle of his keys, made his way out. But before he left, Sanderson turned and said, his expression sincere, "You know this already, but I'll say it again: everyone's with you, Mr. Graham. The whole town. We want to nail whoever did this to Jamie. Anything you need, even if it's a potted geranium to help you get your thinking caps on, just ask."

The detective inspector nodded. "Thanks, Mr. Sanderson. We'll do everything in our power to resolve this."

Sanderson closed the door behind him, and they heard an engine start. "That wasn't all quite true. He was angry with Jamie," Molly said in a low voice. "A few weeks ago."

"Angry? About what?" Graham said, making more notes.

"The job at the Granby place. They worked together on the final costings. Mr. Sanderson wanted to charge a much higher rate, thousands more, but Jamie argued against it."

"Why so?"

Molly sighed. She split her ponytail in two and pulled to tighten it. "They talked about this all the time. Or should I say argued about it." She seemed embarrassed. "'Class warfare,' Adrian called it. Mr. Sanderson has . . . what shall we call it? An *elastic* approach to pricing. Says the richest people on Jersey should pay more than the others. You know, clients like the Granbys or that woman with the ridiculous dog, Mrs. Padalka-Lyons, or whatever she calls herself. They can afford it, Adrian says. Jamie didn't agree, said it was unfair, that everyone should pay the same. He said Adrian was punishing people for being successful. Adrian argued he was just levelling things up, Robin Hood-like, standing up for the little people.

"It was a bone of contention between them. When Jamie was ready, I reckon this would have been the reason more than any that he'd leave and start up his own business. That way, he could have run things the way he wanted. And if he did that, set up in competition with Sanderson Landscaping, things would get tricky for Adrian. The people are the business really. It isn't a lot different from hairdressing in that respect."

Graham made notes, giving Molly time to provide details. "Their arguments were brief and noisy," she said. "And once they had their say, they each seemed to forget about it until the next time. They would get on perfectly fine in between. Of course, Adrian won. It's his business. He can do as he likes. But there were tensions. It was the only thing they didn't agree on."

"Was there ever any violence?"

"No, none. Adrian might look like he could flatten an entire rugby team, but I've never seen or even *heard* of him throwing his weight around. Jamie neither."

Where have I heard that *before?* Some of the most memorable moments in Graham's career involved people finally realising the truth when some utterly trustworthy soul who "was devoted to his friends and family," the same decent, upstanding citizen who "wouldn't harm a fly," was arrested for having bludgeoned someone to death or something equally heinous. It was always "absolutely unthinkable," right up until it wasn't.

"Tell me about your hospital visit, Molly." Graham was beginning to wish he'd brought Harding with him. She would have done well with Molly.

"The ICU was so scary," Molly said candidly. "I was terrified there'd be an emergency while I was there, that someone would die. They all seemed *so* ill in their glass bubbles, strung up to machines and medicines."

"What about Jamie's visitors, the ones that bothered you?"

"Her name," Molly said, "is Paula Lascelles. She and Jamie were a couple for a long time, until about a year ago. I could never see what he saw in her. I thought she was toxic. Spiteful, manipulative."

"What happened between them?" Graham asked, keeping his tone low. "A fight?"

"Not just one," Molly recalled. "Plenty of them, for weeks and weeks. He'd come into work looking so depressed, wouldn't talk to anyone about it at first. But I've been through my share of relationship ups and downs, so I told him I might be able to help."

"Sounds like you were a good friend."

Molly glanced first at the front door, then at the back. Looking down, she stared hard at the carpet. "No," she confessed. "I was selfish."

"Selfish? How?"

"Paula wanted to leave Jersey. She said it was too small. People get all excited about big city life, but when they get there, it's not what they expect. That's what I told Jamie. He had a good job that he enjoyed, there was enough money. People liked him. He had lots of friends here. I told him, 'Making a change like that is risky, expensive in lots of ways you don't expect'. You know what I mean?"

"I do," Graham said honestly. He remembered his first move to the city as a younger man. It had been intimidating. His mind wandered to Roach. He wondered what the young sergeant had really made of his week in London with the Met.

"So, we talked it over, and I suppose I encouraged him to let her go. I mean, if she really wanted to be in London, paying those prices, with all that pollution . . ."

"You discouraged Jamie from leaving," Graham concluded. "But how was that selfish of you?"

Molly looked at the floor again. It was covered in the type of durable carpet tile that could withstand a nuclear holocaust. "I . . . wanted him to . . . stay." She quickly lifted her head, fire in her eyes. "I might as well tell you. I was—am—in love with him."

"Ah."

"Yes," Molly admitted, pain and regret overwhelming her. Her chin wobbled. "And if I hadn't persuaded him to stay, he wouldn't be lying in that hospital bed." Tears cascaded down her sweet, pretty, freckled face. "Now, *all* because of me, he's . . ." She sniffed. "Besides, he never even noticed me. I was just the 'girl in the office.' Just a mate. A helpful one, but a mate nonetheless."

"Molly, I'd like you to listen to me," Graham said. Her bright, tear-gleaming gaze rose to meet his. Behind the upset, he could see her hopes for some form of redemption. "The only person responsible for Jamie's situation is the person who attacked him. And we're going to find out whoever that was. You are not to blame, okay?" Molly gulped, her eyes still on his, her eyelids twitching. "One final thing. Where were you yesterday evening?"

"I was at my friend's house. Catherine Marsh. She was throwing a dinner party. There were six of us. You can confirm with her. I was there till gone midnight. I helped her clear up."

"Thank you. You've been very helpful, Molly. Stay in touch. Call me straight away, day or night," Graham said, "if you think of anything else, or if Mr. Sanderson says something I might need to know about."

Tears forming again, Molly nodded. "Okay." She quickly dabbed at her eyes with her tissue. "The new boyfriend, you should talk to him. Big guy. Very strong, like Adrian, but young and . . . well, Jamie told me about him. That he had been inside for something. Said he was a bit dense."

"Easily manipulated, you mean?"

"Hmph, he must be. Paula wouldn't be with him otherwise. She homes in on the easily manipulated like a heat-seeking missile. If Paula told him that Jamie was still holding a torch for her," Molly said, developing her theory out loud, "he might have done something, mightn't he?"

"And would there have been any truth in that?"

"What do you mean?" she asked.

"That the new boyfriend had reason to feel jealous?"

"I don't think so. But there wouldn't have needed to be any truth behind it for Paula to suggest something. I've known her for years, since school. She was nasty even then. Beautiful, but nasty."

"I can tell you're very fond of Jamie," Graham said. "I know this must be very difficult."

Molly blew her nose. "I won't deny it's been terrible since I heard the news." Graham stood to leave. "Have I helped?" she asked, her hands folded, tight and anxious. "All I want to do is help. I want to catch who did this."

"Yes, you've helped very much."

Graham left her to make his way back to the station. He decided to take a detour that took him through fields. An ascending, bright yellow sun was painting them brilliant colours, and for half a mile, he chose to enjoy the play of light on the grasses of the meadow he walked through.

His phone rang. "Sir?" said Roach at the other end.

Graham knew from his tone that Roach felt he had something. "What have you got, Sergeant?"

"I'm still at the hospital, sir. Been keeping an eye on two of Jamie's visitors. Something just doesn't seem right."

Graham stopped amidst the quiet of the lane he was walking along and took a moment to be grateful for the instincts of his officers. "Don't tell me. Paula Lascelles and her simple bruiser of a new boyfriend."

Roach was silent for five seconds. When he spoke, he sounded indignant. "Well, sir, I have to say, that's hardly fair."

"Eh?"

"It's no fun playing 'cops and robbers' with you, boss. Not when you're bloomin' *clairvoyant.*"

CHAPTER SIXTEEN

WHEN HE GOT back to the station, Graham found Barnwell manning the reception desk. "Did you find those lads?"

"Yeah, I did, sir. They weren't of any immediate help. But I've got my eye on them, and they're looking out for us. I'll follow up with them in a day or so if we need them."

"Fancy doing a bit of interviewing with me?"

It had taken three phone calls and eventually a threat to use his powers of arrest before the haughty and uncoopera- tive Miss Lascelles agreed to attend the police station and speak to Graham on his patch. "Couldn't we have done it down at the hospital, sir?" Barnwell said.

"Wrong atmosphere." The efforts Paula had made to avoid coming to the station hadn't endeared Graham to her or her boyfriend. "I don't need them surrounded by compas- sionate people in blue scrubs making me look like a monster next to a barely alive victim. I want them staring down the barrel of my fully loaded interview technique."

"Going to go hard on them?" Barnwell asked. "Roach said we'd be right to. Reckons he's got a funny feeling."

"He's developing instincts," said Graham. "So, let's respect them. This couple dragging their heels doesn't look good either."

"Right, boss," Barnwell said. The constable, initially very reluctant to get involved in formal interviews, had become sanguine about them. Sometimes he even looked forward to their unpredictability. He didn't consider thinking on his feet a strength of his, but with practice, it was becoming easier to formulate a line of questioning on the fly when presented with new information from an interviewee. He was getting nimbler, but no one would be asking him to perform the police equivalent of the quick step anytime soon.

"This is very inconvenient," Paula grumbled to DI Graham as soon as she saw him. "We had to take a taxi."

"We were expecting you half an hour ago, Miss Lascelles."

"We got lost."

"I find that hard to believe. Every taxi driver on the island knows where we are. Follow me, please."

Graham led Paula and Matthew to the interview room, and the couple sat down at the table. Once they were settled, he closed the door and had a final word with Barnwell. "How many times," he wondered, "have suspects come in, all teed off and indignant, only for us to find . . ."

"That they're the guilty party?" Barnwell said. "I've lost count, boss."

Summoning a smorgasbord of wisdom, Graham said, "Remember, beer before whisky, cart before horse, and thought before speech. Alright?"

"Whatever you say, sir."

"Capital."

Graham swung open the door and found a study in human opposites. One was an attractive woman, sunglasses tucked into her blonde hair. She wore a white A-line dress printed with red tulips, belted at the waist. Around her neck was tied an expensive, bright-red scarf. Before she sat down, Graham had noticed Paula Lascelles wore scarlet shoes. He wondered how she walked in them. They had vertiginous heels. Under the table, Paula crossed her legs, a foot bearing one of the aforementioned heels jiggling furiously. Above the table, she rubbed the fingers of her right hand with the thumb of her left. She looked down at them, her lips pushed together in a pout. She seemed deep in thought.

Next to her was the muscle-bound six-footer with huge hands and a vacant expression who was her boyfriend. Graham had learned that his name was Matthew Walker. He wore a T-shirt with a brewery logo plastered across it and baggy shorts with pockets on the sides. He was as still as a statue as he stared straight ahead at the blank wall.

"Thank you for coming in. As mentioned to you earlier, this is not a formal interview. It will not be taped, and you are free to leave at any time. Now," Graham said, moving on quickly in case Paula felt like another round of complaining, "Sergeant Roach has given me the basics, so I won't keep you long. You are not under arrest—"

"I should think not," Paula interrupted.

"You are here voluntarily, helping us with our enquiries as we fill in some details around the attack on Mr. Reeves."

"Good," Matthew said. He pulled at the neck of his T-shirt. "Kinda cluster-phobic in here."

Ah, excellent, we've identified the brains of the outfit. "I'd like to better understand your relationship with Jamie," Graham began. "And learn where you were last night."

"Why?" Paula asked at once.

"When investigating violent incidents, these kinds of things tend to interest me," Graham replied evenly.

"Wait . . ." Paula said, her jaw dropping, "you think *I* had something to do with the attack on Jamie?"

"I don't think anything, Miss Lascelles. I am simply making enquiries. Can you both account for your where-abouts yesterday evening when Mr. Reeves was attacked? Around ten, ten thirty p.m."

Matthew shifted in his seat, suddenly concerned. "I never even seen the guy before I saw him lying in that 'ospital bed all beat up. What's it gotta do wi' me?"

Barnwell was taking notes on his iPad, but he stopped and squared with Matthew. "Big lads like you and me," he said encouragingly, "get a bad reputation. Isn't that right, mate?"

"Yeah, I s'pose."

"People are always assuming we're brawlers, or rugby players, or the kind of bloke who'll sink nine pints on a night out."

Matthew smirked. "My record's sixteen."

"So, it's best if you remove any reputation you might have, however inaccurate, by answering our questions quickly and honestly."

Graham intervened. "Let's return to the evening in question. Where were you both?"

"At my mum and dad's place in St. Helier. Two thirty-two Trent Road," Paula replied. "We flew down from London for my nan's ninetieth birthday."

"What do you do in London?" Barnwell asked her.

"I'm assistant to the deputy head of European sales' executive secretary."

Barnwell was more concise in his notes: *Photocopying*. "And was Nana's party still raging on Friday evening?"

"It's tonight," Paula said. "I'm supposed to be helping set up, but I've spent the morning at the hospital and now here. My mum will *not* be happy. We were planning to go out last night, but I was tired, had a headache. So, we stayed in, watched some telly."

"What was on?" Graham asked. He was writing continuously.

"*MasterChef*. Semifinal round," Paula said.

"It was really good," opined Matthew.

"Who went through to the final?"

The big lad shrugged. "I went to the fridge a lot. Can't really remember. Not my thing, you know? But Paula's mum loves it."

"It was that woman with the red glasses," Paula said. "The one with the teeth. I forget her name."

"Yeah, her," Matthew agreed.

Paula gave a quick shrug and a small smile. "All those desserts make me want to eat for miles."

"What time did you turn in?" Graham asked, making very deliberate eye contact with them both. It was one of his oldest tricks, and it nearly always worked.

"Before midnight," Paula said.

"After twelve," Matthew said at the same time.

A raised eyebrow. "Could we perhaps reach an agreement?" asked Graham.

"Mum and I were going to take Nana shopping this morning," Paula reminded Matthew, her eyes narrowing, "and we had to do all the party prep, if you remember. It was going to be a busy day. So, I made sure to get to bed before twelve."

"Whatever you say, Paulie." Matthew shrugged.

"*Don't* call me that," she rasped.

"Can anyone verify your movements?"

"Mum and Dad could, but they went to bed at ten." *So, no one then.*

Graham moved on. "Tell us a little about how your relationship with Jamie came to an end."

The two policemen soon learned this was by far Paula's favourite subject. "I applied to colleges only on Jersey because of him. I limited my career choices, turned down interviews in London and Southampton, all for him. I *sacrificed* for Jamie Reeves, and when the time finally came, he just couldn't find it in himself to commit to me. Jersey always came first for him." The bitterness was right there on the surface. "I couldn't stand it anymore."

"So, you left?" Barnwell said.

"We took 'a break,' but I knew I had to move on. Nine years together . . ." she said. Each of those years now seemed to weigh on her, the memories poisoned by the ever-present "what ifs" and "if onlys" that always attend a relationship breakdown. "Nine years. What a waste of the best years of my life." And then Paula broke down, only comforted by Matthew's tree-trunk arm after an awkward delay.

Barnwell watched him closely throughout Paula's performance, and he did think it a performance. He looked for signs of anger or jealousy in the man but saw none. Matthew did seem to be as thick as a log.

In between sobs, Paula made a muffled sound. "I'm sorry, did you say something?" Graham asked.

"Molly was a problem," she said, sniffing. "I shouldn't be saying this, but you're investigating what happened, and you should know everything." Staring at her even as his pen moved across his notebook's page, Paula had the detective inspector's undivided attention. "She was very flirtatious. Jamie's a good-looking guy, it wasn't unusual. I was alright with it. Well, at first, anyway," she said. "If I did say anything, he would laugh it off. Said they were just work-mates, colleagues, you know, just two people having fun, there was nothing to it. But I'm quite sure she didn't see it that way."

"Molly came between you," Graham commented. "That can't have made things easy."

"No, and that's another thing. He was really into Molly for a while. When he and I were on a break. At least that's what I heard. But he stopped it, thank goodness, when we got back together. Before we went on another break. A permanent one. After that, I don't know. It was none of my business."

"Stopped it?" Graham blinked. "Stopped what?"

CHAPTER SEVENTEEN

"MOLLY," PAULA EXPLAINED. "The other kind. Not the girl he worked with. Ecstasy. MDMA. You know," she said, embarrassed. "Pretty stupid to be telling the police, I suppose, but you should know everything."

The couple watched Graham pinch the bridge of his nose and almost laugh to himself, while Barnwell sat up very straight and typed into his iPad as fast as he could.

"So, you don't think Jamie continued taking drugs after you split up?" Barnwell said.

"I just said I don't know, Constable. It was none of my business."

"Did he ever mention selling anything, making any money?"

"No, no, that's not how it was. It was just for his own use, recreational," she replied. Then, more determined, "Selling? No, never."

Graham leant in. "It's very important that you're honest with us, Paula. You won't get into any trouble . . ."

"To my knowledge, he was never involved in the dealing of drugs."

"When was the last time you saw Mr. Reeves, Paula?" Graham asked her.

"When I saw him in his hospital bed."

"And before that?"

"A year ago, when I left. I haven't seen him since."

"So, no contact at all? No phone calls, texts?"

"We exchanged a few texts, but that's all."

"Anything recent?"

Paula eyed Graham warily but held his gaze. "No."

"Are you sure?"

"She said 'no,'" Matthew reminded the two officers. "More than once. That okay for you?"

"We prefer it when people speak for themselves, Matthew. Maybe we should interview you separately?" Barnwell's temperature had risen with the big man's intervention.

"Perhaps later," Graham said, closing his notebook, "but that'll do for now. Thank you for your time."

The pair couldn't exit the station fast enough, leaving Barnwell to consider events with Graham in his office.

"Turf war?" Graham surmised. "I mean, it's possible. Makes as much sense as anything. But there's no evidence. It's a big leap from knowing he took the odd molly to him dealing."

"Except for the fact he's now lying in a hospital bed in critical condition."

"Hmm. What did you make of Mr. Walker? Molly at Sanderson's said he'd been inside."

"Matthew? He's a big lad," Barnwell said. "Gives a bloke confidence to do certain things."

"Like what things?"

"Like defending his girlfriend during a police interview or against an old boyfriend."

"Very manly of him. But I'll tell you this," Graham announced. "There's more courage still in telling the truth. And I'm not sure if either of them have yet been guilty of *that*."

Graham began pacing between his desk and the office door, as he often did. "For two people who spent yesterday evening together, their versions of events varied a little too much for my liking. A young couple hitting a roadblock when alibiing each other should always be subject to more investigation. It bothers me that they didn't agree when they went to bed."

"It was just that one detail, sir," said Barnwell. "Easily done."

"No, Constable, they also disagreed about who won the *MasterChef* semi."

"Well, Matthew said he couldn't remember . . ."

"Answer me this, Barnwell. What kind of person watches an exciting hour of televised cooking and then completely forgets who finished first?"

Barnwell pulled a face. "Someone who can down four pints in that same hour?"

"Even if he'd been completely felled by drink, he can't have missed the soufflé. I mean, God knows how she did it."

As Graham started another slow, thoughtful perambulation about his office, Barnwell stared at him as he mentally weighed up whether to ask the question that was on the tip of his tongue. "You, erm, you managed to catch that one then, sir? The semifinal?" The very idea of Graham avidly watching a cooking show stretched credulity.

Graham stopped pacing. "Laura likes it. What's the problem?"

"Nothing," Barnwell said quickly. "Nothing at all."

"So, what's your theory, Constable?"

"I can see three possibilities, sir, all involving that goon as the perp." Barnwell's cognitive reflexes had smartened up in the time DI Graham had been his senior officer. He'd anticipated Graham's question and already considered the options.

"Okay, what are they?"

"Paula gets Matthew all riled up about Jamie and how awful he was . . . And then," Barnwell said, "in a moment of weakness, when his defences were lowered and his brains hobbled by drink, he takes it upon himself to defend her honour by bashing her ex-boyfriend over the head with a heavy object."

"Okay, next."

"She tells him to do it, sir. And he obliges because he's as thick as pig—"

"Yep, okay, got it. And the last one?"

"There's still something going on between the girlfriend and our victim, or Mighty Matthew thinks there is, and he decides to put his rival out of the picture." The two men fell silent as they considered the feasibility of these three theories.

Graham spoke first. "What do you reckon?"

"Bit much?"

"I can see it, just about. Neither of them are towering intellects, but he seemed like he had a gap where his brain should be. She seemed petty and chippy. Certainly unpleasant enough to wind him up, set the bomb off, then stand back and watch the chaos. Her mum's house is only five minutes from where Reeves was attacked."

"But are they capable of such a serious assault?"

"They could have overplayed their hand." Graham

drummed his fingers on one of his old filing cabinets. He had a set of two that reached up to his chest. They predated the war and were made of solid oak. When laden with files, the drawers were heavy. Janice, Roach, and Barnwell complained every time they had to retrieve a document from one. The inevitable procrastination surrounding filing case documents would have risen to critical proportions had Janice not implemented a strict rota that, because they were his filing cabinets, even included Graham.

Filing was well below his pay grade, but the detective inspector shouldered the chore because he loved the cabinets, how they looked, and the sense of history they offered. He liked to think that they survived the war because they were hidden out of the Nazi's sight and had played a part in the resistance, storing important documents perhaps. It gratified him to think he still found a use for them.

"So, she's manipulative and resentful. He's a heavy, vulnerable to suggestion or jealousy, and there are inconsistencies in their stories," Barnwell summed up.

"Don't forget that she's lying."

"Lying, sir?"

"Yes, or at least not being entirely honest. Ms. Lascelles said she and Jamie had had no contact recently. Said so twice, decisively. Walker warned us off." Graham picked up an evidence bag from his desk. It contained Jamie Reeves's phone. "This phone, via Jack, says otherwise. Ms. Paula Lascelles has been texting Jamie Reeves in recent days, trying to set up a meeting. I wonder if she mentioned *that* to Mighty Matthew."

"Did Reeves reply?"

"No, and that might constitute a motive."

CHAPTER EIGHTEEN

I T WAS AS picturesque as anywhere on the island. A broad bay swept inland to the south and then curved outward to form impressive bluffs. There at the top, where the tall, white rock was met by cooling onshore winds, stood a two-storey home, palatial both in construction and setting. Up ahead, Janice saw it first, and like most people, felt immediately impoverished and envious.

"Not bad, eh?" she said to Graham, who was driving the station's unmarked police car with his usual care and precision. "What did you say the Granbys do for a living?"

"No idea what the wife does, but he's some kind of high-end investment manager. Friend to the great and the good and the extremely wealthy. The website's still there on my phone if you want to look at it." He nodded at the phone, stuck as if by magic but in fact by magnet onto his dashboard. Graham had come a long way in his willingness to adopt technology. Technically he was a digital native, having been born during the information age, but he didn't act like one. Encouraged by his younger subordinates, however, he was coming along, persuaded by the opportunities technology provided.

Granby Investments' webpage was smartly designed and reeked of affluence and luxury. Janice said, "I don't think my police salary would be enough for them to even open the door."

"Me neither," Graham replied. "But then we don't need money, Sergeant, just our police IDs. Gets us in places we'd never get in otherwise."

"I hope you're not suggesting what it sounds like you're suggesting," Janice said. She didn't approve of the availing of unofficial benefits that came with being a member of the force. She wanted to get places because of her own hard, exemplary efforts, not because of some favour she'd been offered because she was a copper. Although she had skipped the line in Ethel's a few times.

Graham hesitated. "Of course not. Anyway, Mr. Granby should prove a bit more welcoming in his own home. We'll avoid pouncing on him in his office until we need to turn the screws."

"Not sure we could even if we wanted to, sir. I'm fairly sure that one forty-five Marett Lane is an old stone cottage surrounded by wildflowers. Pretty, but small. Definitely not corporate."

"Hmm, just a business address then. Must do all his work from home. Wealth management is an under-the-table business—who you know, not what you know, special handshakes kind of thing. It'll be interesting to meet him."

They followed the quiet coastal road until it forked. The options were to continue down the coast or turn onto a freshly paved track that led to the Granby residence. Now they were closer, they couldn't see the house from their position. It was set lower down on the bluff and hidden from view. Graham turned, and they trundled down the narrow, tarmacked path.

A large, black security gate blocked their way. Graham stopped the car and found the intercom button on a pillar beside the gate. While he waited for a response, he looked around and noticed the discreet black camera tracking his movements. It emitted a slight buzzing sound.

In the car, Harding read more about Silas Granby and his work. His professional profile was littered with photos from all over the world—business meetings in Singapore, Cape Town, Athens, and London, and that was just the first page. In each of the photos, Silas Granby projected a smart, professional, smiling image whether photographed chairing a meeting or on the golf course. Harding wondered whether he would be as equally relaxed in private while questioned by a pair of police officers about a serious attack on someone who had recently completed work at his house.

"Ready to see how the other half live?" Graham said as he climbed back into the car.

Inside the security gate, in the middle of a bright green patch of closely cut lawn amidst an expanse of rough, a small flag fluttered on a pole. "His putting green has more square footage than the house Jack and I are looking for." Harding growled. "We would be happy with two bedrooms and a little garden. And it'd still be smaller than that piece of grass." She gave a strange, dismissive snort. The electronic gate swung open. They kept driving, and as they drove, the house materialised seemingly from the ground.

Two powerful cars—one black, the other a deep violet—were parked on a broad, gravel area in front of the house. They gleamed in the sunshine. Beyond them, more cars sat visible in a garage, a space which could have comfortably sheltered a light aircraft.

"Oh, wow," Harding said. "They *really* went to town, didn't they?" The house—*compound* might have been more appropriate—was perched on the cliff in a blithe defiance of gravity.

"Guess he's not worried about erosion then," Graham said. "This place is only a couple of bad storms away from ending up in the drink."

"Some people don't think they need to worry about things like that," Janice replied.

"Had to have got it through the surveyors and coastal people though." In response, Janice rubbed her fingertips together. Graham nodded. "Maybe. He might have offered them a cash incentive, but if he's that reckless with his private investments, I'm not sure I'd trust him with mine."

Granby's vision for his home was a pair of contoured, semi-subterranean wings. They emerged from the sloping ground, extending toward the cliff's edge. "Wonder how they managed that," Janice said.

"An architect who commands the highest fees in his profession, I should imagine," Graham responded. The walls at the back of the property were comprised nearly entirely of glass, held in place by only the smallest amount of concrete bonding. Even the ceilings of the rooms were made of massive glass sheets. All the light gave the Granby residence an airy, maritime feel, and surely some of the best views in all the Channel Islands. "Oh, I see how it works. It's nice, isn't it? But I can't figure out if the shape might invite people to jump off the cliff or aliens to attempt a landing."

"Either way, looks like a public safety problem," Janice said, thoroughly hacked off and resentful now. "But yes, sure, it's okay, I suppose." Then, a flash of honesty: "I'm just too jealous to admit it's fab."

They parked on the gravel by the two fancy cars and walked down three steps to the discreet entryway. Graham pressed the bell. As he waited for the door to open, he looked around and noticed more cameras—one above him, another at the corner of the house, and two on an outbuilding. From behind the door came a noisy kerfuffle. A woman was arguing with her dog, which was ready either to bolt for freedom the moment the door opened or savage the new arrivals. Graham couldn't tell which.

"The police!" the woman said, opening the thick, wooden door while still trying to calm her overexcited dog, a ball of fluff out of which poked two black, beady eyes, a button nose, and a pink tongue which, due to all the barking, was clearly visible. The dog was tucked under the woman's arm. "Now, why would they come to see us?" the woman asked her dog.

She looked in her early forties, although it was hard to tell. Janice suspected fillers, a nose job, maybe something around the jaw. She possessed a heavy East European accent and was dressed for comfort and exposure—tight, lilac leggings topped with a stretchy white tank top. There was also more gold about her person than Janice had seen in the jeweller's she'd visited shopping for wedding bands.

Graham waved his ID. "Detective Inspector Graham, ma'am. This is Sergeant Harding. I wonder if we could . . ."

Ceaseless in its yapping, the dog was apparently taking a dislike to these two guests. "Enough, Willow!" The woman patted the dog. It growled a warning but stopped barking. The woman looked at the two officers. "Sorry, he's a prize Pomeranian."

Graham ignored the suggestion that he follow up on this statement. He was not at all interested in the dog. "Are you Mrs. Katerina Granby?"

"Katya, please."

"We would like to ask you and your husband a few questions. We called earlier." Graham eyed the dog, which eyed him back as though Graham might suddenly spring at his owner's throat. "It concerns someone who worked on your landscaping."

"Landscaping?" Mrs. Granby said as though the word were new to her. "Ah, you mean the garden?"

"That'd be one way of putting it," Janice muttered before speaking more loudly. "This is quite a home you have, Mrs. Granby." The sergeant had not been quite able to adopt a professional detachment with respect to the interviewee's circumstances, and it showed in her tone. Graham shot her a "do better" look. Harding took the hint. She lifted her chin and lowered her shoulders.

Katya rolled her eyes. "All of this?" she said. "This is all Silas. All his idea. I would have been happy with a cottage, you know? But he says it's for his clients. But of course, please forgive me. You must come inside and sit down. I will tell my husband you're here." As Katya turned, she pressed one of a series of buttons on a pad mounted on the wall by the door.

Graham bid Janice go ahead of him through the marble entryway and into a remarkably spacious, bright living room. Once again, he noted the cameras. They were more discreet inside the house, smaller and recessed into the ceilings. Only someone hell-bent on security would have configured it into the very structure of the building. Far more usually, security measures were tacked on afterward. "Heavens," he breathed, momentarily gobsmacked by what he saw. "The *view*." Beyond the curve of a bespoke, off-white, semicircular couch, through the floor-to-ceiling windows, the English Channel glittered brightly, as calm as a daydream.

"My husband, he likes the ocean," Katya explained, setting down her dog and ushering the officers to the couch. Willow took a few paces then stopped, eyeing the guests from the middle of the room. "His parents had a place on the coast in Norfolk." She pronounced it *Nor-fork*, apparently certain this was correct. "He grew up by the sea." She gestured outside. "It makes him happy. Please, sit."

"Now I know," Janice said quietly to Graham, looking around, "what I want in our living room when Jack and I get our house." She followed Mrs. Granby's direction and sat, experiencing her very first, and probably her last, £30,000 sofa.

Graham did the same while Katya sat opposite on a high-backed chair. Willow sniffed around, still suspicious of Graham but content not to do him violence just yet.

"Now, you said the landscaping?" Katya prompted.

"Yes, I'm afraid one of the young men who worked on your project has been badly beaten."

Katya stared at him. "You mean beating someone at a game? Like, tennis?"

Janice took care of this. "I'm sorry, no. We mean that he was attacked. He was badly injured."

"Attacked?" Katya gasped. "But why?"

On his phone, Graham pulled up the good-quality photo of Jamie his parents had provided Roach earlier. "Do you remember seeing this man around your property? His name is Jamie Reeves." Graham tilted the screen and watched carefully as she took in the picture.

"Tall, yes?" Katya ran her hand from side to side above her head. "A tall man. And strong. They *all* were strong.

There were three of them, and sometimes their manager guy, but I think I remember the man you talk about."

"How long did they work on your property?" Graham asked.

"It was . . . three weeks, nearly. Silas, he had so many ideas. You saw the golf place and the garage and everything? There was *so much* work to do. The young man . . . James?"

"Jamie," Janice said.

"He worked very, very hard. Super strong."

With Katya's memories of Jamie apparently firm, Graham pressed further. "Did you ever speak to him?"

"Yes, a little. I went out with the cups of tea on a tray. Like you English do. Chatted a little."

"What was your impression of him?"

"He seemed a nice man. We didn't speak much. Hallo, how are you? That sort of thing. He seemed a little more, how do you say . . . important than the others." She smiled quickly as she found the right words. "In charge." She shifted in her seat slightly. "Except for the manager guy, of course. He was the most important."

"Did you ever see him speaking to his boss, Adrian Sanderson?"

Blinking quickly, Katya searched her memory, but before she could answer, she was cut off by the bounding arrival of her husband. "I'm sorry to keep you waiting," Silas Granby said as he paced down a connecting hallway. He came from a darkened part of the house that was built inside the cliff top into the light, open-plan living area. "The different time zones, important phone calls, you understand. Ah, I see you've met my wife." Graham and Janice stood as Granby entered. They shook hands. Granby walked to stand next to his wife and took her hand as he leant against the tall back of her chair.

CHAPTER NINETEEN

GRAHAM ESTIMATED SILAS Granby was his wife's senior by about a decade. Looking more trim and fit than most men his age, Silas was good-looking in a silver fox kind of way, like he'd stepped off an aftershave advert. He had quick, curious, piercing blue eyes and wore a crisp, white, open-necked shirt pinned at the wrists by silver cufflinks. He had on navy trousers and tan leather shoes. Business clothes even when working from home. "What can I do for you?"

Janice succinctly explained the case. "Jamie Reeves, one of the landscapers who worked here until a week or so ago, was attacked last night in Gorey. He's in a coma. It's touch and go."

"Just awful," Granby said. "But what does that have to do with us?"

"We're here to find out a little more about him," Graham said. Granby dropped his wife's hand and moved to sit in a matching high-backed armchair. "Please, ask away. Happy to do whatever we can to help."

"Were you happy with the landscaper's work?"

"Yes, yes, I thought they did an excellent job."

"There were no disagreements?"

"Not with us. I have happily recommended them to my friends, and I don't do that with just anyone."

"What about relations between the landscaping team? Did you notice any resentments or arguments between them? Your wife said Jamie was in charge."

"Not between the team, but I did notice him and Sanderson having words once toward the end of the project. They stopped as soon as they noticed me watching them from a window. There was a lot of gesticulating and red faces." Granby paused. "There was even a bit of pushing. They were not happy with each other at all."

"Any idea what it was about? The argument?" Graham said.

"It was about the hours," Granby said confidently. "Jamie was a fast worker; still good, but quick. I've heard that Sanderson likes his workers to take their time, make sure to do a good job so the story goes, but I think it's more likely that he likes to stretch things out so he can justify their charges, which I can assure you are not the lowest."

As before, his wife addressed her question to the dog. "Silas always thinks someone is trying to cheat him, doesn't he, Willow?"

"That's because they *do* cheat me," Granby complained. "I don't hide that I've been successful. Some people try to take advantage."

"But you were happy with the work?" Graham asked. "The grounds certainly look first-rate to me." He looked out of the window at the pool and the sea that met the horizon beyond it.

"They were excellent," Katya trilled.

"Quite adequate," said Granby. "Like I said, I happily

recommend them to my friends. A mainland firm might have done better, but I always try to use local businesses to help the economy, jobs, and so on. If they charge me a bit over the odds, so be it. I can afford it, and it keeps the wheels greased. I made an exception for the security though. I ended up inviting bids on that. I wanted a state-of-the-art system, the very best. Ended up with a Swiss company. Panic buttons in every room linked up to a private security firm. Even out here, they patrol every few minutes."

"We noticed the cameras outside." And inside, Graham thought but didn't add. From multiple angles. For a private residence, it was intense.

"Like I say, some people like to take advantage, but I'm not gambling with our safety."

"Sensible precautions," Graham agreed. "As a matter of routine, we're asking all of Jamie's friends and professional connections to account for their whereabouts last night."

Granby replied without hesitation. "I was coming back from Italy. A flying visit—literally. I was looking at a jet, but honestly, the yachts were more enticing." He turned to his wife. "Got back in the small hours, didn't I, darling?"

A little slowly, Katya caught up and recognised she was being asked to alibi her husband. "He is always flying. Up to London, then to Europe or China or . . . Timbuktu maybe!" she joked. "Meetings everywhere, money everywhere, never stops. Like a rubber baron, no? I told him once, 'Maybe buy your own plane!' It would be easier. Now he's doing that!"

Granby admitted, "It's tempting, honestly. But mostly my clients have their own jets that they send for me."

"Sometimes," Katya continued, "he spends so much time in the air, I think he's maybe a mix of a man and a bird."

"And you, Mrs. Granby?" Janice asked, politely steering her back on topic.

"I don't like to fly. Boat is nicer. The Med is my favourite."

"Your whereabouts, I meant," the sergeant persisted. "Last night?"

"Oh, I was here, at home, making some phone calls. Charity, you know." Graham's curious eyes indicated that he might not. "For the dogs," she said. Graham's expression didn't change. "The Champions Fund." Katya turned to her husband for help.

"My remarkable wife has a lifelong passion for show dogs. She bred Pomeranians in Hungary . . ."

"The north," Katya said. "Near Austria. Our dogs, they are *so* smart, so quick to learn! My family is amazing at the breeding."

Granby chuckled. "But seriously, Katya's had three national champions in five years."

"Oh, my Rufus, my perfect Rufus . . . I miss him so much." Katya sighed dramatically with the anguish of loss, one hand clasped to her chest, the other around Rufus's replacement, the obstreperous Willow. Katya lamented for a moment in Hungarian, as though praying over the animal's grave. "The *best*. Maybe the best *forever*." Janice eyed the puffball Katya was carrying. *Good thing dogs don't understand human.*

"Rufus was the origin of a powerful, new bloodline. A crossbreed which is . . . unique, only from Jersey," Katya announced proudly. "Nowhere else. I've been raising money to mem . . . mem . . ." Katya looked over at her husband again.

"Memorialise."

"Yes, memorialise Rufus," Katya said, still botching the

pronunciation. "We lost him two years ago."

Graham ground his teeth in silence for a moment. "A memorial, you say."

"Yes."

"In what form?" Katya frowned at the detective inspector, not understanding his question or the subtext underlying it. "What kind of memorial?" Graham tried again.

Katya pondered his meaning. "Ah! We are having fundraising activities to produce more champion dogs and fund some prizes each year with Rufus's name on the cups. And a big dinner. Will be fun!"

"Thank goodness," Graham said. "I thought you meant you were going to stuff him!"

"Stuff him? What is this st— Hah! Ah, no. We already have plan for that." Katya pointed to a shelf behind Graham, where eight cedarwood urns stood in a row. "Each one of them is my dog. Here, I show." Katya stood up and brought one of the urns to the detective inspector. Engraved on the front was "Rufus, 2008 – 2020." "You might think this silly, but they are amazing animals. Difficult to train and keep. And others do not take them seriously."

"I'll allow," Granby said, "that it's a little bit daft, but Katya plans to take on some schoolchildren to teach them the ins and outs of the breeding process."

"We have a building we call 'Rufus's Kennel.' Would you like to see it?"

"Maybe later, Mrs. Granby."

"Okay," Katya said, carefully replacing the urn on the shelf and sitting back down. She pulled Willow onto her lap. "Maybe on your way out. Is nice."

Graham turned to her husband. "So, you were returning from Italy?"

"Yes, my assistant Cynthia can confirm."

"And you, Mrs. Granby, were home alone until your husband arrived. What time was that?"

"Uh, really, I have no idea. I was asleep."

"It was around one thirty," Granby confirmed.

"And despite seeing Jamie arguing with his boss, you had no disagreements with him directly?"

"No, absolutely not. Besides, if I had been unhappy, I would have spoken to Adrian Sanderson directly."

"Were you aware of any drug taking at all?"

"No, should I?" Graham raised his eyebrows. "Well, you should really ask Katya. I was away mostly and only communicated with Sanderson."

Everyone looked at Katya. "Drugs? Oh no, no. I see no drugs. Just good men. Hard workers. They do their job well."

On their way out, Granby and Katya led Graham and Harding to an outbuilding. It had a beautiful view of the northern coastline and was strewn with dog toys and an obstacle course. "Willow is in training," Katya said. The outbuilding was larger than Graham's old room at the White House Inn, despite him having had the largest, best-appointed room there. Graham suspected Willow's gourmet canine feasts might even hold a candle to Mrs. Taylor's full English breakfasts and Sunday roasts.

"Well, we appreciate your time. Good luck with your . . . memorial," Graham said, entirely unconvinced of its value. "If you think of anything else . . ."

"Of course, of course. Anything we can do," Granby told him, guiding the two officers to their car. "A terrible thing to happen."

"How might we contact your assistant to confirm your flight details, Mr. Granby?" Janice said.

"Here's my card," he replied. "Call that number and

speak to Cynthia. She's in charge of all that sort of thing. I just show up and board the plane when and where she tells me."

"One last thing, Mr. Granby," Graham said. "Do you have surveillance footage of the incident between Mr. Sanderson and Jamie Reeves? You said it was recent."

"Oh no, I keep only a few days' worth of footage. I wiped it long ago. It has all gone."

"Ah, shame. Well, goodbye, Mr. Granby. If you think of anything, please let us know." Graham gave Katya a nod. "Mrs. Granby," he acknowledged.

The standard police Vauxhall looked comically grace-less juxtaposed next to Granby's two shiny machines of a horsepower and sensuality the Vauxhall couldn't match, even if it was souped up for high-speed chases. Graham and Harding climbed in. "No wonder he went all in on the secu-rity system." Graham counted five cameras trained on them. He'd be overjoyed to have that number spread along the length of Gorey's high street. "You know what these are, Janice?"

"They're cars, sir." He could equally have asked about specialty golf clubs, fine wines, or any of the dozen 'one-percent' hobbies of which Janice knew next to nothing and cared about even less. "The four wheels give them away."

"Maserati," Graham announced. "The coupe, a model from about fifteen years ago. It's got a four-point-two litre engine, drives up to a hundred and eighty miles an hour." Even Janice had to be impressed with that, Graham reasoned. But her expression didn't flicker. "And this little weekend runabout is a Ferrari four-eight-eight. Goes all the way to two hundred if you tell it to."

"I hope he doesn't. In case you haven't noticed, sir,

that's well over the speed limit." Janice tutted and shook her head. "Boys and their toys," she muttered.

"Point is, no insurer would have looked at him twice without a world-class surveillance suite."

"The added stress that comes with riches. My heart bleeds." Janice shrugged. "Makes me wonder why they bother making all that money in the first place, poor dears."

The display of such ostentatious wealth made Graham thoughtful about his career choices. A mind like his could readily have found lucrative work in the corporate field; equally, he could have joined the military and risen through the ranks. The latter would have earned him far less money, but he would have benefitted from a decent pension and a second career based on the first that was far more handsomely rewarded. But he knew nothing would give him the challenges and responsibility that came from a serious police investigation. And he'd made his peace with the trade-offs long ago. He wasn't sure Harding had quite done the same.

CHAPTER TWENTY

JANICE KNOCKED ON the door of 145 Marett Lane, Gorey. She'd dropped Jack off at the farmer's market and decided to follow up on Silas Granby's alibi. The address was the one stated on the Granby Investments website. Cynthia Moorcroft, Granby's assistant, lived there.

The address was as picturesque as any on Jersey. Terraced stone cottages lined one side of the quiet lane. High stone walls that hid large, whitewashed houses from public view lined the other. The lane was so narrow, Janice had parked her car tight against a wall to avoid blocking the road. This particular lane led to the beach, and Janice waited to cross as families carrying towels and other beach paraphernalia, walkers with poles, and cyclists passed her on their way to and from it.

The row of cottages she was aiming for was set back from the lane by front gardens that frothed with late spring blooms. Those at number 145 were especially unrestrained. Janice practically had to fight her way through them to reach the front door as she picked her way down the crazy-paved garden path. This was no conventional office, particularly one touted as the corporate home of a business with the name Granby Investments.

The door opened. Janice found herself looking at a woman's chest and immediately adjusted her gaze upward. The woman was easily over six feet tall in her bare feet. She was aged about sixty with grey, wavy, short hair. She wore a striped shirt waister with an apron over the top. She held her hands high. They were covered in flour.

"Ms. Moorcroft?" Janice said, flashing her police ID. "Did I catch you at a bad time?" The sergeant smiled.

Cynthia Moorcroft smiled back. "Not the best, I admit, but not to worry. I'm not at a critical point. My scones can wait. Please come in. I assume you're here about Silas's alibi. He said you might drop by."

Janice went inside. The rooms were small, the ceilings low, the windows few. It was dark until she wandered into the large kitchen, a modern addition at the back. Light flooded in through a skylight and French doors. The kitchen led onto a patio and walled garden that, like the front, fizzed with flowers, many of them, like the woman who lived there, tall and rangy. In the middle of the room, on a wooden table, lay the reason for Cynthia Moorcroft's floury hands. On a board lay a mound of dough and a rolling pin. A recipe book lay open at a page entitled "Soulful Scones."

"I can't offer you a scone, but I can make you a cup of tea. Would you like one?"

"That's very kind of you, thank you," Janice said. Cynthia pointed to a sofa next to the French doors before reaching for the kettle. Janice took a seat. For a quick moment, she relaxed into the squishy cushions, enjoying the sight of the garden through the windows, the sun on her face.

"So, how can I help you?" the older woman said as she clattered about making the tea. The kettle clicked off, followed by a gurgle as she poured boiling water into a pot.

"I'm just making enquiries. Mr. Granby said you could confirm where he was on Friday night. A young man who had recently been landscaping his gard—"—Janice fumbled for the right word—"estate has been attacked. He's hanging on by a thread."

"Yes, Silas told me."

"Did you meet Jamie Reeves, Ms. Moorcroft?"

"Please, call me Cynthia." Janice would do nothing of the sort. It was unprofessional. "I did not. But I heard they did a good job." Cynthia poured Janice a cup of tea and handed it to her. She brought over a hard chair from the kitchen table to sit on.

"What do you do for Mr. Granby exactly?"

"I'm his assistant. He does all the client facing stuff, but I deal with everything else. I take care of all his admin, his calendar. I schedule his meetings. I also handle many of his and Mrs. Granby's personal arrangements."

"Would that have included dealing with the landscapers?"

"No, Silas handled that himself mostly. He was deeply involved in the whole custom build. He worked with the architects, builders, and landscapers directly. It was pretty extreme. The house is his 'place on the water,' and he wanted to get it right. I didn't have much to do with it at all."

"And what about this cottage? It's listed as the corporate office for Granby Investments." Janice looked around her. "It hardly strikes me as that."

Cynthia blushed. She looked at Janice coyly. "A little convenience. Tax, you know. Perfectly legal. I work from here, and it forms part of my benefits package. Mr. Granby is a very generous employer."

"How did you get the job? It seems a cushy number."

Cynthia smiled, not in the least offended. "It is. A contact of mine knew I was looking for a job and introduced us. I had no experience in the wealth management world, but I'm a fast learner. I had no idea what I was letting myself in for, though. No idea who Silas was or what he did. But it all worked out."

"So, tell me about his movements for the last week."

Cynthia moved over to a desk against the wall and unplugged her laptop. Picking it up, she sat next to Janice on the sofa and placed a pair of half-moon glasses on her nose. She turned the laptop so that Janice could see the screen. The sergeant leant over to see April's calendar. Most of the days were filled with appointments. "He came back from Singapore on Wednesday and flew out to Italy, Turin, the next day. He flew back on Friday evening, arriving around six p.m."

Janice's mind whirred. Granby had told them he hadn't arrived back until one thirty the next morning. "Do you have a flight number and times for the Turin flight?"

Cynthia eyed her over her half-moon glasses. "Oh, no. There's no flight number. There are no schedules. This was a private jet, a private arrangement. I don't even know the name of the client. Silas often uses code names."

"Don't worry, I'll be able to get records."

"I doubt it. These are not the kind of flights you and I catch to Marbella for our holidays. These are discreet, personal arrangements. The planes are often sent by clients for Silas. Private jets are like cars to these people. They very much fly under the radar. Literally."

Cynthia closed her laptop with a click and put it aside.

"You have to understand, Silas deals with people who possess astounding, unbelievable wealth. He knows their demons, their Achilles' heels, their secrets, and their scandals. He also knows where the bodies are buried. His is complex, delicate, highly confidential work that goes far beyond managing money."

Janice's eyes widened. "Like what, exactly?"

"He might have to manage the child who has been arrested or organise rehab for the one with a drug problem, deal with the ex-wife who's demanding more maintenance, or pay off the mistress threatening to tell. He's often asked to resolve family disputes and do the dirty work. More than once he has had to communicate to one child that they have been disinherited, while another receives it all. Much of his work is to do with protecting the image of the client to emphasise the stability of their businesses to the stock market or simply to protect their standing in society, but it often strikes at the heart of intimate and family relationships.

"High net worth individuals are not immune to tragedy, heartbreak, or chaos. Quite the opposite. Invariably, Silas is the person the client trusts most in the world before spouses and family members, sometimes especially them. He has less to gain. Normal rules, the ones you and I follow, simply don't apply. Rules are bent, ignored, or encouraged out of existence." Like Janice had at the Granby house, Cynthia rubbed her fingertips with her thumb.

Janice considered this for a moment. To her, a member of the police force, the idea that rules weren't followed was unfathomable and simply plain wrong. It upended her heightened sense of justice. She thought about the sacrifices she and Jack were making to save up for a home—the nights spent in, the value packs Jack bought at the grocery store, and the cheaper-priced, oddly shaped vegetables he scavenged at the farmer's market. They both put in so much overtime that they, a couple soon to be married, barely saw each other.

Cynthia closed her laptop and returned to her seat. She leant forward confidentially. "Between you and me, he barely needs a passport. Sometimes he doesn't even get off the plane. There's a whole world out there that is inaccessible to you and me. We can't gain access to it because we lack the wealth, class, and status. Almost nothing is handed out on merit, you know. Moving up in life is simply down to who you know and who your parents were." She sat back. "It's just the way it is."

"But how does Mr. Granby get these clients in the first place?" Janice knew there were people with a lot of money on Jersey, but unless they made their way into custody, the reality of them didn't touch her life. Sure, she saw the boats in the harbour, the big houses, the fancy cars, the odd helicopter, but to her it was just part of the Jersey scene. She felt sure there was still room for her on the island, especially if she ignored the house prices. But perhaps she'd got it all wrong. She had spent her early twenties working on boats owned by the rich, for the rich, and having seen them up close, she did not hold them in especially high esteem. But what Cynthia was describing was a world beyond that. No passports? No rules? A world where money meant no checks, no accountability.

"Most of it is done on the hush-hush. Personal contacts, recommendation by a friend of a friend, that kind of thing. The über-wealthy want people like them, people they can relate to and who can relate to them. It's very much a people business. And the most important currency is trust.

These people tell Silas their deepest, darkest secrets. And he's expected to keep them."

Janice wondered if these secrets stretched to crimes. She was almost sure they did. "So, there's no tracking, nothing to prove Mr. Granby was where he says he was. What about the pilot? Aircrew?"

"Huh, good luck with that. They are sworn to secrecy and often don't know who their passengers even are. Many travel with just a pilot. Like I said, it is all done softly, softly; hush-hush. Shadowy figures climb aboard and, at the end of the flight, silently disembark to disappear into the countryside."

Janice frowned. This wasn't at all like her trips to Ibiza with her sister.

CHAPTER TWENTY-ONE

"**I** THINK SILAS Granby might be lying, sir. His alibi doesn't completely check out." Janice was back at the station, congregating with Graham in his office.

"How do you mean, Sergeant?"

"His assistant says he got back at six p.m., yet he says he didn't get back home until one thirty the next morning."

"Can you check with the airline? He probably flew Turin to Paris and Paris to St. Helier."

"That's the thing, sir. There is no record. He was flying on a private jet. Apparently, for people like him, it's all done on the down-low."

Graham straightened. The inconsistent application of laws, especially when it hinged on whether one was rich or not, offended him. He was aware of the fondness for "ghost flights" among certain elements of the Jersey population, and when he first arrived on the island, the chief officer had explained in fulsome detail why he should overlook them, but it didn't make their existence any easier to bear. And now they were interfering in the rigour of his investigation.

"Okay, let's make a note and bear it in mind."

Confused as to Graham's lack of concern over this seemingly important piece of evidence, Janice steeled herself to ask a question that had been playing on her mind. "We still on for dinner next Friday? I mean, if we still find ourselves in the middle of a serious enquiry and all."

"Yes." Graham was certain. "I hope we'll have it all cleared up by then, but if not, we'll make it a working dinner. We can discuss the case." Janice's face showed clearly what she thought of this idea. "I know, I know, but otherwise we'll have to cancel, and Laura's been looking forward to it. If we discuss the case, not the whole evening obviously, it'll assuage our guilty feelings, and you never know, we might have a breakthrough."

Satisfied, Janice returned to the main office. "Whassup, Bazza? That's some face you're pulling." Over the top of his screen, Janice stared at Barnwell's contorted expression as he battered his keyboard.

"I'm searching the databases for info on Matthew Walker. There's something not right there, I'm sure of it. We've heard that he was inside at some point, but I'm not finding anything on him. Will you have a go? You're the expert."

Barnwell stepped aside to let Janice do her magic. Her fingers flew across the keyboard as she cross-examined the database with the digital incisiveness of a top-flight barrister. After several minutes, she paused, then resumed her interrogation of the PNC. Finally, she let out a breath. "Nope, nothing. He doesn't appear, not even a mention of him. Never picked up, never fingerprinted. Not crossed our paths at all."

"I just don't believe it. He must be known to us. I can feel it in my water."

Janice sat back and folded her arms. "You know, only ninety-eight percent of the criminal records are on the database. If it was a while back, or the station that nicked him used an out-of-date process, it's possible there's a record of him somewhere that never made it onto the central system. You could see if that's the case. It'd be a long shot though."

"Hmm, okay, I'll think about it. It's just a hunch." Janice moved from the computer. "Has Jim said anything more to you about the Met? Did he do anything?" Barnwell was pensive.

Janice shook her head. "Not said a word."

"Do you think he's going to leave us?"

"Probably. I mean he has to at some point, doesn't he? He can't stay here forever. It would be a waste. And we can't really support two sergeants in a station this size."

"Hmm, I'll be sorry to see him go though. I thought he was a right ponce at first, but he's grown on me." Carmen, sensing Barnwell's mood, trotted up and put her chin on his knee. He rubbed her head absentmindedly.

"It'll be for the best, you'll see," Janice said. There was a bang.

"Anybody home?" Roach called out from the back.

"And he hasn't gone yet," she whispered.

In his office, Graham's phone rang. It was Tomlinson. "Alright, Marcus. You know what I want to hear."

"Yes, I do," the pathologist answered.

"So, Reeves is awake? Is he talking?" Graham asked excitedly. "Did he say anything about the—"

"No, David. I'm sorry." Marcus's tone carried the worst possible news.

His shoulders sagging, Graham slumped into his seat with leaden despair. "When?"

"Half an hour ago," Marcus told him. "The damage to his brain stem was unexpectedly severe. They did their very best to keep his breathing going, but too many other systems shut down. His family was with him."

"Damn it," Graham swore quietly. "*Damn* it." There was little else to say. "Thanks, Marcus." He pressed a button on his internal phone.

"Sir?" Janice said, walking up.

It took many seconds, but Graham realised he was gripping his desk as though preparing to tip it over. It never, ever got any easier. "Sergeant, we're going to have that working dinner no matter what, but I'm sorry to say that the Reeves case just became a murder enquiry."

CHAPTER TWENTY-TWO

The Gorey Gossip
Saturday, April 16th, Second Edition

Let's say I have a friend who's thinking about moving to Gorey.

On any other day, I'd be full of encouragement. I'd tell them: "House prices won't attract first-time buyers, they are insane, but the standard of living is exceptionally high. There's good weather year-round, the high street is terrific, so is the castle, and there's a new vibe to the historic, working port. The people are wonderful, and you won't find a prettier place to live in the whole world."

But then, I worry that my friend might ask a question that's much more difficult to answer: *Is it safe?*

This week, I'd have to equivocate, and that makes me desperately low. Small towns thrive on trust and generosity but fall apart amidst fear and suspicion. This week, we're left with a lot of questions, a grieving family, and a new headstone at St. Andrew's Cemetery. After battling bravely, Jamie Reeves succumbed to his injuries overnight, less than twenty-four hours after being attacked on Hautville Road, just down from the Fo'c'sle and Ferret. That he was able to provide no assistance whatsoever to detectives only compounds the tragedy.

My police sources have conceded they are no closer to identifying anyone with a reason to attack Mr. Reeves. It seems the twenty-eight-year-old was savagely ambushed; the weapon has not been found. Sudden, unprovoked, violent assaults like these often point to robbery, but this was not the case here. So, do we have a mugging gone wrong or a personal attack? The lines of enquiry appear confused, and there is a worrying lack of evidence. The police are reluctant to discuss specifics.

I know that I speak for everyone in Gorey when I say our citizens deserve to feel safe, and that if we're to witness the next dizzying chapter in DI Graham's increasingly crowded career, we trust this investigation will be brief, successfully concluded, and result in the incarceration of the person or persons responsible for a very long time.

My repeated questions to the constabulary on this subject received no reply; DI Graham, if you read this column, please prepare your team to explain to Gorey's public just what happened on that not-particularly-dark road leading to the pub where Jamie was attacked. Was he simply unlucky? Or was something else going on?

If I told my friend that Gorey is a safe place to be, would the DI and his team make a liar of me? Because the simple act of being about Jersey at whatever time of night one might choose should never come with a penalty. We should be free to walk around at will without fear of our safety being compromised. This is as much a human right as breathing the Jersey air, browsing our shops, or taking tea on the waterfront. It's sad, but sometimes the actions of a tiny minority seem to threaten those rights and make us think twice about doing the most normal of things. Our constabulary is there to restore that peace of mind. The ball is now very much in their court.

CHAPTER TWENTY-THREE

ITHOUT A HINT of enthusiasm, Graham
parked once more outside the converted
suburban home from where Adrian
Sanderson ran his business. They'd called ahead and found
Sanderson returned from his meeting and Molly still there.
He and Janice had just come from the hospital, having
interviewed Reeves's distressed parents. It had been a
draining experience but had not elicited any information
that felt pertinent to their son's murder.

"So, are we going to confront Sanderson about the arguing, sir?" Janice said.

"I think we should ask, see what he has to say for
himself. Bashing someone's head in just for expressing an
opinion about the business's fee structure seems a bit
extreme though."

"Money does the strangest things to people," Janice
said.

"Did you follow up on their alibis?"

"Molly was at her friend's dinner party as she told you.
She was there all night and didn't leave until the early

hours. And Sanderson didn't really give us one, did he? Just his wife. She's not going to say different."

"Okay, I'll push him on that." Graham readied himself to tell Sanderson and Molly that a young man they'd liked, respected, even loved was dead.

"Come in," Sanderson began. His top lip shined. His face was flushed. Anxiety dilated his pupils. "Has there been any change?" Molly was beside him, anticipating news, her hands clasped.

Graham's face did much to convey the reason for his visit. "Could we sit down? I'm afraid I have some very bad news." Molly whimpered, and Sanderson led her to the sofa. "Jamie's injuries were not survivable. He died two hours ago."

Sanderson sat down in a rush. Molly cried out and brought her hands to her face, sobbing. Graham went to boil the kettle as Janice provided comfort and solace. When they'd coaxed the pair to take at least a few sips of sugary tea, Graham explained that some questions in the case were still pressing. Janice led Molly away so that Graham could talk to Sanderson privately.

"I'd like to ask you again about drug use," Graham said. "Did you ever see signs of Jamie using? Probably nothing heavy. Just party pills, that kind of thing."

Sanderson rejected the idea. "Impossible."

"Mr. Sanderson, everyone likes to cut loose a bit . . ."

"No, I mean, Sanderson Landscaping has a strict drug testing policy. Alcohol levels too. Random tests, the whole lot. My cousin overdosed. Wrecked the family. I'm very strict on that sort of thing. Jamie was perfectly fine with it and always clean."

Graham made a note. *Drugs. Different stories. Sander-*

son. Lascelles. "Now I'm going to ask about arguments you might have had with Jamie."

Sanderson shifted in his seat. "Disagreements," he said. "Not really arguments. And certainly never violent ones."

"Okay, sir," Graham said, "but we've got eyewitnesses that told—"

"Told?" Sanderson said, suddenly furious. "Told by who?"

"I can't reveal that. Sorry."

"Well, what did they tell?" Sanderson demanded.

"That there were arguments—disagreements—between you and Mr. Reeves, even a physical altercation."

"A *fight*?"

Graham pursed his lips. "I wouldn't call it a fight exactly."

"Me and Jamie? He's off his rocker, whoever he is!" Sanderson appealed to Graham, his hands aloft in confusion. "I bet it was Granby, wasn't it?" Graham's expression remained impassive, revealing none of his thoughts. Sanderson was in full flow, however. "How did he see this, then? From his glass house? That huge greenhouse of his?" Sanderson snorted.

"Why would you think it was Mr. Granby?" Graham said calmly.

"Maybe he wanted to get me in trouble for his own sadistic enjoyment," Sanderson said. "Who knows with these rich, clueless idiots? They're never happy unless they can manipulate others, force them into subjugation! This is the struggle of the worker," he cried, "and it is his responsibility to *resist,* Detective Inspector. Listen, I never touched Jamie, not once."

Sanderson ran a hand through his sandy hair and stared at the floor as he clasped the back of his neck. After a pause, he glanced up at Graham. "Look, I might have the arms of a pro wrestler, but I bloody hate fighting. Gave it up when I was a boy. Never the right way to solve problems. Besides, if I had fisticuffs with one of my own employees on a client's property, they'd have cancelled the job and chucked us all off. Word would get out, and the business would collapse inside a month. I'd have enraged landscapers coming at me with gardening tools . . ." His face dropped. "One fewer now, I suppose." Sanderson rallied and sat up straight.

"Are you sure you never had words with Jamie? It's best to tell me, Mr. Sanderson. We can deal with it if it has nothing to do with the case."

Sanderson paused, then sighed. His shoulders slumped. "Alright, we did argue. Once, at the Granby's." His eyes flashed. "But there was nothing physical."

"When was that, Mr. Sanderson?" Graham asked him smoothly. Now he was getting somewhere.

"Three weeks ago. A few days before the job finished. There were rumours Jamie was getting too friendly with Mrs. G. Nothing serious, but they were flirty. Good-looking guy like Jamie, it wasn't unusual. Granby asked me to remove him from the job. I'm sure there was nothing to it, but I did it. It was for the protection of everyone involved. Felt bad though."

"And what was Jamie's response."

"He reacted badly. Told me it was nothing and berated me for believing Granby over him." Sanderson wiped his face with his hand. "Listen, it was awkward and embarrassing, but it wasn't violent, and it definitely wasn't something to kill over. We each said our piece and moved on like the adults we are . . . were. We never spoke of it again."

"There was nothing physical at all about it, not even minor, like poking or pushing?"

"No! And if that posh twit says otherwise, he's lying. Wish I'd never listened to him now. I might have wagged a finger at Jamie, but that was the extent of it."

"Alright, thanks, Mr. Sanderson. That's helpful. I've also heard that you and Jamie sometimes disagreed about the business's pricing structure."

Sanderson sat back, glancing away and batting a hand in the air, dismissing the suggestion behind Graham's words. "Nah, that's also nothing. We just had different points of view on the subject. We were fine. We went out drinking on occasion. He came to my wife's birthday barbecue last weekend. There's absolutely no truth to the idea that we were on bad terms."

"Can you confirm again for me what you were you doing yesterday evening?"

"Now, just hold on a minute," said Sanderson. "You asked me that earlier. You've come in here, I hope you remember, to tell us that Jamie has *died*. Molly's in pieces, I can hardly think straight, and you're asking where I was after already asking me once?"

"Just routine, sir," said Graham. "We do realise how it looks." Sanderson stared out of the window at a postman emptying a red postbox. "So . . . Mr. Sanderson?" Graham said, his eyebrows aloft. The business owner looked at him. "Friday night?"

"Like I said, I was at home with my wife. It was the *MasterChef* semifinal."

"And you were in all evening?"

"Yeah, erm, except when I went to the off-licence."

"And what time was that?"

'Bout ten."

"How long were you out?"

Sanderson pursed his lips. "'Half an hour? My local

shop didn't have what I wanted, so I had to go to the one further down the high street—MacAdams."

"So back at ten thirty?"

"Yeah, *MasterChef* was still on. I mean, that soufflé. How did she do it?" He shrugged. "Look, I'll come down to the station right now if you like. Take a lie detector test. Give my DNA for analysis. Anything you want. But I had nothing to do with what happened to Jamie. You think my wife wouldn't have noticed if I'd come back having just clobbered one of my own employees?"

Graham kept it cool. "We appreciate your cooperation, thank you. If we need you further, we'll let you know. Now I would like to talk to Molly."

"Yeah, well, you be careful. She liked him. Don't know how much, but she'll be in a bad way."

Graham found Molly in the back room. She was staring out of the window. Janice was with her. The sergeant shook her head when Graham came in and warned him, her eyes active and concerned, not to press too hard. She left the room at Graham's nod.

The detective inspector quietly took a seat. "When we talked before," he said, his tone one of mild curiosity, "you mentioned that Jamie and Adrian argued from time to—"

"He didn't do this to Jamie," Molly interrupted firmly. It seemed the only thing she was sure about. "I don't believe that at all. Yes, they got a little cross with each other now and again, but it wasn't hate-fuelled rage likely to lead to murder. They would be laughing and joking ten minutes later. They were more like brothers, not mortal enemies. And . . . Adrian isn't like that. He's a pussycat. Takes care of his mum in the old people's home, charity work, you name it; he does a lot for the local community." Graham didn't tell her that just about every murderer he arrested had defenders like her.

Molly had turned to look out of the window at the yard behind the office. It was full of plants, gardening tools, and building supplies. "Whoever it was who did this," she said, her anger building, "will he go to prison forever?"

This wasn't the moment to explain the various forms of murder charges available under British law and the penalties that ensued from them, but there was no easy, accurate answer. "Probably. Maybe. A long time, certainly."

Molly turned away from the window to look at Graham. "I want to help. But I can't think of anything else I can tell you that might be useful."

Molly was struggling to manage the hot flame of her grief-fuelled anger. Graham knew that over the coming days she would experience a powder keg of competing, conflicting emotions. As far as he could tell, she was both entirely honest and deeply upset. The rest of her weekend would be spent in tears, grieving for someone she'd called her friend. A man she might have liked to have called something more had fate not intervened so cruelly. But there would be frustration, too, at the inevitable slow pace of the investigation, and plenty of that red, unfading anger known only to those who have no way of directing it. Those who have no one—as yet—to *blame*.

Waiting patiently in the reception area, Janice completed her notes. She'd confirmed with Sanderson what he had said to Graham and, having elicited no new information, she wrapped up his statement.

"What did Molly have to say?" she said as she and Graham walked outside.

"Not much. I've wondered if she might have orchestrated something, got someone to do the dirty for her, but on my reckoning, she's either a supremely talented actress or she was genuinely in love with Jamie and can't believe he's dead."

"She has a concrete alibi too, remember? What about Sanderson? He's changed his story with the visit to the off-licence."

"Yes, he has. Please check it when we get back. Technically, he could have done it, but I think he's telling the truth. Could all be a play, but I don't get the sense that his and Jamie's problems went beyond workplace disagreements."

"But what about the thing with Mrs. Granby? Employee fraternising with the client. Could have put his business at risk."

Graham closed the driver's door and sat behind the wheel for a quiet moment. He looked up at the landscaper's premises. Baskets overflowing with pink, white, and blue flowers hung on either side of the door. Tubs with yet more flowers sat on the ground. Nothing else distinguished it as a gardening, or even a creative business. "Yeah, but would you really kill someone over that?"

"He might not have, but what about Mr. Granby?"

CHAPTER TWENTY-FOUR

BARNWELL AND HIS brother were back at their table, sitting in the same wooden seats as Friday evening. It was lunchtime, and the pub was filling with diners looking for a hearty Sunday roast.

"Alright, let's try this again," Barnwell said, "but without the sudden head trauma and pouring blood."

"This is what I wanted you to see," Steve said. He had the family photo album in front of him again, turning the pages. "Look, photo after photo, every few months, no interruption for years. Pictures of you, me, us, all of us. Then"—Steve turned another page—"we skip a whole year. Look, we're much older in this photo. I remember that bike; it was yours, then it got handed down to me and you got a new one." He growled. "You always got the new kit. I had to make do." Steve took a swig of his pint. "In this picture, I could barely reach the pedals." He pointed to a photo three over. "But here, look, I was too big for it. And there are no family photos for two more pages."

The pages were filled with classic family childhood

shots attached to the album with neat, white photo corners. Birthdays, Christmases, family holiday shots. One showed Barnwell in costume as a police officer. He looked about six, maybe seven. "Even then, you were determined to arrest people for a living," Steve said.

"Can't really remember wanting to be a copper," Barnwell said honestly, "until I spoke to a bloke at a school careers fair in my teens. I signed some things, went for an interview, and then everything happened at once. Look, what's the point you're trying to make?"

"Don't you think that's odd? That there's a big jump in the photos and none of the family for two whole pages after loads of them in quick succession?"

"Not really. I mean, so what? A few photos fell out."

"But then there'd be empty slots."

"The camera broke then? Lord knows we weren't flush enough to make buying a new one easy. Perhaps they had to save up."

"But cataloguing family memories with photos is a basic parental duty. It was a priority for Mum. After she died, I went through all their things, remember? Took me ages. There were boxes and boxes of photos from our childhood. You know what Mum was like, so organised. Date and place on the back of every photo. Our ages. What we were doing. She left nothing to chance. And yet for the years 1993 to 1994, there are some photos of us, a few of her, but none of Dad or all of us together."

"Maybe Dad just got tired of being in them, or he was behind the camera. Hey, don't look at me like that. It's possible. Selfies weren't a thing then." Barnwell turned to the album, flicking back and forth between the pages. The Barnwells had been a tight unit, their dad a stern, uncompromising man and their mum acting as the perfect foil. She had given Barnwell and his brother the hugs and love they needed, and despite often straitened circumstances, magicked birthday parties, Christmas presents, and holiday fun seemingly out of nowhere. Barnwell had adored her. "What about Uncle Pete and Auntie Elaine? Remember their study? All those little mementos of this and that? Perhaps they know something if you're looking to fill in some gaps."

"Uncle Pete didn't know who I was when I called," Steve said. "He's not well, mate."

"Poor sod. What is he now, eighty?"

Steve puzzled it out. "Four years older than Dad, so eighty-three."

"Was Auntie Elaine more helpful?"

"Not really. Kept talking about her knees."

"Shame. It's a pity we can't get her to take to technology. It would really help with keeping in contact. It annoyed me that Mum and Dad were so reluctant to use it."

"I could have taught Dad to type and use the internet on his own. But you know what he was like . . ." Steve said.

"And Mum told you not to," Barnwell remembered. Basically, once Mrs. Barnwell realised the internet was a pipeline for pornography and gambling, she put as many roadblocks in her husband's way as possible. Their retirement was spent almost entirely together, mostly in the kind of content-to-rub-along happiness people work all their lives to finally enjoy.

"She told me," Steve recalled, summoning an exaggerated but hilarious impression of their mother's voice, "'I won't spend our twilight years bothering an old man to get off the internet or stop playing a game. I'll take a sledgehammer to the thing before . . .'" He broke into laughter, which was mostly Barnwell's fault; he'd always loved Steve's impression of their mother.

They were brought back to earth by a curious and unexpected presence at the bar. "Oh, you're kidding," Barnwell muttered. "Look what the cat dragged in."

"Cat?" Steve asked, reluctant to turn away from his reminiscences. He glanced over to see who his brother was talking about. "Mr. Muscles there?" Steve was thrilled. "Am I gonna get to see you *arrest* someone finally?"

"I'll arrest *you* if you don't pipe down. Give me a second, alright?" Barnwell rose. "Just want to check in with him." Steve raised a glass to salute his brother's diligence and turned back to the album.

The constable covered the distance between him and his quarry before Walker had time to react. "Now then," Barnwell said cordially, inserting himself into a small, conveniently open stretch of bar next to the man.

"Eh?" Matthew looked tired and a bit unsteady. "Oh, it's you."

Barnwell assessed the amber dregs of the pint in front of him. Matthew's eyes were rimmed in a similar colour. "Stinky Bay IPA, if my eyes don't lie." Barnwell estimated that Matthew was on his fifth or sixth pint. He signalled to Lewis that his latest should be Matthew's last. "Rather sophisticated, isn't it? I'd have wagered you were more of a lager man."

"Doesn't really bother me," said Matthew. "Gets the job done, dunnit? You 'avin' one?"

"Not right now," Barnwell said. "First, I wanted a little chat if that's alright with you."

Matthew wobbled; to Barnwell, the collapse of such a mighty frame spelled certain disaster. There was no telling where he might land, or what—or who—he might take with him.

"Wotcha wanna know?" Matthew's face was flushed and fleshy with booze. Barnwell could smell fish and chips on his breath. "Something about the poor bloke what got himself beat up? Then kicked the bucket. Paula's"—he swayed—"*ex*."

"Yeah. Can you help us a little bit more, mate?"

"Am I a 'person of interest'?" Matthew seemed buoyed at the thought.

"That's what the Americans call it, Matthew. To us, you're just someone we want to speak to 'in connection with a case.'"

Matthew nearly spat out a mouthful of beer. "You need to get something a bit snappier than that."

"Alright," Barnwell said, a little more steel in his tone. "Let's just call you a 'person helping us with our enquiries.'"

"That's hardly any better." Matthew wiped his mouth angrily with his hand.

"Until we prove you aren't one."

"And 'ow do I—?"

"Can you assure me," Barnwell said, pausing to make sure he had Matthew's undivided attention, "that you were with Paula all evening?"

"Yeah!" he blurted. "We told you, we watched the—"

"Yeah, yeah, *MasterChef* semi. But convince me. Tell me you didn't go out and whack Jamie because Paula asked you to."

Continuing to sway slightly but saying nothing, Matthew paused to process the question. "Me, like?" he asked quietly. "Wallop some posh girl's ex-boyfriend? *My* posh girl's ex-boyfriend? Because she told me to?"

Barnwell's worst expectations were of a violent reaction,

but Matthew seemed more offended by the accusation. "Am I under arrest?" he asked a little too loudly. Watching yards away, Steve Barnwell set down his pint in hopeful expectation of seeing his brother swoop into action.

"No, you pillock," Barnwell said. "Keep your voice down."

"Where I grew up," Matthew said at only a very slightly lower volume, "people didn't make friends by throwing acc-acc . . . things around."

Barnwell raised his hands. "We're just having a friendly chat." His eyes hardened, and he leant forward. "Aren't we?"

Matthew recoiled and glared at him. His corpulent, aggrieved expression reminded Barnwell of a baby who was seconds from bursting into tears.

"What can you tell me that will force us to eliminate you and Paula? So we won't need to think about your connection to the case anymore."

"We ain't got no bleedin' connection," Matthew promised. "Only that Paula used to go out with this digger bloke . . ."

"Landscape architect," Barnwell said.

"He sticks trees in the ground," Matthew argued, "'cos a computer told him to. That ain't *architecting*, mate." He grinned with satisfaction that he'd got his words out right this time. "Look, I never even met him, alright? Not when he was alive," Matthew continued, keen to clear things up. "Not until he was laying there in 'ospital, looking as sick as a dog. Paula said he loved livin' in this out-of-the-way place in the middle of the sea for whatever reason. I don't get it. Do you? Why'd you want to be stuck out 'ere? Miles away from civ-civ . . ." Matthew screwed his eyes up with effort. "*Civilisation*."

Never slow to stand up for his adopted home and seeing a chance to take some of the drunken aggression out of the atmosphere, Barnwell turned to the windows which faced the marina. "Look at that. Sunset on the water, fishing boats. Paradise. Anyway," Barnwell said, turning back, "what else did Paula say?"

CHAPTER TWENTY-FIVE

"**R**EMEMBER WHEN YOU told me, like, us big lads, we're always gettin' into trouble 'cos people think we've been fighting?" Matthew belched with commendable discretion. The pub would have been at risk of destruction by the sonic wave otherwise.

The remains of Matthew's drink had somehow disappeared in the few seconds Barnwell's back was turned. *All the signs of a competitive drinker.* Barnwell had lurched in the same direction himself long ago, to his cost. But in Gorey, since working with Detective Inspector Graham, Barnwell had lived a life so different that he might have believed he was carrying around someone else's memories.

"Yeah," Barnwell said.

"Opposite with little blokes like Jamie, innit?" Matthew said. "The ones that look like . . . what do they call them? Metrosexuals, that's it. No one ever thinks they'd be up to bad fings."

"But you think Jamie was?" Barnwell asked. "Did Paula say that?"

"She just kept saying he could be difficult, hard to be around, you know?"

Barnwell most certainly didn't. Thus far, Jamie Reeves's character references had confirmed only that he was thoughtful and decent, and that he appealed to the ladies. "What do you think she meant?"

Matthew shrugged his shoulders. "I dunno. She says a lot of things. I don't listen to half of it. She was always going on about him. Jamie this, Jamie that. Sometimes she'd be nice about 'im. Other times . . . She never said he hit her or nothin', just that she couldn't stand him. If she wasn't my girlfriend," he said, bashful for a second, "I'd be a bit susp—" Matthew gave up trying to express himself with long words. "Ugh, you know what I mean."

Barnwell blinked a few times. "Mate, men don't normally incriminate their girlfriends in serious crimes."

"It's just the things she's said. I'm sure she didn't do nuffin'." Matthew picked up his glass before seeing it was empty. "But she does go on. Bears a . . . what is it?"

Barnwell waited. He didn't want to be putting words in Matthew's mouth. The heavyset man searched his brain and finally found what he was looking for. "A grudge, that's it. Yeah. But then she couldn't say enough nice things about 'im in the 'ospital. Said he was charmin'. And very good-lookin'. Usually."

"Tends to happen when a person's at death's door." Barnwell stuck his hands in his pockets and rocked back on his heels. "Alright, you're done here. Stay out of trouble and get yourself home."

"Righto, ta." Matthew pushed himself away from the counter. He wobbled again but remembered to pick up his jacket. Barnwell watched him walk precariously to the door, half expecting to need to leap forward to catch him if he fell. Matthew successfully crossed the room to the heavy wooden door. He even negotiated the process of grasping the handle, opening the door, and manoeuvring himself outside in the right order.

Satisfied that Walker would make it home, Barnwell returned to his table. "Sorry about that," he said to his brother.

"Were you laying down the law," Steve asked, "or lending him a tenner? Seemed a bit chummy."

"He's just someone on the periphery of a murder enquiry. Probably just a well-meaning, average bloke," Barnwell said, starting to relax. "Well, perhaps a bit below average, but someone who's got himself caught up in something beyond his comprehension."

"Through no fault of his own?" Steve probed.

"I wouldn't go that far. Guys like him are mostly unlucky. Or hanging out with the wrong crowd. Some are complete idiots, granted." Barnwell thought again of the rumour that Matthew had been jailed for an offence that he couldn't find any record of. "Anyway, enough of that. Where were we?"

Steve tapped the photo album. It took a second for Barnwell to adjust his focus. "What?"

"These photos." Steve leafed through the album again.

Barnwell watched snapshots of his childhood parade across his vision in a tiny evocation of what had been surely a full and complex life thus far. "It's just a few missing photos, bruv."

Steve shook his head, still staring at the photo album. He looked up with dark, serious eyes. "I don't think so, Bazz. He was away."

Barnwell searched for a memory, but nothing bubbled up. "Away?"

"When we were little," Steve said.

"How long? When?"

"For about eighteen months. When you were nine and I was five." Steve added some other family details to accelerate Barnwell's train of thought. "We were in that flat above the chippy, remember? Before we moved to the house on Palmerstone Street."

The wheels of Barnwell's mind were moving, but accumulated rust was slowing things down. "I've got almost nothing, you know, from before that move." Barnwell tapped his temple in disappointment. "I do remember the smell though. Who knew living above a chippy would follow you around for the rest of your days?"

Steve kept trying. "Mum worked at that building supplies place, the one with the big yard out back."

Wait. "The place with the shed where we used to play on Saturday mornings?"

"Remember the manager would tell us off for playing tag around the concrete slabs?"

"Yeah, well, I don't blame him. One slip and it'd be all over for us. It was a dangerous place for kids, especially as young and feral as we were." Piled-high bags of cement and stacks of bricks had provided the perfect cover for their childish games.

"But don't you see? We were there because Mum had no one to look after us. Dad *wasn't* there. Just like he wasn't in the photos."

It took longer than Steve had expected, but then Barnwell said, "Hang on . . ."

Steve gripped the table as though threatened with being whisked away against his will. "It's coming, I can tell! We're off down Memory Lane!"

"The North Sea!" Barnwell exclaimed.

"Finally, mate. How's that Sherlock Holmes detecting thing coming along, eh?"

"He was on the rigs."

"That's what they told us, yes."

"Highly skilled work, good money." Barnwell pursed his lips. "Pity we never saw any of it."

"Right. How long do you reckon he was gone?" Steve said.

"Well, if this gap in the photos is anything to go by, about eighteen months I reckon. Look, there's a photo of us all under the Christmas tree. Tough work on the rigs," Barnwell said. "Stuck out there in the North Sea. Living in confined quarters with other blokes. Limited entertainment. They didn't have phones or the internet back then."

"But," Steve said, closing the album, "doesn't it strike you as funny that he did that?"

Barnwell shrugged. "No."

"Really? You're telling me that Dad took off for months to go hundreds of miles away to live and work the middle of the North Sea, leaving his missus with two small kids, to do something he'd never done before or since? For what?"

"Money," Barnwell said simply. That was the history he'd always understood. "Can't have been fun. Perhaps they had money problems and this was a way to fix it. Or maybe it was a short-term stint to build up savings for a deposit, buy a house, get a leg up." Barnwell was warming up now. "They always were good with money. Remember when Mum would mash up end bits of soap into a pocket she'd cut in the side of a sponge? Makes perfect sense. Thrifty. Waste not, want not; that's what Mum always said." Steve looked at his brother like he'd gone mad.

"But money was *tighter* when Dad came back from wherever he was, not easier, Barry. Don't you remember?

He had a steady job before, he worked at the factory, the one at Box End before he went away to the rigs. When he came back, he was out of work, hanging around the home for ages. We were particularly skint as I remember it."

"You were only five, you can't trust your memories at that age."

"Oh yes, I can. I remember we had to keep moving and we'd do it late at night. Mum'd make it into a game, but I distinctly remember being fed up about it because one day I'd be at a school with my favourite teachers and friends, the next I'd be somewhere new, knowing no one. I'd have to make friends all over again at the new school, then it would happen again. And remember when those men came? They took the TV, the microwave, even the iron. I heard Mum crying to Grandma. They thought I was playing in the other room, but I heard them talking. They called them a word I'd never heard before—'bailiffs'. Why would they be coming around if we were flush with oil rig money, eh?"

"I can't remember any of that."

"You were always out with your mates. I was too young. I was with Mum."

"Look, what are you trying to say, Steve? That something was going on? That things weren't all that they seemed? That he didn't go on the rigs?" Steve didn't say anything. "D'you think Dad left Mum or something? Had a fancy woman and ran off with her and spent all his money until, seeing the error of his ways, he came back, and nothing was ever said about it? And they made up the story about the rigs as a cover?"

"That wasn't exactly what I was thinking, no."

"Then what?" There was a disturbance behind them. Barnwell took his eyes off his brother and turned to see what was going on. "Ergh, it's them again."

Steve turned. "Who?"

"Duncan Rayner, Kevin Croft, and Neil Lightfoot, otherwise known as DKN, otherwise known as a trio of oiks." Duncan, Kevin, and Neil had rolled in, laughing and pushing as they came through the door, disturbing the quiet, convivial hubbub of the pub.

"Like a handful of bad pennies, they are," Barnwell said. "They take up far more oxygen than they deserve."

Disturbed for the second time that lunchtime, the look in Barnwell's eye was one of determination mixed with barely restrained aggression. He stood to engage the unruly group. His brother grinned and rubbed his hands. "Watching you do your thing, bruv, is life. Have at it."

CHAPTER TWENTY-SIX

"EASY FELLAS," BARNWELL said, arriving at the bar where the three young men gathered. "No need for us to be rushed or uncivilised, is there? Not in a place like this."

"It's a *pub*," Kevin Croft sneered. His tracksuit was as sloppy and low-slung as it had been the day before.

"In Jersey's history, pubs have always been known as centres of discussion and moral improvement," Barnwell said, repeating something he'd heard Graham say. He'd committed it to memory, suspecting it might one day come in useful. "And today, the Fo'c'sle will be a place of honest recollection and unstinting public service." It was not an invitation but an instruction. Barnwell was in no mood for any messing around.

"Oh, bloody 'ell. Does that mean I have to clean out the bins at the marina again?" Neil moaned.

"*Public* service, not community service, you plonker," said Duncan Raynor, who seemed almost as tired of his friend's plodding manner as Barnwell. Bazza noted that

Raynor's poorly judged haircut didn't look so bad today. It didn't accentuate his unattractive features quite so much.

"I trust you've all had your ears wide open like I asked?" Barnwell said.

"Wider than a mile," Kevin confirmed. "Ain't heard nothin'."

"A man is brutally attacked, yards from one of the busiest parts of town," Barnwell marvelled, "and people who literally spend their entire lives in just that same area, they're . . ." He chuckled as if he found it funny just how *unlikely* it seemed. "They're telling me they've heard *nothing whatsoever* about the case?"

Duncan set down his pint and made one of his more cogent points. "Look, mate, I have to ask you this. What is it about the three of us that makes you so sure we're best friends with all of Jersey's finest muggers?"

"Reputation," Barnwell said honestly. "Past encounters with the constabulary," he added, leaning heavily toward Neil Lightfoot, Roach's second arrest. "Dress sense. Daytime schedule. A few other things."

"That's like us asking you if you know Sherlock Holmes just 'cos you're a copper," Neil countered.

"That's not a real person, dimwit," Duncan said, not smart enough to understand that Neil's analogy was spot-on.

"Oh, I don't know," Barnwell said. "We actually have a Sherlock Holmes type back at the station. He's very keen to meet the three of you."

"I'm not going back to the police station," Neil stated firmly, "unless you slap me about, zap me with a taser, and put me in 'andcuffs."

"And I won't go," Duncan said, equally sure, "until I've taken a nice close-up video of you zapping Neil. After that,

I promise I'll cooperate. Right after I've loaded it onto my socials."

"Calm down. No one's zapping anybody," Barnwell said. "Focus. What about drugs?"

"No, thanks. I'm trying to give them up." It was Duncan who couldn't resist.

"Should you really be encouraging that kind of thing?" Kevin wondered.

"Shut it, all of you," Barnwell said. "I'm here bothering you lot because some poor guy is dead. We've got a public who's scared witless and a tourism industry that relies on low crime and high cleanup rates. Work with me, fellas. It's in all our favours. Less banter, more intel. Give me something useful."

Thoughtful and quiet, the three went into a huddle. There were hisses of disagreement, mutters of concern, an "oooh" of appreciation. The three parted once more. "My learned colleagues and I," Duncan announced, pompously, "have concluded that it's in your best interests, in this particular circumstance, to speak with Beetle."

Seventy-three percent sure he was about to hear a cart-load of rose fertiliser, Barnwell managed to say, "Beetle. Really. Do say more."

"He's plugged in," Duncan promised.

"To the matrix," added Neil for some reason.

"*Connected*," Kevin said. "Like, you know, to the *network*."

"You mean he's a seasoned and accomplished drug dealer," Barnwell said, his patience near breaking point, "or that he's just had new Wi-Fi installed in his house? I've never heard of him."

"The first one," Neil said. "No. Yeah."

Barnwell rolled his eyes. "And how would one communicate with this Beetle?"

"I'll give you his digits," Duncan said. Barnwell gave him a card. After scratching around, Lewis Hurd found him a pen. Duncan laboriously transcribed a number from his phone, curling his arm around it like a six-year-old answering a math problem.

"Too kind."

"But he can't know it came from us."

"Don't worry, fellas. This isn't my first rodeo." Barnwell gave the bemused trio a quick salute. "Stay out of trouble. If," he added before turning back to Steve, "that's possible."

"This is on our trip to Pembrokeshire." Steve showed his brother a stretch of pristine beach on which they were the only two walking. He moved to another photo, a group of people in front of a fireplace. "Mum, you, me, Uncle Oliver and Auntie Catherine, but no Dad."

Barnwell's mind was being hauled by a team of horses, laboriously and painfully, over rough terrain, in the direction of an unknown destination. He folded his arms and glared at his brother. "Yeah. Look, I'm bored of this. Do you want another drink?" He half rose from his seat.

"Sit down." Steve paused, sighed, and closed the album. "You're not getting it."

"Getting what?" Barnwell threw his hands up in the air. "You're right. I've no idea what you're on about. Spit it out or give it a rest and forever hold your peace, for crying out loud."

An acidic ache rumbled in Steve's gut. "I'd hoped to not have to spell it out, but it seems I'm going to have to. There's one other thing I want to show you." Steve reached into the back of the photo album and slipped out a folded, creased piece of paper. He slid it across the table to his brother.

"What's this?" Barnwell eyed his brother nervously.

"Open it."

"But . . ."

"Just open it will ya?"

With the tip of one finger, Barnwell flipped the paper open and stared at it. After a few seconds he quietly flipped it closed again. "It's a charge sheet."

"Yes, from 1993. I found it as I was going through Dad's things."

"Okay . . ."

"I don't think he went anywhere near the oil-rigs. I think he was inside. I want to know why."

Barnwell looked at the folded piece of paper again. It was creased like someone had scrunched it into a ball, then carefully smoothed it out. "I think we should let sleeping dogs lie, Steve."

His brother's eyes sparked with anger. "Well, I don't!"

Their eyes locked, the younger's gleaming with passion and fury, the elder's searching and doleful. "You're going to ask me to do something I shouldn't, aren't you?" Barnwell said.

"I'd be an idiot," Steve replied, "if I didn't at least ask. I've done an internet search but it's too old."

"Look, I'd help if I could, but . . ."

"It's just once . . ." Steve argued. "And it does affect you."

"Mate, we're not *allowed* to . . ."

". . . and it would clear everything up, wouldn't it?"

"It *might* make everything a lot worse," Barnwell cautioned. "Have you thought about that?"

As if to emphasise the point, Steve allowed some silence. "Yeah, I have," he said. "A thousand times."

"And?" his brother said.

"Even if you don't, Bazza, I remember Dad going away and coming back a bit different. I want to know what happened."

"Why? How would it help?"

Hands aloft, Steve admitted defeat. "This won't leave me alone, Bazz. I want to know what he did."

Too mired in weighing the problem to answer at once, Barnwell pursed his lips. "We might regret it, mate."

"I know. I feel the same way," Steve said. "But it's worth the risk."

CHAPTER TWENTY-SEVEN

BEETLE, AKA JONNY Hughe-Gordon, couldn't have looked less like an insect. He was in his twenties, tanned, blond, and athletic. He wore an emerald-green polo shirt, shorts, and deck shoes that were worn just enough to prove to Barnwell that he sailed the yacht the constable found him on.

"Afternoon," Barnwell said.

"Hey there, er, Officer." Hughe-Gordon raised his eyebrows. If Barnwell hadn't already formed an impression of the man from his name and appearance, the message these few words conveyed and the accent with which they were spoken would have fed his imagination. As it was, they sealed the deal. To Barnwell, a working-class lad from the East End of London, Hughe-Gordon was a "moneyed, upper-class twit." His precisely enunciated consonants and elongated vowels told Barnwell so.

"I called earlier."

"Indeed you did. How can I help you?" Hughe-Gordon had been polishing the deck when Barnwell walked up. He wiped his hands with a cloth. The white decking and hull gleamed in the bright sunlight, making Barnwell squint. Aware that this put him at a disadvantage, Barnwell pulled out his sunglasses and self-consciously put them on, trying very hard not to look like an American cop off the TV, but also not like a prat either.

"I wanted to have a little chat with you. About the murder of a local man, James Reeves. I was told you might know something."

Hughe-Gordon held his gaze. He had sparkling blue eyes. Barnwell suspected he was a babe magnet. He could just imagine it.

Hughe-Gordon turned down the corners of his mouth and shook his head. "Ah, no. Can't say I know anything about that. Ah, should I?"

"I was told that you are well connected. That you know things, people. Perhaps in your line of work?"

"What line of work would that be, Officer?" Hughe-Gordon flashed a huge smile, revealing uniform, brilliant-white, straight teeth. They were a testament to advanced and expensive dental care that had nothing to do with the barbaric medieval practices that passed for dentistry in Barnwell's youth.

Barnwell decided to lob a missile and see where it got him. "Drugs, mate."

"Drugs? Moi?" Hughe-Gordon widened his blue eyes and opened his mouth in mock astonishment. When Barnwell's stony expression didn't change, he said, "I don't know anything about drugs. Never touch the stuff."

"I never said you did." Barnwell got out his phone and flashed a photo of Jamie Reeves in front of Hughe-Gordon. "Have you ever seen this man among the circles you move in?"

Hughe-Gordon glanced quickly at the photo. "No, can't say that I have."

"You sure? Look again. Longer this time." The younger man took the phone and looked at the photo carefully. "Well, maybe he looks a bit familiar. I think I've seen him at the yacht club."

"Does he sail?" Nothing like that had turned up in Jamie Reeves's profile.

"No, I don't think so."

"I thought you had to be a member to drink there."

"You do, but he might have been a guest if he knew the right people. Might he have?"

Barnwell ignored the question. "Did you see who he was talking to?"

"Hmm, I'm not sure. I didn't pay too much attention, to be honest. He was just another guy in sailing circles. It's not like he stood out. Now, can—?"

Once again, Barnwell stonewalled what he considered Hughe-Gordon's efforts to derail the conversation. "And? What else can you tell me?"

"Nothing really." Hughe-Gordon beamed as though he were offering a substantial piece of information. "Look, what has this got to do with me? I don't know the guy, never spoke to him, barely even noticed him. I'm terribly sorry he's been murdered, but that has nothing to do with me."

Barnwell walked slowly down the side of the yacht, examining it carefully. He picked up a rope and regarded it like it was a precious artefact he was considering buying for a huge sum of money. Hughe-Gordon waited, his jaw working.

"Is this yours?" Barnwell said eventually.

"No, it's my father's. We hire her out. I manage her." Barnwell nodded. "Got a group coming for a few hours sailing shortly; the team taking them out will be here any minute. So if you don't mind . . ."

Barnwell grunted. He did mind. He minded a lot. Anything could happen on the open seas. Anything at all. And it would all go unseen and unnoticed.

"Mind if I take a look? Onboard, I mean."

"Er, yeah, sure." Barnwell climbed aboard, something he'd never have spontaneously dared a while back. But he was a lot nimbler and sure-footed than he had been forty pounds ago.

Barnwell walked about the deck, then poked his head into the cabin. He levered himself down the steps and glanced around. On the floor stood two crates of champagne. Platters of food lay on the work surface. Barnwell suspected that the fridge would be full of more of the same. Hughe-Gordon's boat was merely a vehicle, the open sea a backdrop. The purpose of the yacht's outing was to facilitate relationships and negotiations, deals for those for whom sailing meant hot and cold running attention, not tacking, jibing, and seasickness. It was a world Barnwell had no experience of or interest in. He climbed back on deck.

"How do DKN know you? They don't seem to be your sort."

Hughe-Gordon blushed. Two pink spots flushed his cheeks. He pressed his lips together and squinted, lines fanning out at the outer edges of his bright-blue eyes. He seemed uncomfortable, but nevertheless, beamed that toothpaste ad smile.

"They've done a bit of work for me."

"What kind of work?

"Bit of this, bit of that. Odd jobs, casual. They clean up the old girl, you know, from time to time." The cloth he waved over his shoulder indicated he meant the yacht. "I hardly know them really."

"How long have you lived on Jersey, Mr. Hughe-Gordon?"

"All my life. Born here."

"For someone who's lived on this island all your life, you seem to have only a passing acquaintance with more people than I would expect for someone who is supposedly *connected*." Barnwell, after a rough start, was quite enjoying the disconcerting effect his sunglasses were having. "Why do they call you 'Beetle'?"

"Ah, I really have no idea. You'll have to ask them."

Barnwell surveyed the young man, tanned and taut from hours on the water. "Right, well, I'll leave you to it. Keep your nose clean."

Hughe-Gordon beamed again. If the sun hadn't already been high in the sky, he'd have lit the harbour up. "Certainly, Officer. Have a great day." The clean-cut, preppy young man climbed back on board, the soles of his deck shoes squeaking on the dry, laminated surface of the deck. He leant on the rails leading to the cabin.

As he was about to leap down, Hughe-Gordon paused and turned to Barnwell, who was still watching him. "I might have seen that Reeves chap talking to a woman at the yacht club. They were leaning in close, laughing. Looked like they were having a whale of a time."

"Oh, yeah? And who might that have been then?"

"I can't remember her name, but she's been out with us on occasion. She was recently a guest of a big-time money guy with some fabulously wealthy clients. He's chartered the boat a few times."

"And? What's his name?"

"Hold on." Hughe-Gordon disappeared below deck and

came out shortly afterward, flicking through a large appointment book. "These are details of our bookings. Yeah, here we are. Last time was a couple of weeks ago. A party of eight. Granby, Silas Granby and Katya Granby." He ran his name down the list of names. "There was only one other woman on board. A Molly Duckworth."

If Hughe-Gordon could have seen inside Barnwell's brain, he would have spied sparks as brain cells crackled like lightening. Barnwell wrote the details down and put his notebook and pencil back in his pocket.

"Can I go now?" Jonny Hughe-Gordon said.

"Yes, you can," Barnwell replied.

"Good show. I need to get ready for our guests. They're expecting a good time."

"Cocktails, sunbathing, and being waited on hand and foot, no doubt," Barnwell grumbled as he watched the man disappear below deck. "But as sure as I'm a copper, I bet there's also alcohol, cocaine . . ." He thought for a second. "And orgies. Yeah, I bet that's what they do on them yachts out at sea. Far from prying eyes. Drugs, drunkenness, and debauchery."

CHAPTER TWENTY-EIGHT

"**T**HANKS FOR COMING in, Ms. Lascelles."
Graham regarded the surly, unkempt woman in
front of him. Her hair was lank and dirty, her
face bare of makeup. She wore grey sweats and scruffy
trainers. She looked nothing like the Audrey Hepburn-
esque figure that had pouted and fussed in Graham's interview room the day before.

"I don't see why I should have to, especially by myself."
Paula swept her lap with her hand, brushing off some imagi-
nary fluff to communicate her disapproval of the situation
she found herself in.

"I want to talk to you alone about something you said in
your last interview." Paula's expression didn't change. "I
thought you might prefer it this way."

"Oh? Why's that?"

"It's about some texts we found on Jamie Reeves's
phone. You said you'd had no communication with him
recently."

"That's right. None in months."

"And technically that might be correct, but we found

unanswered texts from you to him on his phone dating back just to the last week or two. I want to talk to you about them, honestly, without anyone present."

Paula's mouth twitched. Her eyes filled with tears. Haltingly she spoke, her voice wavering. "What I said was true. I'd had no contact with Jamie in months."

"But you tried to contact him. These texts prove it."

Paula lifted her chin, attempting to reclaim some of her dignity despite the circumstances. "Yes, but he didn't want to speak to me, did he? He never replied."

"But you wanted to speak to him?"

"Obviously."

"What about?"

Paula stared at him incredulously. "About getting back together of course! What else would I contact him for?"

Graham pressed his lips together and his hands opened reflexively. He gently shook his head. "I find it best not to guess."

"Do you really think I want that thick mammoth of a boyfriend? Matthew 'Muscles' Walker. Darlin' this and darlin' that. Spare me. He's not a patch on Jamie. He's embarrassing." Paula passed a hand over her face.

It crossed Graham's mind to wonder why she kept Matthew around if she thought so little of him. "So, when Jamie didn't reply, what did you do?"

"What do you think I did? I cried, beat my chest, and then I did absolutely nothing, Detective Inspector. Jamie ghosted me. He was telling me something without telling me anything."

"And did you tell Matthew about these texts?"

"Of course not!" Paula was almost spitting.

"Did he know you were still in love with Jamie?"

Paula leant forward, clearly believing Graham to be a

simpleton. "Do you really think I would tell my six-foot-four, meathead boyfriend that?" She sat back, throwing her hands in the air. "Who knows what he might have done?"

"So, you sent texts to Jamie hoping to reconcile, and when you didn't receive a reply, you carried on as normal?"

"Yes, Detective Inspector, that's exactly what I did. I like having a man around. Matthew is a plonker, but he's better than nothing. He doesn't hold a candle to Jamie, who was kind, good-looking, intelligent, and a good laugh, but he's all I've got now. That might sound callous . . . but that's how I am. Besides, Matthew gets something out of our relationship too."

"How's that, Ms. Lascelles?"

"Me, of course! He couldn't do better. To him, I'm a prize, however imperfect." Graham regarded the woman in front of him and marvelled, not for the first time, at the human capacity for delusion.

"And Matthew has no idea that you were still in love with Jamie Reeves?"

"No, I'm certain of it. He isn't that bright, Inspector. It's not difficult to pull the wool over his eyes."

"And he didn't leave your side on that Friday night? Didn't pop out anywhere?"

"No, the only place he went was outside for a smoke. My mum doesn't allow smoking in the house."

"And how long was he gone when he did that?"

"About a quarter of an hour I suppose."

Graham mentally calculated whether fifteen minutes was long enough for Matthew to have travelled to Hautville Road from Paula's mum's house, whacked Jamie over the head, and got back in the time it took to reasonably smoke a cigarette. It was possible, just about. He roused himself with a deep breath. "Okay, that's all for now, Ms. Lascelles.

Thanks for coming in and being honest. You can go home now and . . . do what you do."

Paula placed a hand on the table, halfway between her and Graham. She tapped the surface with her forefinger. "You know, Jamie was a decent guy. He didn't deserve what happened to him. I hope you catch whoever did this. And you put him, or her, away for a very long time."

"Yes, I went on the yacht with the Granbys for the day. It was just a bit of fun. I went to even out the numbers a bit." Janice had been assigned to interview Molly Duckworth at the Sanderson Landscaping office following Barnwell's report of his meeting with Beetle. "All the clients were Japanese businessmen, so Mr. Granby asked me if I'd keep his wife company. It was a nice day. Nothing improper went on. Why?"

"I'm simply interested in the relationship between you and the Granbys. I didn't know you had one."

"Really, it was nothing. I had spoken to Mr. Granby on the phone a couple of times when Adrian was out, and one day he came into the showroom. As he was leaving, Mr. Granby invited me on the yacht, and I said yes. I'm not averse to a little luxury. Goodness knows, I don't have much of it in my life."

"But why didn't you mention this earlier?"

"No, well, I didn't think it was relevant." Janice waited. Molly clasped her hands tightly in her lap. "And I didn't want Adrian to know, you see. He doesn't like us fraternising with the clients. I don't think he'd sack me, but he wouldn't like it. He'd give me a warning and tell me not to do it again." She looked up at the ceiling.

Janice waited. "Is there something else you'd like to tell me?"

"I . . . I said something I shouldn't while I was there."

"While you were on the boat?"

"Yes, I'd probably had a little bit too much champagne."

"What was it, Molly? What was it that you shouldn't have said?"

"I . . . er . . . shouldn't have said that Mr. Sanderson sometimes raises his prices for . . . certain clients."

"Ah, so Mr. Granby knew about that." Molly nodded. She bit her lip. "Probably. I said it to Mrs. Granby, but he might have overheard or she might have told him about it later. I don't know, but either way, I shouldn't have said it."

"Okay, and what did you do on the yacht?"

"Just hung out, chatted to the clients, but mostly to Mrs. Granby. We got on rather well. It was a lovely day, so nice to get out of the office. And there was as much to eat and drink as I wanted. I didn't have to lift a finger."

"What about later? You were seen with Jamie Reeves at the yacht club."

Molly sighed. Her eyes filled with tears. "Yes, it was a lovely evening. When we got back to shore, I went straight there. It's members only, you see, but Mr. Granby saw to it for me. I don't get that kind of opportunity every day. I wanted to enjoy it. I could take a guest, and I asked Jamie to join me. We had a great time eating, drinking, and dancing. And I"—Molly took a deep breath—"I hoped it might lead to more." She sighed. "But no. We went home separately at the end of the evening."

"Do you know if Jamie had been there before?"

"Er, no, I don't think so. I'm sorry I can't help you, Sergeant. I shouldn't have gone on the yacht, but it was all innocent really. A bit boring to be honest. I can see why

Mrs. Granby needed a bit of moral support. I think she's lonely, perhaps sad. All that money and all she's got is that fluffy dog for company."

"What was your impression of Mr. Granby?"

"He's nice, kind. Made sure my drink was continuously topped up and I had enough to eat. And it was nice of him to get me into the yacht club. I could get used to that life. It was a bit of a bump to come back to Earth. Especially without Jamie."

CHAPTER TWENTY-NINE

JACK STARED AT Janice in amazement, a tote bag in each of his hands. They stood just by the big wall which ran down the side of the churchyard. "Romantic?" he said quizzically. Above him was the tower of St. Andrew's, the charming parish church which gave the quiet street its name.

"Yeah," Janice said. "Ask anyone. Classically romantic."

"A graveyard," Jack said, some way short of convinced. "Romantic."

"Alright, it's a shortcut," Janice admitted.

"How many steps have you . . ." Janice had borrowed Jack's Fitbit two months ago. She'd wanted to walk herself into her wedding dress. It was a size smaller than she normally wore.

"Mind your own steps," she said, pulling down her sleeve to cover the device. "I've made my goal for today. And, well, I suppose I wanted to see where they buried that poor lad, Jamie Reeves." The few days surrounding Jamie's funeral had been gloomy and marked by a frustrating lack of progress in the case.

"Oh, great. That'll cheer us right up," said Jack. "We've gone from romantic to morbid in less than ten seconds. That'll put us in the right mood for the evening."

Jack was looking forward to dinner at Laura's, but Janice was tetchy. It was their first time socialising with the other couple on their own, and she wasn't sure how she felt about it.

"Oh, sorry. I feel a bit peculiar about tonight. I mean, what am I supposed to call him outside the station? Detective Inspector? Sir?"

"How about David? That is his name," Jack said.

Janice shivered. "Hell, no. That just sounds weird."

Jack rolled his eyes and shook his head. Janice was being irrational. "Come on. Let's go. Don't you normally go to the funeral when there's an investigation connected? Fly the flag. See who shows up, who's crying and who's not."

"The DI went with Roach," Janice reported. "He said it rained, and it was very sad."

"Not much of a poet, David Graham, is he?"

"It was a funeral, not a Highland sunset." Janice rolled her eyes. "Besides, you're expecting an elegy from the wrong man."

"I think you mean eulogy."

"No, I mean elegy. *'Tis better to have loved and lost, than never to have loved at all.'* And all that. Laments for the dead. I learned about them when I was choosing readings for the wedding."

"Good grief. Better not get mixed up or the vicar'll be sending us off into the afterlife for all eternity instead of asking us to forsake all others for as long as we both shall live."

"Alright, alright, clever clogs, come on, let's go. We'll never get there at this rate, shortcut or no."

This premarital sparring on Janice's part had been increasing. Jack wisely put it down to pre-wedding nerves. He put an arm around her shoulders and pulled her into him, determined to not let their exchange disintegrate further. "So, what are we here for exactly?"

Janice looked around at the rows of headstones, some dating back three hundred years. "I'm looking for Jamie Reeves's plot. But this business of *dying*," she said, scanning the graveyard that wound around the church, "seems to be all the rage. Have you got an app for finding recently buried corpses in graveyards?"

"I haven't." Jack eyes found someone—or a pair of some-ones—who might be instructive. "But those two guys over there might." Jack strode over to a bench under an ancient poplar on the periphery of the graveyard. Two men sat there eating their tea. A modest, yellow mechanical digger stood nearby. "'Scuse me, do you dig the graves?" Jack asked.

One of the men brushed off his hands. He was short and stockily built. He squinted as though he'd never seen a young man in a freshly ironed button-down shirt and clean pressed trousers in a graveyard before. He frowned, looking Jack up and down before he pointed to his mate and said, "That's Clip. *He* works for the church. I just stand and watch."

"Nah, Fred stirs himself sometimes to press the red button," Clip replied. "And I press the green one. We're for equal opportunities here. What can we do you for, young fella?" Clip had glasses on and a flat cap despite the warmth of the early evening.

Janice caught up with Jack and quickly introduced herself without mentioning her police connection. She asked about Jamie's funeral. "The local news said it was well attended."

"Aye, well enough, I suppose. Varies a lot. Sometimes you'll get an old granny who had relations from here to Khartoum, and there's a big to-do. Sometimes it's just us and the vicar," Fred told her.

"I remember that one because there were that journalist fella hanging around, asking questions when he thought no one was looking. We stood around the back of the church. We wait for everyone to leave before filling the plot in. He didn't see us, thank goodness."

"You'd have given him what for if he had, wouldn't yer, Clip?"

"Was anyone especially upset?" Janice was equally interested in the opposite but had no way to ask without revealing more about herself.

"People," Clip said simply, "go through *a lot* at funerals."

"Some show up, then turn away because they can't bear it," his mate said. "Some folks, they stay at the grave, sobbin' or prayin' or whatever until someone drags them away. We've seen all manner of screamin' and carryin' on. Others," he continued as though talking about fascinating local birds he'd recently seen, "come and go in complete silence, like they're going through the motions, but you know they're all cut up inside. Others prefer to leave it all on the field." Standing and rubbing his fingers together as though fine-tuning something, Fred searched his memory. "Hang on, Clip. Weren't that the funeral with the mob wife?"

"The one who came late, after everybody had gone?" Clip stroked his chin. "You might be right there, Fred. The one with the fancy black car. After they left, we did old Mrs. Hitchins from the nursing home."

"Mrs. Hitchins . . . They all run into one another after a

time," Fred said, thinking hard. His face relaxed, his eyebrows popping up to where his hairline used to be. "I remember now. A Maserati, I thought it were, but Clip here, he reckoned it was a Jaguar."

"Ain't neither of us ever gonna afford one, Fred, so who bleedin' well cares which it were?"

"Anyway, we get all types around here," Fred said. "Shell-shocked investment banker husbands, trust fund kids, mobster wives . . ."

"Second wives who stand there blubbering and first wives who grit their teeth. . ."

"'Desperate housewives', he calls them," said Fred. "Every time he tries to get me to bet with him."

"On what?" Jack asked.

"How long it'll be before they're on some new bloke's arm," Clip replied. "We choose a date, note it in our note-book." He pulled out a small, grubby pad, the corners curled over. "Then ask around. I was right to within a week one time. Felt I'd scored a hole in one."

"And I remember telling you," Fred said firmly, more aware of the sensitivities of the situation than his colleague, "that the game were in extremely poor taste."

"Didn't stop you playin' though, did it? Anyway, young Jamie had a visitor who arrived after everyone else had gone," Clip said. "She didn't arrive until even that pretty young lass with the red hair left, and she were the last of the mourners to leave."

"He always remembers them. The pretty, upset ones," Fred said.

"He must have been one for the ladies, that Jamie. There was the petite blonde one with the neckerchief," Cliff said.

"The one with the boyfriend who was built like a brick 'ouse?" Fred replied.

"Yeah, she were crying her eyes out. Bit embarrassing for the boyfriend, I should imagine. There were the one left at the end . . ."

"The one with the red hair?" Janice sought to confirm.

Cliff took a big bite out of his sandwich and spoke through his food, his cheek bulging. "That's right."

"And the mobster's moll," Fred finished.

"The poor fella must've had the gift of the gab to string those three along," Cliff said, swallowing loudly. "Impressive."

"P'raps one of them did it. Jealousy," Fred summed up. He sat back and folded his arms, quite sure of himself.

"Mrs. Mobster didn't stay long."

"Why call her that?" Janice asked.

"Well, she were like a woman from a film. She were all dark hair, big hat, high heels, sunglasses. Dressed all proper she were, too, in polka dots, but only arrived after everyone had left. Perhaps she got the time wrong."

"We would never strive to overhear human suffering . . ." Fred explained, as if reciting a poem. *Perhaps an elegy.*

". . . But we happen upon a good deal of it purely by accident," finished Clip. Almost unnervingly comfortable, the two gravediggers were clearly aficionados of human behaviour *in extremis*.

"The woman, the one who lingered after the funeral, the one with the red hair, what was she like?" Janice asked.

"Oh, she were completely different, poor lass. She were more upset than most of the mourners. Properly let it all out, she did." Clip spread his arms outward like he was introducing an act at the circus.

"Can you describe her?"

"Er, yeah. Why do you want to know all this?"

"Just curious," Janice said.

"Huh. She were slight, ponytail, red hair like I said, proper upset she was."

"Interesting. Seems like you get to see all sorts in your line of work."

"We sure do, don't we Fred?"

"Yep, we sure do." The two old men sat back. When there were no more questions, they tore bites from their sandwiches and stared at Janice and Jack like silent hamsters, big bulges in their cheeks as they chewed. Clip swigged from a bottle of water.

Janice thanked them and left them to their tea. Her mind was churning, Jack could see, but she was content to walk silently onward through the northern part of the churchyard and to the main road beyond. Five minutes on was Campbell Street, Laura's, and the promise of dinner.

CHAPTER THIRTY

"READY TO TRY Detective Inspector Graham's cooking for the first time?" Jack said when they arrived at the address they had been given.

"What? Oh, yeah," Janice said, distracted.

"Sergeant Harding, are you alright?" Jack bent over and waved a hand in front of her face.

"Just . . . well, thinking, I suppose."

"I try to do as little of that as I can. Gives my brain wrinkles. Especially during my time off."

Janice gave Jack an apologetic squeeze around the waist. "Love, if dinner with Laura and the DI happens to go a bit, um, *operational* tonight . . ."

"I should just go with the flow?" Jack suggested. "Yeah, okay. I mean, once you coppers get going, there's no stopping you. Isn't that right?"

"It's this case, Jamie Reeves. He wasn't exceptional, just a regular bloke who seemed to live a perfectly normal life— no priors, no nothing really. He'd worked on Tomlinson's garden, Barnwell had seen him at the Foc's'le, Roachie had played against him at five-a-side . . ."

"I fixed his computer."

"Yes, just normal stuff in a small place like this. It seems such an ordinary crime, a bash over the head, but someone lost their life, someone who was intertwined intimately with this community, and we can't find out who did it or why."

Jack held Janice at arm's length, waiting until her frustration died down a little. "The tyranny of incompleteness," he said, reaching for the philosophical. "No case is closed until it's *closed*. Halfway doesn't count, and 'nearly' is no good. I understand that frustration."

"We should make you a constable and be done with it," Janice said, giving him a lingering kiss. Which, of course, was exactly when Laura opened the door to welcome her guests.

"The thing about engaged couples," Laura tutted, "is that they can't keep their hands off each other."

Sergeant Harding straightened her jacket. "I make no apologies," she said. "It's Jack's fault for being the best-looking man in the Channel Islands." Behind Laura, Graham walked up. "Present company excepted, of course," Janice added hastily, then wished she hadn't.

"Good evening. Welcome to our small and humble abode," Graham said, smiling. He hadn't been entirely comfortable with the idea of having Jack and Janice to dinner when Laura had suggested it, blurring the lines between the personal and professional as it did, but now the evening was here, he was quite looking forward to it. The couple were good company, and if he were honest, he knew he needed to loosen up. It was all part of "the project."

Jack grinned and handed over the pair of bags he'd been carrying. "Starter and dessert, as instructed."

"Thanks." Laura smiled as Graham turned back to the kitchen, weighed down by bags. "I knew he'd be alright making the main course in our tiny kitchen," she confided to them, "but I didn't want to push it." She ended on a whisper and grinned. She too was looking forward to the evening. It was the first time she and David had been "coupley" with another pair. It felt like the milestone it was.

The living room of Laura's cottage was slowly transforming into a place which represented them both. Graham hadn't given up his house yet, but more and more he gravitated to Laura's. It was more homely, comfortable. His own place, while bigger, was rather sparse, clinical.

Laura's books dominated the living room in a large set of bookshelves which occupied half the available wall space. Two small paintings of the countryside near Graham's parents' favourite holiday place, a cottage on an island in the Outer Hebrides, hung on another wall over the top of a tall, blue vase. A telescope stood in the corner on its tripod, pointing skyward in expectation. There was a guitar, too, though whether it belonged to Laura or Graham wasn't clear. Two boxes of CDs were stacked by Laura's tiny media unit as if trying not to get in anyone's way.

"Has he read Freddie's latest?" Janice asked Laura in an equally hushed tone. "I don't want him forgetting the oregano or boiling the pasta sauce down to a sticky mess."

"He's read it, but said he had 'better things to do.'"

"I wanted to try faggotini," Graham called through, "but there were some tricky challenges." From the doorway, he held his hands up, his fingers splayed wide. "Very 'hands-on.'"

It was Jack who opened the conversational door. "How did you get into making pasta?" From the doorway—the kitchen was far too small for them all—the trio were treated to a display of David Graham's ability to unconsciously juggle several things at once. While his hands found the saltshaker, then the red chilli flakes, Graham launched into a slimmed-down version of one of his favourite stories. "Little *trattoria* in Herculaneum just a few streets from the ruins. Not far from Naples, on the Italian coast," he said. "Perfect place, small and family run. Incredible mussels, simmered with cherry tomatoes and *so much garlic*." He grinned. "Lots of good local wine, of course. And then"—Graham stirred the thickening, deep-red pasta sauce with a wooden spoon—"the owner brings out this plate of faggotini."

"The little parcel things?" Janice said. She'd never heard of faggotini, but not wanting to appear as unsophisticated as she felt, she had quickly looked them up on her phone while hiding behind Jack.

"Normally, they're made from thin pasta rolled out like pastry. Kind of chewy," Graham said. "But in this case, the pasta surrounding the filling was paper thin. So delicate, I couldn't imagine how they'd stayed intact in the boiling water. You just slid a whole one onto your spoon and . . . I'm serious, it was like eating a garlic and cheese infused cloud," he said, reminiscing happily. The occasion had been his honeymoon with his ex-wife, though only Laura knew that.

"How long were you there? In Italy, I mean," Janice asked. She was testing the waters. How far could she probe?

"Ten days, but I'd have stayed there to become an apprentice pasta maker if they'd let me."

"Think of the crime we'd have!" Laura exclaimed. "The world would have better pasta but more unsolved murders."

"Sounds like a reasonable trade," Jack said. Not bound by Janice's sensitivities, he'd squeezed around Graham and rummaged in the kitchen drawers to find a corkscrew. He set to work on a bottle of Chianti.

"One of our citizens would have conniptions," Graham

commented. "The crime rate is high enough. Or so he keeps saying on his blog." His tone was one of disdain and concern; Freddie Solomon provided Graham with most of his public relations problems while, in the detective inspector's opinion, repeatedly threatening the integrity of his investigations. "Or maybe he'd prefer it if I *was* a pasta maker. Seems I'm not doing nearly enough."

Janice got there first. "He's full of it, boss."

"Meh, Freddie's entitled to his opinion," Graham said. "No laws were broken in the writing. Well," he added, "not exactly."

Laura exchanged places with Jack and began grating Parmesan. She stood shoulder to shoulder with Graham as he stirred the sauce. "'Not exactly'?" she said.

"Kind of."

"Freddie's *kind of* fallen afoul of the law?" Laura wanted clarity. It wasn't like Graham to equivocate on things like this.

Janice took over. "It's illegal to tamper with a jury. Influence people, coerce them, threaten them, that kind of thing. By writing about cases in the way he does, Freddie is potentially influencing the pool from which a jury will be pulled. It's been the case with previous investigations, and it will be the same way with Jamie Reeves."

"But you haven't charged anyone," Jack said. "We can't know who the jury will be."

"Not yet, but when we do arrest someone and the case comes to trial, they'll be citizens of Gorey and the surrounding area," Graham told him. "Which is precisely the intended audience of Mr. Solomon's diabolical screed. If I were a lawyer, I'd have no trouble putting together a case which proves Freddie's writings prejudice potential jurors.

But his readership is so wide, we would be in danger of not having any jurors if we excluded them."

"How so?" Laura wondered. "Even if they worshiped Freddie, they'd never be silly enough to ignore the clear facts of the prosecution's case."

"If they're worshiping Freddie, they're silly enough to do pretty well anything. And I do wish he'd stop putting himself at the centre of things. He's not qualified. He's never done so much as a ride along with us, let alone been trained in evidentiary procedure."

"Perhaps we should try it, sir, I mean, David, er, boss." Janice suppressed a wince.

"How do you mean?"

"I mean perhaps we should invite him to come out with us, shadow us, see what we do, what we deal with on a daily basis. He might be more understanding, less confrontational. Hell, just some appreciation of what we're up against would be something."

"Hmm, perhaps so, but I suspect that he understands that negative stories sell, positive stories not so much, just like any tabloid. I mean, it's not the criticism I object to so much as the uncalled-for undermining of the trust the public have in us . . ."

"Wine anyone?" Jack said loudly.

"I'll get the glasses!" Laura said, almost as loudly.

Graham stopped short. "Right." He turned back to stir his pasta sauce, which was almost thick enough. "Going to drain the pasta in a moment. Why don't you all sit down and try Jack's antipasti?"

Jack quickly laid out a selection of pastrami, Italian cheeses, and spiced, pickled vegetables along with a baguette. He'd picked them up from the farmer's market. "I skipped lunch," he explained to Laura as she set about slicing the baguette. "I'm starving."

"Yeah, me too," Laura said. "Some days, the distribution desk is more like reception at A&E, and sometimes equally as life-threatening." She laughed. "I just never know what I might be faced with."

"Really?" Jack said. "I didn't know being a librarian was quite so exciting."

"You'd be surprised. The other day, old Mr. Hetherington showed up looking pale and very out of sorts. I thought I was going to have to call an ambulance for him. Turned out he'd just had a slice of the pizza we lay on for the 'book of the month' group. He'd never had pizza before. It didn't agree with him."

"Aha, his digestion was more used to overcooked greens and grey meat, no doubt."

In the kitchen, Graham tasted the sauce for a final time. "A fraction more sweetness," he said, quickly finding the sugar container. "Thanks for bringing the antipasti," he told Janice, who was standing in the doorway watching him. "I tend to get a bit overambitious with my cooking. Laura's always telling me to scale things back. She's right." He smiled. "She's always right."

CHAPTER THIRTY-ONE

J ANICE WATCHED GRAHAM check his sauce, the clock, his pasta, and clear his work surface. She noticed the same precise, considered movements she'd have recognised anywhere. The hard surface of the fridge door felt cold against her skin as she moved to lean against it. Something caught her eye. A photo of Graham with his arms around a young girl sat in a frame on the kitchen windowsill.

"Hey, you two, come and get some antipasti before Jack and I eat it all," Laura called out.

"I was asking him about the case," Janice responded. "Was that alright, or . . ."

"It's fine," Laura said, walking over. "If I objected to David discussing work out of hours, we wouldn't have got very far. He puts things aside when I tell him to though, don't you?" She leant over to give Graham a peck on the cheek. "But I'm pretty sure his mind is never still under that calm surface."

"Wish I could leave it all at the station sometimes," said Graham, turning away from some intensive chopping to grab a hunk of black truffle Pecorino cheese. "Most of my time is spent *thinking*. Pinning down details that we've missed, trying to make connections. It mostly goes on in the background. I try not to let it affect things," he told them all, but his eyes were only on Laura. He popped the cheese into his mouth.

"*Mostly.*" Laura chuckled. "There was that time you put yogurt in my coffee."

Graham returned to his chopping. "And what's wrong with that?" he called over. "The Vietnamese have added yogurt to coffee for generations." Another glance at Laura, then a smile meant just for her, one she understood.

"So, sir, I'm learning a lot here, but, um, can I ask about the Reeves case? What are your most recent thoughts?"

"I'm considering the possibility that Paula Lascelles' boyfriend might have done it. She did say that he was outside for fifteen minutes having a smoke. Do you think that would have been long enough to do the deed?"

Janice turned down the corners of her mouth. "I mean, maybe, if he ran. Does he look like a runner?"

"That's not the sport I'd have in mind for him, no."

"What about the boss, Adrian Sanderson? He has a shaky alibi too."

"Hmm, I still think his motivation is rather weak."

"What about Granby? His alibi's questionable. And, you see, on the way here I—"

"Excuse me, Janice. Can I get by?" Graham squeezed past her, holding his chopping board covered in chives above her head. "It's just the damnedest case. No one saw anything of the attack until Jamie staggered into the pub. Nothing on camera," he added heavily, rolling his eyes at this continued hindrance to effective and efficient Gorey policing. He scraped the chives into a pan on the stove.

"The gift that keeps on giving us bugger-all when we most need it."

"But sir . . ."

"And Marcus could provide only the most basic details. Not his fault," Graham conceded. "We were unlucky with the evidence."

"Rain," Jack said, walking up, "can *really* muck things up. Couldn't it have been a run-of-the-mill robbery? One that went sideways?"

"It could," Graham said, dipping his head to accept a pitted green olive from Jack's antipasti tray that Laura popped into his mouth. "But if it was, they failed spectacularly. Not only did they not get anything from him, they killed him to boot. In a moment they went from an opportunistic common crime to the prospect of a life term."

"Maybe he was seen as a rival. He was a good-looking guy. Maybe one of his paramours has a jealous boyfriend, and he flirted with someone who was a little too flirty back," Laura speculated.

"Which, in a manner of speaking, brings us back to Matthew Walker," said Graham.

"And Silas Granby, sir," Janice added.

"Let's not be hasty," Graham replied.

"When I spoke to him, Bazza reckoned Matthew wrestles bison for a living," Jack said.

"Doesn't make him a murderer," Graham countered. "Constable Barnwell is also a man of considerable . . . Well, he's *considerable*, but I'd never think of him as a killer. In fact, I'd trust him to babysit a child in a heartbeat. And he's pretty soppy over that dog of his. No, size has very little relevance."

"Walker has to be among the field of suspects though,

surely," Jack reiterated. "Top of the list, maybe. Perhaps the girlfriend incited him."

Graham thought back to the woman who'd sat across the table from him a few days ago. "Hmm, I don't know that she did that."

"But what about Silas Granby, sir?" Janice was becoming breathless. "I mean, Adrian Sanderson denies Granby's story about having a physical confrontation with Reeves, and if he's telling the truth, why is Granby lying?"

Her boss appeared to not hear her. "Right now," Graham said, setting down his knife by a neat pile of chopped garlic, "our field of suspects includes almost the *whole of Gorey.* All because, basically, we don't have any good ones."

By general consent and to everyone's relief, dinner party talk veered toward Janice and Jack's upcoming nuptials. With the remains of crumbly Italian cheese and smoked meats now scattered around the antipasti plate, Graham was in the kitchen preparing to serve the faggotini into bowls, though he promised to lend an ear to the discussion.

"People talk about wedding nerves, you know," Jack was saying, "but it's not really *us* that's anxious. It's the other people who are getting hot and bothered, causing us second-hand stress in the process."

"My mother," Janice summed up in a tone of heavy foreboding.

"She's decided to . . ." A year ago, even less, Jack would never have risked a negative comment about Janice's family. Even now, his impulse was to avoid offence, but he and Janice were a team, and both knew it was best to face the inevitable awkwardness of family occasions by sticking together. "Actually, she's trying to decide pretty much *everything.*"

"Everything except the husband. She's happy with him." Janice started listing the issues. "She's got opinions on the venue, the service . . ."

". . . the flower arrangements, the bridesmaids' dresses . . ."

". . . even the date. She actually phoned me a couple of weeks ago," Janice said, nudging Jack, who only vaguely remembered this singular conversation but who nodded in agreement, or possibly sympathy, "and asked if we could bring the wedding forward by two weeks. Just like that!" she exclaimed. "And all because she found a great deal on a package holiday to Greece and needed to book it before it was sold out!"

"What's her problem with the venue?" Laura wondered.

Eyes closed, sighing, Janice couldn't even find the words. Jack stepped in. "Our proposed venue 'suffered from an absence of Holy Spirit.'"

"We said no initially to a church wedding," Janice explained. "Got nothing against the idea, not really . . . But as soon as we looked into it, the complexities doubled, then doubled again. I mean, some of my family are atheists. There are hymns to choose, the processional and recessional music. Readings to be selected and approved. Banns posted. But Mum was so insistent."

"I'd just as soon scrap all that, have a ten-minute wedding right on the beach, and then repair to the Foc's'le for a slap-up lunch," Jack said.

"Make it the Bangkok Palace," Graham added, ferrying through four bowls of faggotini from the kitchen, "and I'll be your best man, no charge."

"And *this*," Laura said, admiring Graham's professional presentation of his culinary efforts, "looks amazing." The faggotini was topped with grated Parmesan and a sprinkling of fresh parsley.

"Well done, sir. Could be on the cover of a food magazine," Janice said warmly, forgetting again to drop the "sir" for one night.

"Just keeping things simple," Graham said. "Sorry about the kitchen though. Looks like a toddler tried baking for the first time."

"The mess is worth it," Laura said. She leant over to give him another kiss on the cheek. Jack and Janice exchanged a glance, mutually aware that they were seeing something rare and special: David Graham putting aside his responsibilities and stresses just long enough to be *human*.

Graham popped one of his faggotini into his mouth, making a point of enjoying it before delivering his verdict. "You know, I'm not transported into ecstasy, and my dough could be a hairbreadth's thinner, but these are pretty bloody good for a first try."

"Well done, Dave," Jack said.

While the DI enjoyed his pasta, Janice silently mouthed to Jack, "*Dave?*"

"Remember, it's your wedding day," Graham said. "It's all about you two. Others will have their views, but they don't matter. I recommend you sit down, agree what you want, veto almost everything other people suggest, and have a fantastic time."

"'Almost everything'?" Jack asked.

How was it possible, Graham found himself asking himself later that night, for him to delve back into those memories so easily? His wedding, his honeymoon in Italy. Those gold-flecked days—dozens upon dozens if one is lucky—which sweep by when a new marriage is just *perfect*.

Eight years together, as happy as any man could expect, until that one moment when everything fell apart.

"The car," Graham said. "Get a nice car. You and your bride must leave for your new lives together in something *showstopping*. And I don't mean a paddy wagon waiting outside the church with its lights on."

Janice laughed. "I can just imagine me, dress every which way and furious, having to clamber into a vehicle that recently transported our most recent murderer. I would not be impressed. Are you listening, Jack?"

"Yes, ma'am. Got it, loud and clear. No paddy wagon."

"An Aston Martin would be a good choice."

"Or one of Silas Granby's motors," Janice added. She sighed wistfully.

Graham didn't answer. He was working on his final faggotini, admiring its proportions. "I'm not going to be competing in *MasterChef* any time soon, but these are gratifyingly edible."

"Like eating at a restaurant," Jack said. "Do I detect a dash of fish sauce?"

Eyes closed, absorbed in his faggotini, Graham failed to reply, so Laura stepped in. "A tablespoon. Just isn't the same without it." She watched Graham for a moment. The others worried briefly that they'd overstepped but were not sure how. Before the conversational momentum could dip, Laura did the sensible thing and steered things back to the wedding. "And the flowers? What are you choosing for the flowers?"

CHAPTER THIRTY-TWO

ONCE EVERYONE HAD eaten and retired to
the living room, Graham brought through a
steaming cafetière of coffee and, of course, a pot
of tea. "Now, where were we?"

"Means, motives, and opportunity," Janice reminded
him. "Matthew Walker, Adrian Sanderson, Silas Granby, or
some unnamed individual we have no idea about."

"Matthew might not be the brightest," said Graham,
"but Barnwell maintains that Walker denies everything.
Was genuinely offended at being accused. He even tried to
inform against his girlfriend. I don't completely trust either
of them, but she was still in love with Reeves, and his opportunity was slight."

"Perhaps they are double bluffing," Jack suggested.

"That would require coordination and brains the likes
of which I simply don't think they possess."

"Adrian Sanderson, then," Janice said. "You met him
twice, didn't you?"

Graham nodded "And both times he was angry about

what had happened to Jamie. Even considered him a protégé. Maybe someone whom he might give the business to when he calls it quits."

"But if Jamie threatened the stability or future of his business . . ."

"Yes, I agree it's possible, and he did have that small window of opportunity when he went to the office, but again, it's hardly conclusive."

"Then what about Silas Granby, sir? His story differs from Sanderson's. Granby says there was pushing between Jamie and his boss. Sanderson denies it. Granby said the argument was about the cost of the job. Sanderson said it was about flirting with Mrs. Granby. One of them is lying."

"Yes, that is problematic, I agree. Did you get anywhere looking for the murder weapon?"

"No, sir. Unfortunately not." Refusing to be deterred again, Janice pressed her point home. "Suppose Sanderson is telling the truth. Maybe Granby felt threatened by Jamie. Maybe he decided to do something about it, coshed Jamie over the head when he was supposed to be in Turin, and made up the story about the costs and the pushing to put Sanderson in the frame."

"Hmm. Maybe. I can't see it, can you? I mean, why would he? He has far too much to lose."

"It might be nothing, but on our way here, we were talking to two gravediggers. I spoke to them about Jamie Reeves's funeral."

"Oh?" Graham poured Janice another cup of coffee.

"Apparently after everyone had left, another woman arrived. They said she was distressed."

"Did they say who she was?"

"No, but they said she had dark hair, a big hat, high heels, and sunglasses."

"She wore polka dots," Jack added helpfully.

"Katya Granby, sir."

"How can you be sure?"

"She arrived in a black Maserati. It must have been her. Maybe she was closer to Jamie Reeves than we thought. I'm sorry, Laura." Janice found her host's arm with an apologetic touch. "We've turned dinner into a briefing."

"Not a bit of it!" Laura replied. "I want to catch the attacker as much as you do. Besides," she said, "I find it rather thrilling. I can enjoy the mostly peaceful life of a librarian while living vicariously through you lot. It's fascinating to me how you develop theories and go about interpreting people and their behaviours."

"People are quite predictable. I mean, most of the time, we can take basic information, make some simple deductions, and then just depend on people to be *themselves*," Graham said.

"They'll surprise you sometimes, though, given enough provocation," Jack pointed out. "I mean, I'm basically a very quiet person, and I've got most of the characteristics for an introvert. But," he added, "I also managed to ask a beautiful woman to marry me when I didn't know what she was going to say."

"Yes, you did," Janice argued, quite certain.

"*You* knew, but *I* didn't. It was like walking over hot coals," Jack recalled.

"You sweet little lamb," Janice said. She squeezed his waist.

"And while we're talking about people surprising us," Laura added, "Barnwell dangled from a helicopter."

"And someone got me to jump out of a plane," Graham said. "More than twenty times, but that doesn't change my basic, cautious self."

"When on earth did you . . . ?" Jack was surprised.

"Back when I was younger and had too much energy. I used to skydive. I found it relaxing," was all Graham said. "But you're right, given sufficient provocation, people will act out of character. I still think Granby's a poor fit for the attacker though, and he'll stay that way unless something significant crops up. Walker? Not so sure."

"And what about Sanderson? What would it take for you to change your mind about him?" Janice wondered.

"Corroboration of Granby's story about Sanderson physically struggling with Jamie. Them having words is not enough. Or some proof that he was lying about the content of their argument."

"I think the Granbys are definitely worth another chat," Janice said. "I thought they were a strange couple. The dog thing is just weird."

"I know about the dog memorial thing," Laura said. "Mrs. Granby asked to put up some posters in the library inviting donations. There was an article in last week's local paper about it too."

Laura saw Jack was confused. "We've still got it, haven't we?" she asked Graham, getting up from her seat. "The paper."

"I think it's in the recycling," he said.

"Yeah," Laura soon called from the corner of the kitchen, "here it is. They're building a memorial to their top dog, and they're establishing a fund to help build a new one for each fallen champion." She stopped, puzzled by something, but soon handed the paper to Jack. "Here, next to the article about the exhibition we went to last week. Everyone finds their contentment *somewhere*, I suppose."

Jack read from the article, which was accompanied by a

photo of Silas, Katya, and the prancing Willow playing in their sunlit living room.

"For those who love dog shows and the breeding of champion dogs, the Granby and Padalka-Lyons families are a guiding light. Determined both to encourage participation in dog trials and to memorialise the great prize-winning pooches of the past, a small group of women have found a calling in a cause which is often overlooked."

"Overlooked," Graham grunted, "because it's a complete waste of . . ."

"Everyone has their hobbies," Laura reminded him. "You might not agree, but then I can't imagine any of those ladies enjoying early twentieth-century classical music or researching British prime ministers from the century before that." Graham had developed a fascination with the life and times of George Canning, who until recently possessed the distinction of holding the shortest period in office of any British prime minister. His sole term lasted one hundred and nineteen days, from April 1827 until his death in August 1827.

"And then there's this." Laura gestured at the telescope setup—a stout, black cylinder atop a tripod. "Birthday present," she said.

"Wait, he has *birthdays*?" Janice exclaimed.

Jack leant forward, interested. "What are you seeing out there?"

The night sky wasn't yet dark enough for a practical demonstration, so Graham launched into an explanation instead. As he gave them a rundown on the Messier objects —distant, faint nebulae and galaxies—Laura found her attention wandering. It didn't normally; she'd learned a lot about bird migrations and magnetism the other day, and just last week, she received an upbeat, savagely comical critique of the Police Act of 1964. There was no dissuading Graham from these mini-lectures it seemed, and so Laura resolved merely to steer him toward greater conciseness. It worked for them both.

But something was bothering her, and it wasn't Graham regaling Jack and Janice about the "rapid," many million-year cooling of ancient gases around failed stars hundreds of light-years away. Laura poured more coffee, served little dessert mints, and laughed along with Graham's overly enthusiastic hand gestures as he depicted a distant super-nova. But she wasn't with them, not really, and for the rest of the evening, she found herself quietly distracted by a thought. At first, it refused to properly form, and it took most of the rest of the evening, but an idea began to perco-late through the fog.

Later that evening, after Janice and Jack left and Graham had insisted on cleaning up, he walked out of the bathroom, wiping his face on a towel. He'd just cleaned his teeth and smelled minty and fresh. Laura sat on the bed. "All yours," he said. She didn't move and stared pensively at the light from the lamp across the road. He sat next to her. "What is it? Did you not enjoy yourself this evening?"

"What? Oh no, no. I really had a good time. I was thinking about something else." Laura shifted to face him. "You know that night you refereed the under-fourteens?"

Graham rolled his eyes. "How could I forget?"

"Janice and Jack and I went to the exhibition at the council offices, remember?"

"Hmm."

"On the way out, a man bumped into an elderly couple on the steps so hard they fell into Jack. The man was in a huge rush and didn't stop; he just kept on going. It was exceptionally rude."

"Okay."

"Well, that man, I recognised him from the paper."

"Love, you're not making much sense."

"Oh, sorry." Laura shook her head. "The man who ran out of the exhibition. I'm sure of it. His picture was in the paper. It was Silas Granby."

CHAPTER THIRTY-THREE

O NLY ABOUT A third of the council building's
   employees were at their desks when DI Graham
   strode in and made the strangest of requests
with respect to the paintings exhibited there earlier that
month. "The exhibition's finished, Detective Inspector," the
office manager, a well-turned-out woman in her early fifties
told him. "We replaced it last week with a selection of
computer-aided drawings of the—."

"I know that. I just walked past it." Heartfelt and
commendable, however amateurish they may have been, the
local artists' paintings from the Wordsworth retreat had all
too quickly been replaced for Graham's liking. As far as he
could tell, the lobby now hosted an exciting debut exhibition by R2D2. In fact, it was a collection of blueprints
depicting the council office's renovations. "Here's what I
want to know," Graham said. Since Laura had told him
about Silas Granby rushing out of the exhibition, he had
been anxiously waiting for the offices to open on Monday
morning. "What happened to them, the paintings?"

Some of them were gone for good, he soon found, deliberately destroyed by one of the artists as part of an "Activist-Performative Gathering." "I think her name was Belinda. A young girl with weird ideas. Really got her head in the clouds," the office manager said. Graham was strangely and hypnotically drawn to the woman's bright, glossy peach lips that stood out in her otherwise unadorned face, spouting words he didn't want to hear.

"Destroyed? How?" Graham asked. His notebook opened in his hand almost unbidden.

"'Ritualistic purging,' I think she called it. She put it on YouTube. You might find it there."

"What does ritualistic purging consist of? Did you watch it?"

"A bunch of teenagers stood in a field, staring in different directions, while a small pile of terrible paintings got what was best for them, if you ask me. A good, hot barbecue."

Graham fired off an expletive fractionally too loud. "Sorry. It's just . . . I need to get hold of as many of them as possible." He handed her his card and began looking around. "Is there a list of the artists somewhere or promotional stuff for the . . ."

"I'm not sure, I wasn't involved in the planning or take apart. But I know where the remainder of the paintings are now. Shall I take you to them?"

Graham's heart jumped. "That would be most kind."

The woman led him through the warren of cubicles, odd corners, and converted rooms which formed the main body of the council building. The public facing part was bright, clean, and new. The rest was a depressing collection of rooms that owed nothing to the best architecture and even less to interior design.

Councillor Zara Hyde, still only days into her role, was

on the phone in her office, a large but still undecorated space at the end of the broad hallway. "All those windows," Graham wondered aloud, looking at the huge sheets of glass held in place by old steel frames, the yellowed white paint peeling off them. "How does she cope when she needs to jump up and down in a searing rage?"

"Oh, I don't think she's that kind of a person," the office manager told Graham. "Very into"—she paused, searching for the right word—"'esoteric' practices, I think she called them. She wants us to begin meditating. Can you imagine? She even brought in a design company to assess the 'flow' of our offices! Now she's considering expensive changes." The office manager tutted. Profligacy, her expression said, was a vice not to be entertained at Gorey Council. Her peach lips pouted.

"Can we please just get the rest of the new cameras first before we throw money at other things?" Graham said. "I've a local man murdered just round the corner from here, and the only thing to witness it was the pavement he landed on."

"Terrible," the woman agreed, leading Graham into a suite of dingy rooms which reminded him of the sets of a Scandi noir crime drama he sometimes watched. "Here we've got some expansion space for when new projects come in," she said as though describing a modern, slick multi-use office rather than an unused, windowless room that hadn't seen a mop or a cloth in quite some time. "And back there is the storage. That's where you'll find the paintings. We've given the artists three months to pick them up." Her expression and crossed arms told Graham that she thought that was being far too generous. "And then we'll throw them out."

"Magnificent," Graham said, heading straight for the stacks of frames he could see propped against boxes. Some were placed neat and vertical, but others had been left higgledy-piggledy, as though certain of their imminent disposal. "These works are going to have a surprise second exhibition," Graham announced. "But could I trouble you for some help? Do you have any photos of the assembled exhibition?"

"Freddie Solomon took a huge number of photos at the—"

"I'd prefer the council's official shots, if you don't mind," Graham said, making a note all the same. "And can I borrow one or two of your people?"

The office manager stared at him, her mouth open slightly, her peach-slicked lips catching the light. Suddenly, she smiled as she chose to convey some of the town's respect toward their lead police officer. "To help out Gorey Constabulary and the famed Inspector Graham? In a murder case, no less?" She reached for a white, internal phone. "I think we can manage that."

The artists arrived at odd intervals, called from their homes by the enthusiastic efforts of the assistants the woman with the peach lips had seconded to the job of helping Graham out. Fergus, the agitated Scot prone to hissy fits, walked into the room with a perplexed but curious look on his face. He seemed to be hoping for a spectacle, or at least something to justify the hassle of being suddenly called down to the council offices. He'd not been particularly happy with his paintings in the first place, and now they would begin a second life as . . . evidence?

Argumentative on the phone, Belinda refused to attend until Graham threatened to compel her through legal means. "What do you want from me?" the young woman kept asking from the moment of her arrival. "Burning *The Crescent Bay Quartet* was always the plan. It completed the cycle. That was how it *had* to be." Her passion rose quickly to the surface, leaving her ruffled but unapologetic about her art and its demise. "It's a concept I'm drawn to. You probably wouldn't understand," she pronounced, clearly conveying she thought Graham far too old, conventional, and uncool. "You don't feel about them like I do. The immolation was a sign of *hope*."

"Well, right now," Graham told her, "my hope is that you're the only artist who's burned evidence before I could see it."

"Evidence?"

It was the most common question from the artists, all of whom had gathered by midmorning. Philomena Courthould-Bryant arrived second from last, despite living eighty yards from the council building. She was accompanied by her husband, all-round art snob Percival Courthould-Bryant, whose presence was unnecessary but the result of being in possession of an overactive curiosity and having nothing better to do. Mrs. Courthould-Bryant clutched four of her canvases. "Can you believe it, Percy? My little paintings being significant in a police enquiry," she said proudly.

"That's good," her husband muttered, "because they were never going to be significant in art history."

"Stop being rude about my art," his wife snapped. "Look at it; really look." She held one of the canvases up.

"Oh, right. I see!" her husband said, standing back to look at what she was holding up. "I get it. Sorry, Philomena. I was being slow." Courthould-Bryant had no idea what he was looking at but hadn't stayed married to his wife for fifty-five years without understanding when he needed to smooth things over now and again.

"See? Just because I'm not one of your classical artists doesn't mean I have nothing to offer." Philomena stalked off to talk to a more sympathetic soul, Dr. Ramachandran.

Abandoned, Courthould-Bryant looked around. "Detective Inspector, good day to you."

"Mr. Courthould-Bryant," Graham exclaimed. "A very good day to you too."

"A very *strange* day, I'd say it is," the elderly man continued. He'd lost none of the sergeant-major vigour he'd shown at the review of a historical miscarriage of justice months earlier. He still had the air of a man who always wanted to be in charge of any situation, his lack of comprehension with respect to its nuances notwithstanding. "Are you investigating forgers, then?" Courthould-Bryant asked. "Is that it?"

"Is what what, Mr. Courthould-Bryant?"

"Forgeries. You reckon one of these students is knocking out fakes? Selling them on the what's-it-web. You know, on the FreeBay." Courthould-Bryant leant in close. "You can tell me," he said, tapping his nose. "I'm a super confidant."

CHAPTER THIRTY-FOUR

GRAHAM SUPPRESSED A laugh only with effort. Courthould-Bryant was a super confidant for Freddie Solomon, more like. "No, we're not chasing forgers. Was your wife able to find all her paintings from the exhibition?" he asked.

"Yes." Courthould-Bryant leant in conspiratorially. "Unfortunately. One might rather she'd joined that young gel in a purifying immolation ceremony, or whatever she called it." Graham raised an eyebrow.

"Alright, alright." The elderly man raised his hands. "I'll be nothing but polite about Philomena's splashes of colour. Beauty in the eye of the beholder and all that."

"You could try being her *muse* from now on. Talent should be nurtured," Graham told him. "And especially later in life, we should all seize opportunities to bring plea-sure to others and ourselves." Before the stunned septuage-narian could respond, Graham reiterated his main point: "Be nice to your wife. It'll do you good."

As Graham walked away, the elderly man decided to follow the detective's advice and headed off to help

Philomena with her paintings. Graham had arranged for a conference room to be made available, and the artists were busy selecting their artwork and arranging it around the room.

Graham found his way to a small, pleasantly plump woman with thick-rimmed, round glasses who wore an elegantly draped saree in a bright-yellow batik print. "You must be Dr. Ramachandran," Graham said. He extended a hand. "Thank you so much for coming over."

"Please call me Dr. Hiruni. Everyone else does." Dr. Hiruni was affable and gracious, and though bemused by the situation, intrigued as to where it might lead. "When they told us the paintings might be useful to the police," she said, "I assumed they meant an artistic crime had been committed, not a violent one." Like the other artists, she had propped up her paintings against an uncluttered wall. Fergus banged nails into it so they could be hung.

"One never knows," said Graham, "where vital evidence is going to come from. And we have to try everything. Are your paintings in the same order as before?"

"Yes, but I can't see how they'll be of any help. They're just landscapes, and not especially good ones, I confess."

"They're very attractive," Graham said. "And as for whether they are evidence, leave that to me."

Rumours had spread quickly, and by the time the last artist from the retreat, Magda Padalka-Lyons, finally showed up with Pom-Pom the Pomeranian trotting along behind her, the five-person artists' collective understood the seriousness of the case and their role in it, even if they didn't understand how their paintings mattered.

"Mine were here and here." Philomena was pointing as the exhibition took shape once more. "And over there."

Graham helped her hang the pictures while her husband held his wife's handbag.

"I suppose," Belinda said, considering the space, "that my pictures occupied these four gaps. But they're not here now."

"Of course they aren't here now," Fergus said. "You burned them, remember?"

"I mean," she said, "that their *resonance* isn't here anymore. There can't be *harmony* now."

"Ah," Fergus said, and left it at that.

Sheets of card were fixed to the walls to represent Belinda's pieces, and she eventually consented to providing rough sketches of them, quickly done in pencil. They became ghostly in their incompleteness, as though the artist had tired of the work and given up or met with some terrible fate.

"Thank you, Belinda," Graham said, mindful of her prickly character as he sought to sustain her cooperation. The others were largely bemused by the whole thing except Fergus, who was enjoying himself, this second exhibition, and the inevitable attention *far* too much, all the while muttering about the inconvenience.

"Don't be daft, lass," Fergus was saying to the stupefied Dr. Hiruni. "Yours were *here*, and mine were next to these other ones *here*."

"That's not how I remember it," Dr. Hiruni objected. Clearing up their conflicting memories took only five minutes using the council's promotional photos, at which point Fergus offered a grudging apology.

"What does it matter, the order?" Fergus asked as Graham paced steadily around the room, fixated on the L-shaped row of pictures that spread across one wall and part of another. "I mean, why do we have to recreate it exactly as it—"

"Because exactitude is a virtue, Mr. Barr," Graham answered, unwilling to share his thought process with the artists. "Whatever Peregrine Wordsworth believes." Graham had seen Wordsworth's show on TV once and only once, vowing never again to spend his time in such a manner. He had been relieved to hear that the leader of the retreat had disappeared off the island immediately after the public viewing of the paintings was over. Wordsworth was currently somewhere in South Asia.

Once Belinda's reconstructions were complete and Dr. Hiruni was content as to the arrangement of the pieces, Graham labelled each painting with the date and the artist's name. He began his 'survey.' "I hope you won't mind me asking for complete quiet," he said, his back to the artists. "I'll call on you if I need to, alright?"

Roach pulled his pole out of the back of the patrol car and grabbed Carmen's lead as she jumped down. He'd parked the car at one end of Hautville Road, and now he stared down the row of houses to the Foc's'le at the other. He knew Janice had already searched the front gardens of these houses, but she'd encouraged him to have another go at finding the murder weapon.

"Right, Carmen, old girl. Let's give you a good old sniff."

A car pulled up and Janice got out. As she walked across the road to Roach, she took a call. "Hi, Laura . . . Uh-huh . . . Council offices, okay, I'll look him up. . . I will, take care." She hung up. "What have you got there, Roachie?" In his hand, Roach held a bloodstained shirt. Janice recoiled at the sight.

"It's Jamie Reeves's from the other night. I'm going to let Carmen sniff it and then see where she takes us."

"Is that even allowed?"

"I don't see why not. I considered using Bazza's shirt—he had a load of blood all over him—but I thought his scent *and* Jamie's would confuse her. Let's see what she can do, eh? If it doesn't work, we'll resort to the sticks." He raised the pole in his hand.

Roach crouched and held out the shirt for Carmen. She gave a little bark but seemed uninterested in it. "Come on, girl. Take some notice, will ya?"

"She's too young and untrained, Jim."

Roach tried again, but Carmen turned in a circle, unsure of what was expected of her. He sighed. "Okay, it was worth a try. Poles it is then—whoa!" Carmen took off. She ran to a spot in the pavement two houses up.

"That's where the trail of blood started. It's where we think he was hit," Janice said. "He then staggered or crawled his way up the road to the pub." As if to confirm what Janice was saying, Carmen started to pull on her lead in the direction of the Foc's'le.

Roach let her follow the trail as he and Janice jogged behind her. When Carmen reached the pub doors, Roach gave her a treat. "Good girl, Carmen, *good* girl. Alright, what shall we do n—" Carmen strained on her lead, but this time in a new direction. She led him down the side of the pub. "She's heading for the bins, Janice!"

"Could be nothing, but let's see." Carmen ran up to a green industrial skip and stood on her hind legs, whining and pawing at it.

"I'll grab that pallet," Roach said, leaving Carmen with

Janice as he manhandled a crate over to the side of the skip. Janice climbed up to peer over the top into the pile of bottles, pizza boxes, and other detritus generated by a lively pub one day away from collection day.

"Give me your pole." Roach handed it over and watched Janice carefully as she poked and prodded. Her eyes lit up. Carmen was still whining. "Shush, girl, shush. I think she's got something."

From her pocket, Janice pulled out a pair of gloves and reached into the skip. "Aha!" she said, holding up her find for Roach to see, her eyes shining.

"What is it?" Roach cried.

"This, Sergeant Roach, is a bloodstained chunk of pebbled concrete of the exact kind one will find to excess at the Granby house."

CHAPTER THIRTY-FIVE

THEY HAD PRODUCED sixteen exhibit-worthy paintings in all, but Graham immediately eliminated seven of them: all four of Belinda's, two of Dr. Hiruni's three, and one of Magda's. He politely asked each artist to retrieve their works. "Very good," he said of them. "Please don't be discouraged. They simply don't possess the relevant evidentiary features."

The muttering began, encouraged by an overly excited Fergus. "We should be filming this, you know. It'd make a great documentary."

"Shh," advised Dr. Hiruni. "He's thinking."

"He's barking mad," Fergus hissed. "Are you sure he's a real detective and not just a local crank who's, like, a 'consultant,' or whatever?"

Ten yards and many worlds away, David Graham was assessing . . . But then the rude distraction of Freddie Solomon's particularly annoying voice wrecked his concentration. As certain as the sunrise, Freddie Solomon had somehow arrived in the conference room. "Upsetting to see your art utilised in this way, isn't it?" he began sympathetically to the group. "Who feels like sharing?"

"Solomon!" Graham cried. "Who let you in? Are you *trying* to get arrested for interfering with witnesses? Is that what's going on?"

The artists all took three steps back as though Freddie were radioactive. "Let me guess. You're planning a special article called 'Inside Gorey Constabulary,'" Graham continued, "where you blog from one of the cells. I can imagine it now. 'The conditions are appalling, but my fight is just. Please send donations to . . .'"

"I have every right to speak to members of the public."

"Blog on down the road, Freddie. Steer clear of this one."

"This is intimidation of the press!" Freddie cried. "The latest in a long history!" He turned to appeal to the artists, but there was no sign of them. They'd disappeared like mist over water at sunrise. "It's like being a journalist in a police state!"

Freddie stalked off, leaving Graham alone. Once he'd gone, the confused gaggle of artists showed their faces again. "I apologise for the interruption," Graham said. "Now, where were we? I have questions about the paintings."

"We weren't really supposed to be exact about everything," Dr. Hiruni explained.

Graham summed up what he understood of Wordsworth's philosophy and process: "You were instructed to produce gusty, colourful gestures to celebrate one's joy in the creation of art, yes? Precise details of people and things half a mile away, not so much."

The lack of detail bothered Graham acutely, and this worsened as his study of the exhibition reached its conclusion. "This," he muttered to himself, "is going to be tricky.

Did you make anything up? Paint things that weren't there?"

There were a lot of furrowed brows. "I think the scenes were pretty much as I painted them, certainly as I interpreted them," Philomena Courthould-Bryant said.

"I don't have enough imagination to put things in that aren't real," Magna simpered. "If I did, there'd be dragons and shapeshifters everywhere."

"For me, Peregrine helped make a good container for my practice," Fergus said, finding such buzzwords irresistible despite his dislike of them when uttered by anyone else. "But I didn't need all his advice. The stuff about letting the details go and what have you. 'Breathe through the painting,' he said once." Fergus shook his head. "Anyway, what did you want to know about my work?"

Graham kept his questions direct. "Did you paint this one on Friday?" He tapped the frame of a particularly vibrant pastiche of swirls and loops. Over these, Fergus had painted in contrasting colours a series of dots.

"They signify details. I thought the precise colour coding provided an evocative contrast with the surrealism of the background. Sort of like life—a series of adventures imprinted over a lifetime."

"Er, right. So . . . Friday?"

"Yes, I think so."

"In the morning or afternoon?"

"After lunch. Does that matter?" Fergus asked.

Graham ignored his question and continued to stare at the paintings, pondering the many elements—the depictions of the water, the small strip of beach at the foot of the cliffs, the grey complex of low clouds which signalled another incoming rainstorm. Instead, Graham brought his full attention to the right-hand side of each picture, where the cliff face swept upward and out as though sculpted by the wind, leaving a plateau of land which jutted into the Channel.

Janice appeared at his elbow. "Boss? Everything alright? Laura said I might find you here." What Laura had actually said was "David might be on red alert today. You might want to keep an eye on him."

Thus far, Janice found, Graham had succeeded mostly in confusing everyone, including the staff at the council offices, several of whom kept peeking into the conference room to see what was going on. They saw only a man dressed in a dark grey suit standing thoughtfully in front of the paintings. "Boss?" she asked again.

"Good day, Janice," Graham said without turning round.

"You, um, think you've found something, sir?" Janice watched him for a reaction, but his face was impassive and focused. "In the paintings?"

"Maybe." Graham stepped right, becoming absorbed again in Fergus's painting from the Friday lunchtime.

"I've got some news, boss."

"Okay." Graham didn't look up from peering closely at Fergus's dotty composition. Janice blew out her cheeks. She looked around. She'd save Carmen's find until she had the DI's full attention.

"You'd have thought," Fergus whispered to Belinda, a few yards away, "he'd seen enough the first time around."

Unconcerned with plaudits but fascinated by the inspector and his process, Belinda shrugged and watched the detective work. He moved steadily through the space, always aware of everything, his eyes constantly in motion. "What's he *doing*?" she whispered.

Dr. Hiruni had depicted the Granby home almost like a kind of mushroom exploding upward out of the rock.

Graham stared at it, his nose almost touching the canvas. *Friday morning, purple van and one black vehicle.*

Graham moved along to the next painting. *Friday, early afternoon, no van, no black vehicle . . .*

One after another . . . *Friday late afternoon, man and woman beside pool, purple shirt, bikini, no van, black vehicle.*

Next . . . *Saturday morning, man, woman sunbathing. Black vehicle only.*

The paintings were of varying quality, and some were mere compilations of splodges of colour on canvas, but viewing the paintings side by side multiple times, Graham layered the pictures in his mind. He built a composite image of what they conveyed even though when viewed individually, their meaning was near impossible to determine. It was almost like flicking through an old-fashioned flip-book. They only made sense when viewed together, comprising an uncommon witness to events otherwise unseen. He closed his eyes, encoding the images into his memory.

There were more questions, highly specific and direct. "Magda, come and look at your third painting with me," he said. "Can you remember how many people you saw around the house?" As Magda ransacked her memory, Graham also brought Fergus forward. "Cast your mind back and convince me you painted *exactly* what was there."

His cheeks puffed out; Fergus was nervous at this challenge to his accuracy. Would his work be sufficient to help the police? Might he be partly responsible for catching a violent criminal?

Belinda remained silent. She sat on the floor, leaning against a pillar sketching the scene. Harding glanced down to see a hastily sketched row of people pointing at the artwork, a taller, imposing man at the centre. He appeared to be directing them, organising their work. "I don't think the DI's been commemorated in art before."

"I'm just trying something out," Belinda said, barely restraining her first impulse to shield her sketchbook from view.

"It's great," Harding said, smiling. "I just hope you don't feel the need to burn it this time, that's all."

"Fantastic." Belinda snorted. "I'm typecast. Am I to be forever 'The Girl Who Burns Her Work'?" She sighed, still young but already weary of the world.

"Alright, love. As you were," Harding muttered. She moved on and eyed Freddie. He had scuttled in again when she'd arrived. "Takes all kinds to make a world, doesn't it, Freddie?"

For once, the blogger was fascinated by DI Graham and didn't care who knew it. "This is his process! Right here in front of us!" he whispered to the others excitedly. "I *wish* I could interview him right now."

"Don't you dare," Janice advised. "He'll likely make sure you end up in a Category-A prison, sharing a cell with a terrorist."

"Best not then," Freddie said, crestfallen. "Still, I might be able to press Laura for a few details later."

"Come on, Sergeant," Graham called over. There was a note of urgency in his voice, a quickness to his stride like he'd suddenly plugged into an energy source.

"Where are we going?" Janice said, trying to catch up as they travelled along a dark corridor. Graham hadn't even said goodbye to the artists.

"The Granby place," Graham replied. "I enjoyed their topiary. Fancy myself another look."

CHAPTER THIRTY-SIX

"TOPIARY?" JANICE SAID, diving into the passenger seat before she was left behind. They were soon driving at a speed which would have left Graham liable to arrest were he a regular person. "You've got a theory then, boss?" she asked, holding on tight and hoping Graham hadn't lost his mind.

"A theory? We'll see," said Graham.

"Care to share it? Something? Anything?"

"When Mozart was nearing the end of a composition, did people barge into his studio and ask to see the incomplete manuscript?"

"Probably not," Harding admitted. "But, sir, I mean, comparing yourself to . . ."

"My manuscript is ninety-six percent finished, Sergeant. With a little bit of luck, you'll be witness to its completion." He turned right onto the newly laid, single-lane track. When they reached the security gate, Graham stayed behind the wheel while Janice gained them access. The moment she shut her car door, Graham raced around the edge of the Granby's putting green and past the two superb sports cars resplendent in the sunshine.

The car stopped. Graham was in a hurry to get out and speak to the Granbys. "What was that news you mentioned?" He was already tripping down the front steps. The deep *bong* of the doorbell could be heard within, followed by hysterical barking.

"Oh, God, not again," Graham muttered. "Give me a golden retriever any day."

"Jim and I had another poke around for the murder weapon. And we think we found it."

Graham's eyes widened. "What? Where?"

"In the bins behind the Foc's'le. Carmen found it."

"Well, what was it?" Graham could hear footsteps getting louder behind the door.

"A bloodstained lump of concrete . . . of a particular type that matches that holding up this precise residence. Jim's testing it as we speak."

"Well, hello again!" Katya Granby looked shiny and radiant. Janice suspected an intense multistep skincare routine involving products that cost the equivalent of her monthly salary. "Look who it is!" Mrs. Granby said to the dog under her arm. Willow had the suspicious, aggressive eyes of an animal prepared to square up to anyone. "It's the police again. What do they want this time, hmm?" she asked her dog. Willow licked her fragrant, sticky face appreciatively.

"Might we come in please, Mrs. Granby?" Graham said. "We have a few more questions. Won't take long." Invited in, he walked past Katya, who continued uttering childish nonsense to her dog. Once he reached the living room, Graham rather brazenly took a seat in the middle of the living room couch.

"Make yourself comfortable," Katya said, setting down her dog. It patrolled around her feet, hoping either for scraps of food or, Graham suspected, an excuse to finally bite someone. "The news," she said, abruptly changing her tone, "about Jamie. Very, very sad. So young. So *tragic*."

Graham supposed he'd gone through the usual motions of bringing out his notebook and pen but couldn't remember doing so; they were simply in his hand, ready. "I'm afraid I have to disagree with you there, Mrs. Granby."

"I'm sorry?" she said. "You know, English is my second language. Maybe I make many mistakes."

"About it being a tragedy. Do you know the origin of the word?"

Katya looked at her dog, then at Harding, then at Graham. "Is it an English test?" She laughed. "I didn't prepare."

"The Greeks," explained Graham, "would call a story a 'tragedy' when our main character is headed for disaster, but one which is inevitable, one that cannot be forestalled."

Katya struggled to catch up. "Cannot be . . . what? Like, cannot be stopped?"

"That's right. A person is walking into disaster—another Greek word, by the way—and can do nothing about it."

"But . . . it's *tragic*, no? Jamie. Bad news. The worst, the most terrible!"

"But not inevitable," Graham reiterated. "Actions could have been taken to avoid such an outcome."

Harding was no help, despite Katya's pleading eyes. "I really don't understand. Maybe you should talk to my husband."

"That sounds like a good idea," Graham said.

"But . . . I need to tell you, he's very upset today." Katya's slick face fell. "Very angry."

"Why's that, Katya?" Janice asked gently. She might as well play good cop. Graham was clearly doing his damnedest to be obtuse.

"A problem," Katya said, heading down the hallway to her husband's study, "at the airport. Very big trouble. Was a . . . how do you say? A *fiasco*."

Silas Granby answered the knock on his study door with a gruff expletive but was soon persuaded by his wife to greet their guests. "'Fiasco' is right," he said, coming through to shake the officers' hands. "First time it's ever happened to me. They behaved as though they'd never seen a British passport before. Problems with my visa. Highly unusual."

Graham took in every detail, as usual, from the man's tousled hair to his comfortable, expensive carpet slippers. "Where were you heading, sir?"

"New York," Granby answered. "Three days of meetings, then onward to Beijing. Honestly, some years I reckon I do more air-miles than a migrating bird. Makes it even harder to understand the problem this morning. I mean, I've been through immigration about a million times. They even gave me two different reasons, and they couldn't both be true!" He threw up his hands. "Typical government idiocy. I've had to delay my trip."

"Terrible," Janice trolled. Granby looked at her sharply. She gazed back and smiled sympathetically.

Graham motioned to the couches, a strange gesture perhaps in someone else's home but symbolic of what would come next: this was now his show. Part of him craved a more generous crowd, but he knew the moment had come, and he could not delay.

"Sergeant, let's begin with what we know," he said, standing now while the others sat, experiencing varying degrees of concern.

"Before you launch into something, can we please talk about why you're here?" Granby said, unwilling to relinquish control of the situation in his own home.

To Graham's surprise, Katya rolled her eyes at him. "Darling, the Jamie Reeves situation? Remember? They're investigating."

"Still?" Granby said.

"We've been developing some lines of enquiry," said Graham, "and they took time to bear fruit."

"Splendid," said Granby. "I hope you catch the monster. But how can we help?"

"Sergeant Harding, why don't you tell Mr. and Mrs. Granby what you told me?" he said to her. "About the graveyard."

"Jan told me that some records aren't always in the database. That some get 'lost' in the process of digitising." Barnwell was in the office talking to Jack, who'd popped in at Janice's behest.

"Yeah, they're not 'lost' as such, they just aren't in a compatible format. It takes time to convert them, and some never make it. They're somewhere, but not always available on the main system." Jack stood behind Barnwell, who sat in front of his computer screen, a mug of tea warming his hands.

"See, is there any way to find them?" Barnwell twisted his head to look at Janice's fiancé. "I've got a feeling about this Walker guy. He has 'ex-con' written all over him. But I can't find him in the system. And he's not saying nuthin'. I'd like to go a step further to see if we can winkle him out."

"If you get me the records, I can see what I can do. I

might be able to rip them and even roll them into the system so they are there for the joy of every police officer in the land."

"That would be fantastic. But to get them, who would I talk to? I've no idea. Walker's from London, so most likely someone in the Met."

"I know someone," Jim piped up from behind his screen. He was typing up a report on the forensic findings on the lump of concrete found in the skip next to the Foc's'le. "I met him when I was there. Let me give him a call."

CHAPTER THIRTY-SEVEN

"T HERE WAS A sighting of one of your cars, Mr. Granby," Janice said.

"A 'sighting'?" he said. "How do you mean?"

"Someone drove your Maserati, Mr. Granby. It was seen. And the driver wasn't you."

"Impossible," he said brusquely. "Only I'm insured, and I never let friends borrow . . . Oh," he said, with a look of concern. "Oh, wait." He turned to his wife. "You mean . . ."

"Mrs. Granby," Janice said, "could you please tell us about the visit you made to the graveyard at St. Andrews church?"

Blinking, Katya forgot about her dog, which ran sniffing around the edge of the room. Eventually it toddled away down one of the hallways. "She means the cemetery, yes?" Katya said. "The place for the dead peoples?"

"One dead person in particular," Graham said. "Could you tell us why you chose to visit Jamie Reeves's grave?"

Three pairs of eyes observed her every movement as she struggled to retain her composure and simultaneously answer a question which was difficult emotionally and linguistically. "It is normal, no? To say goodbye to someone. At home, it is like this. You have it here too."

"We do," Janice said. "The thing is people who quietly visit gravesites alone are usually loved ones."

Katya's face reddened. "*Love?*" She glanced around the room. "Please, you misunderstand. Was not 'love.' How could it be?" She reached for her husband's hand, finding it cold. "I am married lady, after all. Just, I was . . ." She made several false starts before saying, "You know, just sad for the young man, sad for his family. Is normal, no?" she asserted again. "I was passing and thought I would pay my respects."

"But you chose not to join the other mourners at the funeral," Graham pointed out. "His parents, his colleagues, his friends."

"Of course, of course." No further explanation was forthcoming.

"You didn't want to be seen there," Janice said. It wasn't a question. "One might wonder if coming late, alone, was a good way to remain unobserved."

Through all of this, Granby kept absolutely quiet. He sat back on the couch, his legs crossed, his fingers interlocked over his knee as though watching a solemn scene at the theatre.

"The family would be so sad, no? Was a tragedy, even if the Greeks don't agree." Katya smiled politely at Graham. "I got the time wrong. Was late was all."

"Very considerate," Graham said. He held Katya's gaze for a moment before dragging it away to look at her husband. "Now, if I could ask you, Mr. Granby, about one thing you told us?"

"By all means," he said. He smiled briefly, spreading his hands.

"You claimed that you witnessed an argument between

Mr. Adrian Sanderson and his employee, Jamie Reeves. Do you still make that claim today?"

With a little shrug, Granby asked, "Why would I want to change what I said? I remember it distinctly. They disagreed about the fee they would charge me."

Graham let the bitterness slide. "It was Sanderson who wanted to charge you a higher price?"

"Certainly. Everyone who's worked on this place has done their share of price gouging. I'd have taken half of them to court except . . ." He raised his hands before letting them drop in his lap. "Eh, I can afford it. I see it as a way to contribute to the local economy in the wider sense."

"And you maintain there was pushing."

"I do."

Abruptly rising and striding to the front door, Graham took them all by surprise. "I want to conduct a little experiment. Ears open, ladies and gentlemen. Please be ready to repeat back to me everything I say when I'm outside."

"He's leaving?" Katya stood, perplexed. Willow sensed the same. The Pomeranian suddenly appeared and chased Graham to the door.

"Bugger off," he hissed.

Katya retrieved Willow from Graham's ankles and he headed outside, closing the Granby's heavy patio doors behind him. The transition from the cool, air-conditioned interior to an unseasonably warm, spring outdoors made Graham sweat. Deciding quickly how to proceed, he stood in the centre of the paved area three steps down from the doors, adopted a heroic, theatrical stance, and went for it.

"'Friends, Romans, countrymen,'" he cried, his voice huge and stentorian. "Lend me your ears; I come to bury Caesar, not to praise him. The evil that men do lives after them," he warned with a raised finger. "The good is oft interred with their bones; so let it be with Caesar.'" Graham straightened his jacket, gave a small cough, and threw open the door as fast and as far as its mechanism would allow. "Any notes? Marks out of ten?" he asked his audience of three.

"You are back?" Katya cried, entirely confused. Granby stared up at Graham from his unchanged position on the sofa.

The expression on Janice's face said it all. She sat poised with her notebook, ready to dictate, but apparently hadn't heard a thing.

"Oh, for heaven's sake," Graham complained. "I know it's been twenty years since I won the school Shakespeare prize, but please tell me I've still *got it.*"

Fascinated but now entirely lost, Janice could only watch, wondering what on earth William Shakespeare might have to do with the Reeves case.

"What about you, Mr. Granby? Did you catch the performance?" asked Graham.

"I'm afraid not," he said, still relaxed on the couch despite Graham's unexpected theatrics.

"I gave it my all," Graham said, deflated. "Well, it's as good a reason as any, I suppose."

"What is?" Janice replied.

"My performance."

"To do what?" Harding said.

"To arrest Mr. Granby."

Katya shrieked, which set off the dog. Above the din, Janice couldn't stop herself from exclaiming, "Arrest him? Because he doesn't like Shakespeare?"

"No, because he didn't *hear* it. I was projecting fit to fill the Albert Hall and not a word came through." Graham turned to Granby, who was sitting forward watching the detective with narrowed eyes and a clenched jaw, his mind working as he tried to anticipate what the detective might say next. "I've got to say," Graham continued, "that's one heck of a glazier you hired, Mr. Granby. These windows are absolutely first-rate."

Predictably, Katya's comprehension was fixated on one word. "*Arrest?*" she asked again and again. "*Arrest* my Silas?" Harding gestured for her to be calm, but it did little to help. "For *what?*"

Annoyed it had taken so long, Harding was, however, finally able to latch onto Graham's floating, cross-field pass and run with the ball. "If DI Graham's Shakespeare was inaudible, you'd have been unable to hear a conversation between Jamie and Mr. Sanderson as you state."

"Perhaps," Granby said, still quite relaxed. "If they were closed. But one of the back windows was open. It's been so warm for April."

"I realise that you have money to burn, Mr. Granby," Graham said, "but only a fool runs their air-conditioning *and* opens the windows."

"You wouldn't be the first to call me a fool," Granby said. "Although I'm not sure failing to admire your Shakespeare is grounds for arrest."

"No, it's true," Graham said, putting away his notebook and pen. "They don't let us arrest people for those things."

"Well, there's a happy state of affairs," Granby summed up. "Isn't it wonderful to live in a democracy?"

"But," Graham added, "they do let us arrest people on suspicion of murder."

CHAPTER THIRTY-EIGHT

"**Y**OU'RE OFF YOUR bleedin' rocker!"

"Please be quiet and go inside, sir."

The answer was another noisy complaint. "Ge'roff me, you big twit! I'm already in handcuffs. What more do you want?"

"Sergeant Harding, I present to you Mr. Matthew Walker," Barnwell said to Janice as he succeeded in manhandling Matthew into the reception area. Janice was entering the details of Silas Granby's arrest into the computer. "He has been detained on suspicion of the murder of Jamie Reeves."

Harding watched the two men struggle briefly. It was at times like these that she wished she had a taser on her, something she could call upon easily without needing to complete a bunch of paperwork. She decided to threaten instead. "Mr. Walker?" she said loudly to the enormous, angry man. "Are we going dancing down Electric Avenue, or are you going to behave yourself?" Carmen came running into reception, her nails clicking on the hard floor. Excited by the commotion, she ran between Walker and Barnwell until the constable put his hand on her head to calm her. "Sit! Good girl." He pulled a treat from his pocket. Carmen snuffled it down in a second.

"He's only gone and bleedin' nabbed me!" Matthew howled. "Read me me rights and everything! Been 'elping 'im all week, telling 'im the truth, answering all 'is questions. 'E's got it in for me, 'e 'as!" Walker's London roots were showing.

"Don't be bloody daft," Barnwell rasped.

"Well, I dunno what else to fink." Matthew slumped into one of the plastic chairs set out in reception. The chair was dwarfed by his bulk, the fight suddenly leaving him.

"Afternoon, Janice," Barnwell said brightly. "It turns out that Mr. Walker has a colourful and fascinating past, previously unknown to the Gorey Constabulary, one he didn't care to share with us. Initial searches of the Police National Computer revealed no criminal record for the name, but some sleuthing and a stroke of luck changed the sitch. He's done some *very* bad things."

"That ain't me," the furious man complained loudly. "I'll plead mistaken identity!"

"Plead? You couldn't bloody well *spell* it," Barnwell growled. He turned to Harding, his tone all sweetness and light once more. "Sergeant Harding, I ask you," he said, feeling very pleased with himself, "is there anything that our fabulous computer forensic consultant can't do?"

"How do you mean?" she asked, too conflicted and lost to even begin the arrest paperwork. If Matthew was the killer, he certainly wasn't ready to confess. The anger evaporated off him as he rhythmically knocked his handcuffs against the underside of the chair he was sitting on.

"Police forces throughout the whole country," Barnwell explained, "have been digitising their criminal records. Takes ages, really tricky. Some of the records slot right in, others take longer, and some just never quite make it into the main file. They get stuck in a desk drawer . . ."

"Or shredded by mistake," Harding added, something she'd learned from conferences.

"Or, in this case, left on a form of media that none of our machines can read."

"Ah-hah," Janice said, making the connection. "Couldn't read until a certain technical wizard entered our midst?"

"He's a wizard, alright. Only had sixty records on the disc. London didn't know what to do with it, but they found an 'M. Walker' on the index, and we thought it worth a try."

"Unlucky, Matthew," Harding said. She looked over. "Lying about previous offences won't help your defence, man."

"I didn't lie. I ain't saying nothin' more without a lawyer," Matthew declared, quietly pleased that he'd thought of it. "Never had anyone pin a murder on me. Bloody ridiculous!"

"Oh, come on, lad, there's no need to sell yourself short. You were convicted of beating a man almost to death." Barnwell looked at Janice and paused for dramatic effect. "With a snooker cue."

Matthew was sulking now, beaten. "That bloke was a bloody liar. Exaggerated 'is injuries. Told the police a bunch of absolute rubbish."

"Medical records prove otherwise. And while you were banged up for five years, you got into a fight with a Scottish hard nut who put *you* in hospital for a fortnight. Sound familiar?"

"No."

"Want to show me your back, on the left side, where you were stabbed?"

"No."

"Must have been some fight over something at least one of you thought important."

"Self-defence on my part." Matthew was surly now. "What are you arrestin' me for anyway?"

"Suspicion of murder. Obstruction. A few more we can lay at your door if we have to."

Harding reiterated Matthew's rights under the law. "You do not have to say anything, Matthew, but remember that 'it may harm your defence if you fail to mention something you later rely on in court.' Them's the rules for you, just now."

"Yeah, he told me all that already."

The door to the interview room opened. Graham emerged. "What's going on?"

"Matthew's got previous for GBH, sir. Never mentioned it. Tried to hide his past from us."

"No, I didn't!" Matthew protested. "Was all on that disc thingy in London, you said! And," he yelled at Graham, "no one even *asked* about that!"

Graham was tired. It had been a long day already, and it wasn't even close to being over. Now, he felt pulled in two directions at once. He pinched the bridge of his nose.

"He did it, sir. I'm sure of it. Ten minutes in there with you," Barnwell said, pointing to the interview room, "and he'll sing like Ella Fitzgerald."

"I can't sing, I won't sing, and you lot are off your bleedin' rockers!" Matthew repeated. "I didn't kill anyone!"

"Funny, I've got a chap sitting in there right now," Graham replied, "who's saying the same thing."

"Two of us? What, now?" Matthew sneered. "Are you

just arrestin' anyone you feel like?" He shook his head like a dog with a flea in his ear. "That's what you lot all do, innit? Make it up as you go along."

Determined to let silence reign for a few seconds, Graham gave the atmosphere time to settle. "Finish off booking him in and put him in a cell. Barnwell, step into my office. And Janice, could I borrow you too when you're done with that? We'll leave the door open to keep an eye on reception."

Five minutes later, Graham used dividing gestures to organise his office like a court room. "I'm the judge. Barnwell, you're the prosecution, and Harding, you're defending Walker. Alright?"

"I'll give it a try," said Harding.

"Bring it," Barnwell added.

"Barnwell," Graham began, "set out for me why and how Matthew attacked Jamie Reeves."

The constable listed the sequence of reasons on his fingers. "A violent past, uncontrollable jealousy, rising anger, plenty of lies and deception, and a ton of alcohol. Insanely jealous of Reeves still having command over his girlfriend's affections, he goes out on the night in question and hits Reeves over the head to take him out of the picture."

"Right. Thanks. Harding?" Graham nodded at Janice. "Over to you."

"Do you have a confession from Mr. Walker?" Harding asked.

"Quite the opposite. But . . ."

"Right, so how exactly do you think Mr. Walker committed the offence?"

"He left the house he was sharing with his girlfriend on the Friday night, followed Mr. Reeves, or encouraged him from his house somehow. Either an argument took place, or he simply took a pop at the victim."

"Mr. Walker says he was at home all evening."

"Walker is alibied only by his girlfriend, who has said he was outside for fifteen minutes. He couldn't tell us who had won *MasterChef*. The house he's staying at is only five minutes from where the attack took place. He slipped out to batter Reeves and got back within fifteen minutes."

"Witnesses?" Janice asked Barnwell simply.

"None."

"Corroborating forensic evidence?"

"Unavailable." A gnawing feeling formed in the pit of Barnwell's stomach.

"Certainty about his motivation? That Matthew knew Paula wanted to get back together with Jamie?"

"Not established," Barnwell said, losing traction by the second.

"Did you know that earlier we found a bloodstained lump of concrete matching that found at the Granby house in a skip next to the Foc's'le?"

"I did not. Drat."

"But you had a *feeling*," Graham said. "Didn't you? Something in your gut told you, *insisted* to you: 'This is the only thing that makes sense. This *must* be the answer.' A confidence that you've *definitely* got your man, even though the evidence isn't quite there yet. Right?"

"Something like that, sir." It was best to be honest, Barnwell thought as his theory shed its wings and tumbled into a terminal descent.

"You were premature, Constable. But I like that you're listening to your instincts."

"Sounds like you know the feeling, sir."

"I do. I'm experiencing it right now, as it happens." Graham rose to put the kettle on.

"Sir?"

"Silas Granby. He's in the interview room," Janice said.

"The snooty chap with the expensive cars, the brunette mail-order wife, and the ridiculous house?" Graham raised an eyebrow. "Sergeant Harding told me, sir." Janice looked at her black police boots.

"That'd be the same man, yes," said Graham. "You see, I've got a feeling. A feeling in my chest telling me that Granby is the only suspect who makes sense. A feeling that he *must* be the murderer. A certainty that I've . . ."

"Definitely got your man," Barnwell said, "even if all the evidence doesn't line up yet."

Graham poured boiling water into his new teapot. It had a Dutch windmill scene on the side, the handle of his old one with the willow pattern having finally become too fragile to be serviceable. He took a few seconds to enjoy the sinuous curls of steam emanating from the waterfall of concentrated heat, the rising of a grassy, optimistic aroma. Every single time it brought him joy and lit up his brain. Especially right now. "That's the thing, though," he said to Barnwell, delighting in the delicate oolong scent coming from the pot. "My evidence *does*."

Janice's phone pinged. "It's Roach, sir. He's got a blood match on that lump of concrete."

"For whom?"

"Jamie Reeves, sir. We've got a conclusive connection between the victim and Granby."

CHAPTER THIRTY-NINE

EFFREY LANGHAM ARRIVED just as Graham and Barnwell finished their planning for the interview with Silas Granby. There was no need for him to introduce himself; the pin-stripe suit, expensive briefcase, highly polished shoes, and superior air marked him as a high-powered lawyer. Graham ushered him into the interview room where Granby sat in front of a cold cup of tea.

"Mr. Shiny Shoes is going to tell Granby to shut up and hope for the best," Barnwell guessed. "Isn't he?"

Graham handed Barnwell a mug of tea, a hot one, and then laid out the standard *modus operandi* for such lawyers in these circumstances. "Find irregularities in the arrest or charging, pick holes in our arguments and evidence, then demand release on bail, at the very least."

"Can't see you going for that, boss," said Barnwell.

"Not in a month of Sundays. Granby's a flight risk."

"Want to keep him downstairs overnight?"

"Maybe."

Barnwell blew out his cheeks. "This case, I tell you, it's as twisty as a snake."

"Good thing then that Gorey Constabulary is staffed by sharp-eyed birds of prey," Graham said, his notebook out and ready.

"You seem very sure Granby is your man, boss." Barnwell was reluctant to let go of his idea that Matthew was the killer. But he had yet to hear the full story about the wealth manager, and he knew that Graham would have solid reasons for arresting him. "No doubts about him at all?"

"We'll see. Got a couple of things to fall into place yet. We've got the wife too. She's not being straight with us either."

Just then, Janice escorted a woman with flowing brown hair perfectly coloured with red highlights into Graham's office. The woman wore large, anonymising sunglasses and heels which were perhaps three inches too high for the occasion. No one was surprised to find that Mrs. Katerina Granby was absolutely furious. Barnwell left to man reception.

"She," Katya said of Harding, "is nice. Is a nice lady. But *you*, Inspector"—she pointed accusingly—"are a devil!"

"I've been called worse," Graham said.

"Where is my husband?" she demanded.

"He's with his representative on the other side of that wall." He pointed. Katya bolted for the door, but Harding caught her forearm. "We'll be speaking to you separately, and due to evidentiary constraints, you may *not* speak with him alone." Graham's hard eyes held Katya's, and some of the steel in hers faded. She yanked her arm away from Harding. "Would you like some water? Tea?"

"*Tea?*" Katya sang in amazement. "How can you think about *tea*, you crazy man? I swear to heaven," she said, perhaps hoping Granby would hear through the wall, "the *second* we leave this horrible little place, we'll make complainings about all of you! *Official* complainings!"

Behind her, Harding wasn't impressed with these threats. "I can hand you details of our complaints procedure when you leave," she said.

Katya ignored her, focusing squarely on Graham. "We begin, yes?" she said, gathering her resolve.

"Faster we're in, faster we're out," Graham assured her. "All you need to do is to tell the truth."

"Truth?" Katya scoffed. "Truth is created by men and by money. That is the only truth."

"Smash the patriarchy, eh?" Harding muttered under her breath.

"Fascinating notion, but I haven't time for it right now." Graham clicked his pen. "Ready?" Katya nodded gravely. "Please sit down." Katya sat in the chair across the desk from Graham, crossing her legs and clasping her linked fingers around her knee. "Mrs. Granby, I wonder if you'd characterise your marriage to Mr. Granby for us?"

"Character . . . Oh, you mean what kind of marriage? Is nice!" she said. "Is love and happiness."

"The marriage hasn't hit any trouble recently?" Graham asked. "Any extramarital issues? Infidelity?"

Katya glanced at Graham, whose expression was hard to read. "Every couple has troubles. But we are good, thank you."

"Mrs. Granby, lying to investigators is a criminal offence. You could go to prison."

"What?"

"Let me ask you again . . ."

"No!" Katya insisted. "No troubles. I don't know why you ask this!"

"Calm down, love," Harding said to her. "Just answer the question truthfully." This did nothing but ignite Katya's anger further until she was bouncing in her seat.

"You think . . . you think I'm a criminal!" she shrieked. "What have I done? Did I break a crime . . . I mean break the law?"

"That depends," Graham said, "on whether or not you know that your husband killed your *lover*."

Katya's face tightened into such a rictus of scorn and anger she couldn't speak. Graham waited for some response to his trial balloon. When none was forthcoming, he asked her another question. "Did anyone from Sanderson's come back to check on their work after the project was finished? After sales service, that kind of thing?"

"I can't remember a visit," Katya said.

"You can't remember, or you don't want to tell us about it?" Graham pressed.

"Is a new house. Is a . . . ah, *complicated* place. People come and go all the time," she said. "Maybe Mr. Sanderson, maybe not."

Graham paused for a few seconds, just to be sure in his own mind. "One more time, Mrs. Granby. Did Jamie Reeves attend your house after the landscaping was finished?"

Katya was silent, then shook her head. "For the benefit of the tape, Mrs. Granby has indicated in the negative," Graham said. She trembled slightly.

Graham leaned on his forearms, facing Katya squarely. "Look, Mrs. Granby, we can prove that you are not speaking honestly about your relationship with Jamie Reeves. If you continue to do so, I will have to arrest you on suspicion of conspiring to pervert the course of justice. Now, would you like another try?"

Katya's eyelashes fluttered as her eyes flitted around the room. Her hands twisted in her lap as her mouth opened and closed several times. But no words came out.

"Mrs. Granby, what do you seek that money can't buy?" Graham asked when Katya had settled down. She was impassive now and, with her lithe body and long neck, strangely insect-like.

"Something that money can't buy?" She pulled her sunglasses from her hair. Thick, lustrous tresses now unbound fell around her face. "A dog masseuse who really *gets* Willow. One who makes dogs their life, their *calling*, you know? Who puts dogs before *everything*."

"I'm not sure I . . ."

"I have no idea what you are talking about!" Katya cried. "I don't understand these questions, so many questions, all in English. It's like a terrible river!" she said, miming a torrent overwhelming her. "All English, English, never a word of Hungarian. And *he*," she said, standing now and pointing at Graham as though unmasking a traitor, "is a crazy, *crazy* man! He is the most English of all! It's like he has teas"—she mimed—"coming out of his ears!"

Graham's voice cut across the interview room. "Almost, Mrs. Granby, but not quite." Except he said it in Hungarian. "*Majdnem*, Mrs. Granby, *de nem egészen*."

Pulled in three directions at once—raging anger, sudden amazement, and delight at the sound of familiar words—Katya was speechless again. Graham, his objective accomplished, saw that Katya was back in her shell, hermetic and silent. She was near motionless.

Graham took the tablet that laid on his desk and turned it so that Katya could see the enlarged image of one of the paintings from the exhibition. "Please look at this, Mrs. Granby. Do you see anything familiar?"

Katya gazed at the painting but shook her head. "I don't understand" was all she would say.

"Let's try another one." Fergus Barr's painting was the most detailed of them all. "The pool, once more. What do you see?"

Katya leant over to look. Her hand faltered as she spread her thumb and forefinger to expand the image. She began to cry, her sob subtle, almost silent. Harding, even from behind, heard it and, showing a sharp degree of sensitivity, sent what felt like a telepathic wave in Graham's direction. A tear rolled down Katya's face. The detective inspector wrote in his notebook.

When he looked up again, Katya was still staring at the image. Something about it had grasped her attention, and she picked up the tablet. She held it close to her face as though perhaps wanting to dive into the painting, into a simpler reality, and be rid of this chaos she now found herself amidst.

"Who is that? In the painting, Mrs. Granby."

"It's me." Fergus had painted her lustrous brunette hair, white skin, and the little black dots on her red bikini. "And Jamie. Sweet, sweet Jamie." Abruptly, Katya pushed the tablet away, more tears streaming down her face. "It was scandalous. What I did. What *we* did." She flicked a hand in the direction of the tablet. "I cleared the cameras, but I did not know about *this*."

CHAPTER FORTY

"I WELCOME THE opportunity to defend myself," Granby said in a strikingly mild tone. He was in the interview room with his lawyer. Graham and Barnwell sat across from him. "If you have evidence, sir, I hope it's more convincing than your Shakespeare charade."

"You only failed to enjoy it," Graham argued, "because you were deprived of my finely crafted oratory. And yes, it will convince twelve members of the public. It's a perfectly valid piece of evidence. A reconstruction should do it."

Barnwell glared at Granby, pained that his own theory was crumbling. He already felt the urge to slip next door, apologise to poor Matthew, and let him go home.

"Lying to us about hearing that argument," Graham said, "badly damages your defence. I suggest that you wanted to incriminate Sanderson in Jamie's murder by convincing me that they were at each other's throats."

Granby smiled, a snake taunting its prey. "Now, why might I do that?"

Graham leant forward, his elbows on the table. "Revenge, Mr. Granby, for one. Payback for being exploited. And deflection for two. I put it to you that after you returned home from your trip to Turin, you confronted Jamie Reeves and attacked him, injuring him so severely that he later died." As the detective inspector waited for a response to his accusation, the atmosphere in the room became thick, noxious, almost solid, like a knife wouldn't cut through it and they'd need a hammer and chisel.

"Listen, I did not kill Jamie Reeves. Okay, so I wanted to cause trouble for Sanderson. So what? He deserved it. But I did not, I repeat, did not kill Jamie Reeves."

"Mr. Granby, you are a man of considerable means. In the last week or so, I've tried to put myself in your shoes. To see the world from the perspective of someone with fabulous wealth, money to burn. I thought to myself, 'If I were filthy rich and I could already buy anything I desired, what *else* would I want in my life?' Which of those special, elusive things that money can't buy would I covet?" Graham turned to Barnwell like they were running a seminar. "Constable?"

"Erm." Barnwell thought quickly. "Partnership? You know, love, that kind of thing?"

"Mr. Granby is a happily married man though. As far as we've established, anyway."

Barnwell twirled the pen he used for his tablet between his fingers. "It can't be travel that he's short of. How about career satisfaction?"

"Mr. Granby appears very satisfied. He's at the top of his profession by all accounts. Why don't you tell us, Mr. Granby. What might *you* be looking for that money can't buy?"

"Faith? Is that it? Now I'm rich, am I supposed to get religion?" Granby said sarcastically.

"What about stability?" Graham said. "Predictable

patterns of life. Markets are volatile, and the people you work with doubly so. But a contented domestic life, well, that's priceless! A welcoming kitchen, dogs to fuss over," he said with a glance at Barnwell. "A beautiful, charming, *accommodating* wife at your side. A wife you can depend on, trust to be there for you. Your career is built around managing risk, but you must want a counterbalance at home. Yet recently, perhaps you saw signs in your wife's behaviour that posed a genuine threat to that stability and peace of mind."

Granby folded his arms and sat back. "You have a modest flair for psychoanalysis," he said, "but nothing you're saying makes sense to me."

"Well then, let's leave Freud behind and talk about Peregrine Wordsworth instead. What did you make of the art exhibition? Must have been quite a thing seeing your own home rendered a dozen different ways." He watched Granby with pixel-sharp intensity.

"Amateurish, but yes, enjoyable," Granby said.

"Unflattering in places?"

"How do you mean?"

"You left the exhibition early, sir," Graham spelled out, "and by all accounts, in a fury. In fact, you barged into an elderly couple standing near some other visitors on the steps as you left. I have witnesses. Strong ones." When Laura had told him that she recognised Granby from his photograph in the local paper as the man who had bumped into Jack at the exhibition, Graham's synapses had lit up like fireworks on Bonfire Night.

Granby laughed off Graham's suggestion. "Maybe their depictions of my house left something to be desired. They were hardly flattering, often unrecognisable. But I lay that at the door of their artistic abilities, not my architects. I wasn't angry." Granby glanced over to his lawyer, who remained stone-faced.

"Let's take one more gander around the exhibit, shall we?"

"If we must," Granby said, "but I have to say, this is all rather—"

"Friday morning," Graham said, producing from a file a photograph of one of the paintings from the retreat. "This was created on the first day of the workshop. What can we see at the Granby house?"

Granby pulled a face. "God alone knows," he said. "I suppose it could be my place, but it's a very confused representation."

"I've learned a lot about art interpretation recently," Graham said. "Look at this." He pointed to an uneven black splotch the approximate breadth of a thumbnail. "You know what that is?"

"Creative licence?" Granby guessed. "I saw a BBC thing about Peregrine Wordsworth once. He sounded like he'd lost his marbles. This only proves it."

"Looks to be a vehicle, doesn't it?"

"Perhaps, but I wouldn't recognise it," Granby said.

"And look at this?" Next to the black splodge was another one around a similar size, purple this time. Four dark shapes under a rhombus of purple could have been tyres.

"Constable, please describe Sanderson Landscaping's livery to Mr. Granby?"

Barnwell jumped. "Eh?"

"The colour of his vans."

"Purple," Barnwell replied. "And gold. Looks very smart."

"It's distinctive," Graham agreed.

Now as perplexed as he was angry, Granby said, "The firm was doing some work for me. They have a purple van. I have a black car. So what?"

"The landscaping was finished over a week before these canvases were painted." Graham showed him a second painting.

"Same day the black splodge is still there, but the purple one has disappeared. And there is another series of splodges over here by the pool. What do you see, Mr. Granby?"

Granby rubbed his eyes and shook his head before answering. "Scrawled, basic approximations," he said, dismissing the images. "Could have been painted by a child. Quite worthless."

"Then let's try something else. Later on Friday afternoon. Quite late, about five p.m. the artist said." Graham showed Granby a third image. The photos were now lined up next to each other on the table. "Here, this artist is more traditional. Less, oh, I don't know, impressionist. It's clear what's in this painting; it isn't just a series of swirls, swoops, and curlicues."

"You're certain they weren't drunk? I could do better, honestly."

"The artist is a seventy-four-year-old woman without the least shred of humour, and a complete teetotaller."

"Seventies, eh? Eyes like a hawk then," Granby scoffed.

"Actually," Graham said, "you're righter than you know. Look more closely."

"What am I looking at?" Granby asked, frustrated.

"Do you see the swimming pool at the front there?" prompted Graham.

"Yes. I know where it is. I helped design the damn thing."

"And do you see anything next to the pool?"

Granby peered. "Birds?" he guessed. "Or something created from the artist's imagination?"

Graham quickly slipped Fergus's less impressionistic, most representative painting, the one he had shown Katya, in front of Granby. "The pool, once more. What do you see?" Graham said.

"I see some people, like stick figures," Granby said. "Probably to make the painting more realistic. Or something. There is no telling with these types of people."

Graham raised an eyebrow. "Are you sure, Mr. Granby? Look again. There's meaning in those depictions."

CHAPTER FORTY-ONE

"SO WHAT?" GRANBY shouted. "This is a whole cartload of nonsense, and nothing more. You've got yourself all frustrated at not catching anyone, and so you've invented this flight of fancy. What am I seeing? I don't know! What am I meant to be seeing? I don't know!"

"What we're looking at is your wife lying by the pool on Friday afternoon with a man. A man that isn't you. A man in a purple shirt who drives a purple van."

Granby was aghast. He laid both hands flat on the table as though ready to stand up and take someone on. "What . . .?" He looked at the picture. "She . . .?"

"Oh, come on, Mr. Granby. How long are you going to spend imagining that we're a bunch of idiots? I put it to you that at the time you walked into that exhibition, you already suspected your wife had a history of cheating on you with Jamie Reeves. Perhaps you'd noticed them being over-friendly, or you'd heard rumours. But we know that you were concerned because you asked Adrian Sanderson to take him off the job."

"You are making things up. Jamie was becoming too

familiar with my wife? *My wife* asked for him to be removed. Really, you people." Granby folded his arms again and looked away.

"I suggest you went to the exhibition and found that you'd been duped. The artist made it easy, didn't he? Purple van. Purple shirt. Tall, distinctive young man by the pool. Your wife in a bikini. Where were you when this was painted? On a business trip, no doubt."

"Sydney . . . I . . . I was in Sydney." Granby couldn't seem to drag his eyes away; they were drilling furious holes into the painting, at the representation of his home and the poolside as depicted by the brushes of Fergus Barr.

Graham pressed his point home. "When you attended the exhibition, I suggest you saw what was happening and realised that your wife was cheating on you. You subsequently lost your temper and stormed out. As you did so, you bumped into the elderly couple and caught the attention of a witness."

Granby broke his focus and sat back, folding his arms. "So, you think I killed this Reeves fellow because he was having an affair with my wife? Well, I did nothing of the sort. I left that exhibition in a hurry because I had to take an important phone call. You can check my phone. It was from a client in Manila. This is all news to me." Granby waved his hand at the table.

"A lump of concrete that matches the kind used at your house was found with Jamie's bloodstains on it close to where the attack took place."

Granby shrugged again. "It isn't unique. I'm sure you'll find plenty of it at any builder's yard."

"Constable Barnwell, let's review things. What do we have so far?"

Barnwell checked items off his fingers. "Motive," Barnwell replied. "Revenge for the affair. Means, the blood-stained rock . . ."

"And what else?" Graham watched Granby closely.

"Opportunity, sir. There is no proof that Mr. Granby was where he said he was when Jamie Reeves was attacked."

Granby's eyes flickered left and right as he searched his memory. "What? I was on my way back from Turin." He made a show of calculating the time difference. "I was in Swiss airspace when the attack took place."

"Can you prove that?" Graham said.

"I told you Cynthia, my assistant, has all the details about . . ."

"But where's the proof?" Granby was silent. "Ghost flights, Mr. Granby. Isn't that what they call them?" Graham leant forward. "Your assistant was very helpful. Turns out that few of your flights are trackable. Isn't that correct? And therefore, no one really knows where you were on that Friday night."

Granby's pale cheeks flushed. "It is not uncommon in my line of business."

"Say nothing, Silas," interjected Granby's lawyer. He'd been silent this whole time. "They're guessing. There's nothing there. They just want a quick collar. And all the more satisfying to take down a 'one-percenter,' eh, Detective?"

Graham pushed away his notebook and stood. "Mr. Langham, is it? We have procedures for lodging complaints. You are free to make use of them. In the meantime," he said, glaring at Granby, "I suggest Mr. Granby think long and hard about telling us the truth."

"What the . . ." Graham came out of his office. He'd been preparing to go home for the night when he heard shouting. Janice had taken Katya Granby home. Barnwell was releasing Matthew Walker. Roach was en route to the cells with Silas Granby.

"This is a travesty! Are you on someone's payroll? Dirty cops? Don't you understand? Money isn't enough for some people," Granby railed. The reality of his situation seemed to have suddenly hit him. "They need to deceive you, to get one over on you, to watch you fall. In the end, everyone wants their pound of flesh!" Roach manhandled him just enough to persuade Granby that he was the stronger of the two and waved away Barnwell's offered assistance.

Dazed but genuinely entertained by the spectacle, Matthew was leaning on the reception desk as though he were about to ask Barnwell to pour him a pint. "So, is this, like, a regular day for you lot, then?"

"What's that, Matthew?" Barnwell said, still enjoying the memory of Roach's strong hand on Granby's shoulder; there was something authoritative about it, even if Granby had ruined the moment with fearful complaining.

"Arrestin' people for murder and such like. Bangin' people up. Regular sort of day?"

Barnwell slowly swivelled his gaze from his computer screen to regard the big lad; he looked tired and sweaty, but there was the sense that after five pints and a couple of packets of barbecue-flavoured crisps, all would be well. "It happens from time to time," Barnwell said. "You should know, though, that we generally don't cause the murders, so we can't predict when they'll happen or the subsequent arrests."

Nodding, Matthew said, "Yeah, suppose that's right. Anyway, is that it?"

"Is that what?"

"*It?*" asked Matthew. "This whole thing with the dead boyfriend and the expensive wife and the rich idiot? 'Coz I'm off down the pub, if that's alright." Barnwell appeared at his shoulder. "And if you see me there, you won't ask me any more questions, will you? You could buy me a pint, though. Wouldn't want a complaint on your record, eh? For wrongful arrest or whatever they call it," Matthew said, wagging a finger.

"Get outta here, lad. Stay out of trouble."

Matthew laughed and bashed open the double doors with his hefty body. "I'm not the one chasin' thieves and murderers!" He had a thought and turned. "I could apply, though, right? To be a fuzz. I'm not too old or nothin', and there's a limit on my convic—"

The reception's lights went out. "'Night, Matthew."

The next morning, Graham whistled to himself as he bounded up the steps to the station. He had come in early, eager to press on with questioning Silas Granby. "Morning, Barnwell!"

"There you are, sir." Barnwell came around from behind the reception desk. He flapped a notebook against the palm of his hand.

"How did things go overnight?" Graham nipped around the desks on his way to his office.

Barnwell ignored his question. "I'm waiting for a call from Sergeant Roach, sir." The constable looked weary. He had completed an eighteen-hour shift, some of it spent on a camp bed in the break-room.

"Good stuff. Off you get home. You must be exhausted."

Graham was light-footed and looking forward to his second cup of tea of the morning. He'd already enjoyed a perfect cup of Oolong with his breakfast, and now he planned an equally perfect cup of Assam. It would get him in just the right mood to verbally spar with Silas Granby and hopefully nail down his confession. Graham was in such a good mood he was almost skipping.

"He's been called out to the Granby house."

"Who has?"

"Roach, sir. I've been trying to call you. The cleaner was hysterical." Graham came to a halt. He took two steps backward, bringing Barnwell into his field of vision.

"Hysterical?"

"Roach's on his way there now. To the Granby home."

"Oh?" A cold hand clutched at Graham's heart. "Why?"

"Katya Granby, sir. She's dead."

CHAPTER FORTY-TWO

"CLEANER FOUND HER, sir," Roach informed Graham as he put on paper bootees. SOCOs were beginning to arrive. "At about seven thirty this morning. Called it in as soon as she saw her." Roach consulted his notebook. "Which was about half an hour after she entered the house.

"Didn't find her straightaway, eh?"

"No, sir. You'll see why."

"Alright, Sergeant, lead the way."

Roach led Graham through the house, past the sofa on which he'd interviewed Katya the day before, and across the patio where he'd delivered his Shakespearean speech.

It was a cool day, but Katya was wearing a bikini, a red one with little black polka dots. Graham recognised it as the one from Fergus Barr's painting. She was lying on her back on an inflatable, sunglasses covering her eyes. She looked like she was enjoying the morning sun.

"What's she got in her arms?"

"Looks like an urn."

"Jesus Christ, her dog's ashes." Graham looked around. "Where is her dog, anyway?"

"In the urn, sir."

"Not that one, the other one. The live one."

"Not sure, sir. No sign of it in the house."

Graham stared at the slim but pale body floating across the pool, the inflatable swaying slightly in the breeze. Katya's leg dangled over the side, her foot bobbing in the water. She looked like a memorial to the rich, wasteful, and utterly pointless. "So, what are we thinking?"

"No sign of any injuries. We found pills and a bottle of wine on the kitchen countertop, so I'm thinking overdose."

There was a noise behind them, and Marcus Tomlinson appeared around the side of the house. "Morning, lads. What have we got?"

Graham looked from Tomlinson to the figure in the pool. The three men stood mournfully on the side gazing at it for some moments. Roach broke the silence first. "Overdose we think. Pills and wine in the kitchen. I've taken photos."

Tomlinson pursed his lips. "Right, then. Who's going to get her?"

Graham and the pathologist both looked at Roach. The sergeant blinked before straightening his shoulders and casting around for tools that might help him. Propped up against a wall was a wide pool brush. Roach used it to prod the inflatable to the shallow end. Rolling up his uniform trousers, he waded in to bring Katya ashore.

Tomlinson looked her over. "Help me lift her." Graham and Roach moved to tilt Katya on her side. "Okay, you can let her down."

Tomlinson kneeled. "Ah, my creaking joints." He took Katya's body temperature. "Roach, take some more pictures, will you? Get some close-ups." The sergeant moved around the body, taking photographs from various angles, his trousers still rolled up around his knees.

"What can you tell me, Marcus?" Graham asked him carefully. Tomlinson was notoriously stingy with his information until he had done a full examination, but today he was more magnanimous. "Death around fourteen to fifteen hours ago I suspect. She's been here overnight."

"That's not long after Janice dropped her home." Graham's head swam. Had he, by pressing for an admission about the affair, contributed to her death? He closed his eyes.

"And she didn't overdose." Tomlinson sniffed. "I smell Rohypnol. There's some faint bruising around her arm here, but no obvious signs of injury except for . . ." Tomlinson leant over and looked closely at the bruising. "That looks like a puncture wound." Graham stared.

"You mean she was drugged, killed, and then staged like this?" Roach said, horror creeping into his voice.

"Maybe, young man. The urn's interesting. Who's Rufus?"

"Her dog, former dog. A champion apparently." Graham was as stunned as Roach.

"But this means . . ." Roach said.

"Her husband can't have done it," Graham finished for him.

"And if he didn't kill her, who did?"

They stepped back as the ambulance crew arrived to collect Katya's body. "I'll let you have the report as soon as I have it. By the way, I was impressed with your ingenuity earlier, Sergeant Roach. I felt sure you'd show us your aquatic skills." Tomlinson closed his doctor's bag of instruments.

"My what?"

"Your lifesaving skills. Except, of course, there was no life to be saved here. Swimming."

"If I'd tried that, you'd have had another body on your hands," Roach replied. Tomlinson frowned, puzzled. "I can't, sir. Swim."

Tomlinson's eyebrows rose. "Ah. Well, you'd better get that sorted out. You might have to save someone from drowning in the Thames when you get to the Met." He winked at Graham. "Goodbye, Inspector. Speak to you later." Graham continued to study the pool as though he might find the answer to his thoughts at the bottom of it.

"So, what do you think, sir? Are we back to square one?"

"No, not square one. But we've definitely got a conundrum on our hands. Who killed Katya and why?" He didn't say the next part out loud. *And did they kill Jamie Reeves as well?*

Screams sounded from the front of the house, followed by yapping, barking, and shouts. Katya's best friend and artist from Peregrine Wordsworth's retreat, Magda Padalka-Lyons, had arrived along with her dog, Pom-Pom, and Katya's dog, Willow. "Katya left Willow with me. She said she pick him up this morning. She not arrive. Someone say she's dead! Killed herself!" The short woman stood in front of Graham, her hand at her throat, her mouth twisted with grief. "Tell me it is not so, Inspector."

"I'm very sorry to confirm that Mrs. Granby is dead, Mrs. Padalka-Lyons."

Magda staggered back into a patio chair. "Oh my God, I can't believe it." She waved her hand in front of her face, taking huge, deep gasps.

"Did Mrs. Granby tell you what she was planning to

do? Was she going anywhere, meeting anyone? Why did she need you to look after Willow? Mrs. Padalka-Lyons?" Graham pressed after a pause.

"Hmm? Oh, she didn't go anywhere without Willow, but she said he needed better company than she could give him, so could I look after him. I did that sometimes when, well, you know, she needed to be discreet. I never asked her what she was doing. I don't know who she was meeting or where she was going or if she was doing anything. I thought she maybe wanted to be by herself."

"How did she seem?"

"Well, she was upset. Her husband had just been arrested for the murder of her . . . her landscaper. But I didn't think she was going to do a suicide. I would have stopped her!"

At his owner's wailing, Pom-Pom started yapping, followed shortly by Willow, their chorus ear-splitting. "Thank you, Mrs. Padalka-Lyons. I'm sorry for your loss." Graham stalked off. "Roach!" he barked. "Come with me." Roach trotted after his superior. "Let's get out of here. And Tomlinson's right. It's not a requirement, but you need to learn to swim. It's a basic life skill. You never know when you might need it."

CHAPTER FORTY-THREE

The Gorey Gossip
Tuesday, April 26th

It is with consternation and not a little trepidation that I have to announce the death of Mrs. Katya Granby, wife of Silas Granby, CEO of Granby Investments. Mrs. Granby was found floating in her pool earlier today, clutching the ashes of her beloved dog, Rufus. Her husband was not available for comment, detained as he currently is at Her Majesty's Pleasure under arrest for the murder of Jamie Reeves, a landscaper who recently worked on the Granby property and who was battered to death just a few days ago.

Initial reports suggested suicide as the poor woman, her husband cast as a murderer, had been devastated by news of his detention. However, rumours have reached me that

Mrs. Granby's death is now being considered suspicious. If so, this is a most worrying development.

For, should it turn out that Mrs. Granby was indeed murdered, there are two major issues that our local police force needs to resolve as soon as possible. First, whether Mrs. Granby's killer and that of Jamie Reeves is one and the same person, rendering Mr. Granby's arrest a terrible error that gave an unknown person licence to kill. Or, possibly worse, we have TWO killers in our community, one of whom is still at large. This further development in the case undermines considerably the community's confidence in our boys (and one girl) in blue.

Can we trust them to investigate this case to a successful conclusion and restore our feeling of safety? Remember, Mrs. Granby was killed in her own home.

Where are you, Inspector Graham? Another life has been tragically lost. The public needs answers. And our patience is running out.

Correction: April 26th

A previous version of this article mischaracterised Jamie Reeves as Mr. and Mrs. Granby's gardener. He was their landscaping project lead.

CHAPTER FORTY-FOUR

GRAHAM AND ROACH bundled through the station doors. Janice was at reception. Barnwell sat behind her at his desk, sipping a coffee. "Barnwell, you still here?" Graham said.

"Yes, sir. Couldn't leave until I knew what was going on."

"Well, you might be here for quite a while in that case. Janice, call Granby's lawyer. I want him here when I tell Granby about his wife. Then everyone come to my office. Got it?"

"Yes, sir," they cried.

Five minutes later, Graham was pacing. He hadn't even been able to calm himself to make a cup of tea. He took a deep breath and walked up to the whiteboard. "Right, let's go through what we've got. I want to assume that Tomlinson is right and Katya Granby was murdered. We've got a big problem, and I want to get a jump on it."

"A second murderer, sir?" Barnwell said.

"Or Granby isn't our man, and we've got a double murderer on the loose," Janice added. Graham wrote the two options on the whiteboard, placing question marks after each of them. Neither of them gave him any comfort at all.

Graham posed the question they had all been asking themselves. "Why would someone kill Katya? What motive would they have?"

"Lust, loathing, or loot," Roach said. "That's what the textbooks say."

"Let's examine loot first."

"Someone wanted money from her, a robbery that went wrong?"

"Possibly. Argue for or against."

"Maybe it was a house burglary that went wrong . . . or . . . or . . . a kidnapping attempt. They were going to hold her to ransom and demand money from her husband," Janice said.

"Who's currently in a cell under suspicion of murdering his wife's lover?" Barnwell countered.

"Maybe the murderer didn't know that."

"Alright, alright. No squabbling," Graham said.

Roach piped up. "Hmm, I can't see it. She was killed without violence and carefully posed. That suggests a cold, calculating killer."

"What else? Lust. Give me the textbook definition, Roach."

"The motive for someone murdering a romantic rival. Jealousy."

"Who might that be? Someone who's in love with Granby and wanted Katya out of the way?"

"Surely not. We've seen no evidence of that in our investigation."

"Someone who's in love with Katya and thinks if he, or she, can't have her, no one can?"

"Again, wouldn't that be her husband? Or has Katya been playing the field and there's another lover out there?"

"Blimey, I can't keep up."

"Let's move on to loathing."

"Someone hated her."

"What about Molly Duckworth?" Janice said. "She was in love with Jamie Reeves. Perhaps she knew about the affair. Paula Lascelles for the same reason."

"Reeves's mother if she indirectly blamed Katya for his death."

"Someone else who simply didn't like her?" Barnwell shrugged. It was all he had.

"Was there any sign of forced entry?"

"No, sir."

"So, it was probably someone known to her, then."

"Molly knew Katya from her day on the boat."

"Tomlinson has confirmed cause of death, sir." Roach scrolled his phone. "Cardiac arrest. Puncture wound in her right arm. Suspected administration of an unknown drug. Blood samples sent to toxicology."

Graham tapped his pen against the large filing cabinet. "Hmm. Alright, folks, this is what we're going to do. I think Ms. Lascelles and Mrs. Reeves are long shots. They didn't know Katya or about her relationship with Jamie. Let's put them aside for now. Janice, I want you to speak to Molly Duckworth. Check her alibi. If it's weak, look into her background for something relevant—nursing, access to drugs, that kind of thing. Roach, get down the lab. Oversee the forensics. I'm looking for anything that connects Katya to someone linked to this investigation. Barnwell, come with me. We have to tell a man his wife is dead. Lucky us."

"Hello?" Janice called out. She stepped further inside the Sanderson Landscaping office. The place was as silent as the *Marie Celeste*. Nothing stirred.

Janice walked through the office. "Hello!" She peered through the glass patio doors that led out to the yard behind. Sitting on a bench surrounded by young saplings in wooden pots was Molly Duckworth. She leant on her knees, talking furiously into her phone, her free hand gesticulating wildly.

Janice watched her for a few seconds. Molly glanced up and caught sight of her. Her body tensed and she wound up her call. Janice opened the doors and stepped out into the sunshine. "Good morning, Molly."

Molly stood, smoothing down her skirt. "Hi. Are you here about Katya Granby? I read about it in the *Gorey Gossip*."

"Yes."

"I'm very sorry to hear that she died. She was a nice lady."

"Can we go inside, Molly?"

"Yes, yes of course. Would you like a cup of tea?"

"No, thank you. Let's just sit and chat." They walked over to the white sofa. "How well did you know Katya Granby?"

"Not at all, really. A couple of times, I'd run over to the Granby house to take a few supplies that the lads needed. I saw her then, but we didn't speak. My interactions were mostly with Mr. Granby, and then it was only when I answered Adrian's phone to pass on a message. He did come in here once, and that's when he invited me on the boat, like I told you earlier. Before that day, I hadn't spent any time in Mrs. Granby's company at all."

"I understand you thought that Mrs. Granby was lonely, is that right?"

"Yes. She was quiet when she came on board but perked up as we chatted. And I'm sure the constant champagne refills helped. She was quite charming. Talked about her dog a lot. I like dogs so I didn't mind."

"Were you aware of the rumours about her and Jamie?"

Molly's face fell. Colour flushed her cheeks, and she looked down at her lap. "Yes, I'd heard the rumours. She's—was—a very attractive woman. Bit old for him, but some men like that, don't they?"

"What was your reaction to the rumours?" Janice inclined her head to insist Molly make eye contact with her.

"I thought he was a bit mad, to be honest with you. Seemed unlike him too. He wasn't normally reckless. He was risking everything—his job, his reputation—for what? A bit of fun. And look where it got him."

"And what was your personal reaction? How did it make you feel?"

Molly sighed. Her shoulders rose and fell. "It made me sad. Like why couldn't he go for a girl his own age? Someone without . . . baggage. Perhaps he was entranced by her glamour and wealth. He obviously didn't deserve what was coming to him, but what an idiot. He was playing with fire."

"Did you see Mrs. Granby after your day on the boat?"

"No, she said we should get together again, but I'm sure she was just being nice. I went to the yacht club and invited Jamie to join me, and that was the end of it. It was back to Earth with a bump for me."

"Did you know that Silas Granby has been charged with Jamie's murder?"

"I read about it at the same time I heard about Katya's death—in the *Gossip*. Do you think the two deaths are connected? I mean, they must be, mustn't they? But it must have been someone else who killed Mrs. Granby if Mr. Granby was in jail." Molly put her hands up to her face. "Oh, what a mess."

"What's a mess, Molly?"

"This whole situation: Jamie, Mrs. Granby, Mr. Granby. The drama. Being involved in this kind of thing isn't me. I like a quiet, normal kind of life. Friends, family, a bit of fun. Adrian hates all this too. We simply want the person or persons who did this to go away for a long time and for this to be over."

"Okay, Molly, one more thing. Where were you yesterday evening?"

Molly's eyes widened. Janice intervened quickly. "It's just routine."

"I was in France with Adrian. We'd gone on a buying trip. He needed to negotiate with a new supplier. It always looks better if there are the two of us. You can check with him, or even the supplier. I can give you their details. We came back on the late ferry. Got back in around ten p.m."

"It wasn't Molly, sir. She was with Sanderson in France. Didn't get back until late last night. It all checks out. She was on the ferry manifest, as was he."

"So, we have to rule out Sanderson too, eh? Not that I could see why he might wish to do Mrs. Granby harm."

"How did he take the news, sir?"

"Hmm?"

"Mr. Granby."

Graham replaced his cup in his saucer. It had been a gruelling morning. For all his poise and sophistication, Silas Granby had been broken by the news of his wife's death.

His lawyer had made a swift exit after the announcement, and Graham and Barnwell had been left to comfort the new widower as he alternately lashed out and clung to them.

"He's back in the cell, but I don't know how long I can keep him. He's in no fit state to talk, but I can't let him go either. We might never see him again."

"What would you like me to do, sir?"

"Go take a break. Be prepared to interview him this afternoon. We can try tackling him together. Let me know when we hear from Tomlinson. I want to know the drug that caused Katya Granby to go into cardiac arrest."

Janice left, and Graham turned to the view outside his window. Katya Granby's demise had thrown a wrench into his expectations for the Jamie Reeves's case. He needed to keep an open mind. Maybe Granby wasn't involved after all and there was another killer out there who had murdered both Reeves and Katya. Or maybe Granby had killed Reeves and like that idiot Solomon suggested, there was a second murderer on the loose.

Graham squinted. A super yacht made its slow way across the horizon, the sun bouncing off its gleaming white surface. It cost more than he would earn in a lifetime. He admired the sleek curves of the streamlined hull, the three decks at the back, one a helipad. He knew that below deck, the interior would be opulent, all polished walnut and deep, squishy sofas. He was at one moment envious of those like the Granbys whose lives involved such a reality and simultaneously relieved that his did not. No one coveted him or tried to cheat him; his friends were genuine. He could place his feet on the ground and know that it would be solid beneath him.

And yet there was no denying the pull of the lifestyle, the yachts, the private jets. Could he genuinely say he wouldn't want it if it were offered? The tension between the two worlds—that of the superrich and the perfectly ordinary—had collided with this case. It was his job to clear up the mess. And as he stared at the hugely expensive yacht set against the perfectly free sun and sea, he was buggered if he knew how.

CHAPTER FORTY-FIVE

"**D**ID YOU HEAR the latest?" Barnwell walked into the break room to fill Carmen's water bowl.

"No, what?" Janice didn't look up from her screen.

"Roach and the boss are with Tomlinson. Roachie says Rohypnol rendered Katya Granby unconscious, and then she was plied with massive doses of an epilepsy drug which caused a heart attack."

"So she *was* murdered." Janice sat back in her chair. "But who, Bazz? Who could have done it?"

"Beats me. Feels like we're back to square one, and if not, we're only up to square two. Wotcha up to?"

"Wedding research," Janice mumbled, resuming her scrolling. "Taking a break before the boss wants me in with him and Granby. Can't say I'm looking forward to it." Her elbow was propped on the break room table, her head in her hand. "I need to find some shoes. Not too expensive but not so cheap they're uncomfortable. I need to stand in them for hours."

"You could go barefoot if you had a wedding on the beach."

"Tell me about it. But I'd never hear the end of it from my mother. What are you doing?"

"Just covering reception, but if you get a chance, could you spell me so I can take Carmen for a walk? She hasn't been out since this morning."

"Okay, I'll be there in a sec." Barnwell left her searching "satin wedding shoes comfortable jersey uk."

Barnwell returned to reception and placed Carmen's water bowl on the floor underneath the counter. No one could see her down there. When he was manning the desk, she liked to lay across his feet. It was sweet but restricting. He found himself getting cramps from not moving, but he hated to disturb the lady in his life. He bent down to scratch between Carmen's ears. She'd been a great help earlier in the year when he was coming to terms with both of his parents' deaths. He'd had to take some compassionate leave to attend their funerals and, after his mother's passing, to clear out the family home and put it up for sale. While he was gone, the Gorey police team had each taken it in turns to care for Carmen, and Barnwell had been grateful. Roach had even moved into Barnwell's flat to avoid disrupting Carmen more than necessary.

Barnwell's mind wandered to his brother. Steve's time on Jersey was coming to a close. He had just a couple of days left. The constable looked at the clock. He had a few minutes before Janice returned from her lunch break. He took a deep breath and prepared to run a search of his own.

A few minutes later, a door slammed. Barnwell hastily shut down his screen, but there was no need. Janice ran from the break room and grabbed her uniform jacket. As she tapped keys on one of the office computers, she said,

"What was the name of that epilepsy drug? The one that killed Katya Granby?" The printer warmed up and spit out a sheet of paper.

"Eh? Erm . . ." Barnwell scrolled Roach's texts on his phone. "Dexa . . . meth . . . amine. Brand name Elli . . . Ellip . . ." He found the text he was looking for. "Ellipsis, yeah that's it. Ellipsis."

"Bloody hell." Janice hesitated for a second, just one, then came to a decision. "I gotta go, Bazz. Sorry."

Again, Janice parked her car so tight against the stone wall on Marett Lane that if she'd had a passenger they would have been trapped. Before crossing the road, she waited for a couple to walk by on their way to the beach. The pair held hands as they strolled, beach towels under her arm, deck chairs under his. They were chatting quietly. As they passed Janice, the woman threw back her head with a peal of laughter. The sergeant noticed the woman's clerical collar. *A female vicar. Unusual. Wonder what my mother would make of that.* They were followed by three louts in tracksuits, the bottoms of which hung virtually to their knees.

Janice rapped on the door of the cottage a bit louder than she meant to. The door opened, and Cynthia Moorcroft stood in the doorway. She was less poised than before, her hair mussed. She wore no makeup. Dark circles under her eyes aged her. There was a stain on her shirt. "Oh, hello. I wasn't expecting to hear from you again. Come in."

Inside the cottage, Janice looked around. Nothing seemed awry. "Are you alright? After Mr. Granby's arrest?" she said to Cynthia.

"And Katya's death." Cynthia clicked the kettle's on button. "I can't believe it. I would never have thought that Silas would kill anyone, nor that Katya would be next. There's a rumour that someone murdered her too!" Cynthia placed a mug of tea in front of Janice and dropped two teaspoons of sugar into her own. The older woman wiped her pale face and let the kitchen table take her weight as she levered herself into a chair.

"Everything has changed since we last spoke, hasn't it? What will happen to the business, do you think?" Janice said.

Cynthia looked at Janice with only half-seeing eyes before realising what the sergeant was saying. "Oh, I don't know." Cynthia shrugged. She waved her hand in the air slowly. "It's over for Silas. Trust in him is lost, and his business is all about trust."

"But doesn't he know where all the bodies are buried?"

"Yes, and some of these people are gangsters in Savile Row suits. They won't want the whiff of a police enquiry anywhere near them. A lot of the rest will fall away. They won't want to associate with someone on the edge of a double murder enquiry either, even if he is exonerated. They're probably digging up those bodies as we speak, helped by other wealth managers who'll step in like the vultures they are."

"What about you being that person, Cynthia? Can't you take the business over?"

Cynthia laughed. "Me? No chance. I want to get away from these greasy people." She tapped her finger against her lips.

"The thing is, Cynthia . . . can I call you Cynthia?" The older woman nodded. Janice thought how to phrase her next question. She took a sip of her tea. "You told me that you got the job with Granby through a mutual contact and that it was your first experience with the world of wealth management."

"Yes, that's right."

"And that you'd never heard of Silas Granby before that."

"Yes. I had been just a lowly secretary in a firm of accountants."

Janice unfolded the piece of paper that she'd printed out earlier. On it, a copy of a newspaper article was headed:

"Distraught Mother Loses Her High Court
Battle with Pharmaceutical Company."

It continued:

"Frances Macintyre, whose daughter lost her
life one day before she married her
childhood sweetheart, defeated in her legal
fight to bring company she blames for her
daughter's death to justice."

Alongside the article was a picture of a woman holding up a pair of satin wedding shoes and a framed photograph. The article had been written nearly twenty years ago, but Janice saw clearly that Frances Macintyre was a younger version of the woman who sat across the table from her.

"But isn't this you?"

Cynthia peered at the picture. "No."

"She looks just like you."

"Well, it's not. You are mistaken. Look, it's not even my name." Cynthia held Janice's gaze.

"Okay, then tell me this. This woman who looks just

like you. Who has a dead daughter. Who, according to this article, blames her daughter's death on the lack of a drug that might have saved her. Who believes that if the company that manufactured the drug hadn't made it so prohibitively expensive, her daughter might still be alive. Tell me, why does this woman now work for the man who was the CEO of the pharmaceutical company at the time? A pharmaceutical company that made a drug found twenty years later in the body of that former CEO's wife who died while he was held in custody for the murder of her lover?"

Cynthia stood. She smiled. "Let me show you something." She walked over to a dresser that stood against the wall. She picked up a photograph. "See? *That* is the woman in the photo. My sister, Frances. It was her daughter, my niece, Holly, who died. Frances killed herself on the first anniversary of Holly's death."

Cynthia leant down to show Janice the photo. Janice took another sip of her tea. In the photo, a woman in her early forties hugged a very attractive younger woman. They beamed for the camera. In her hands, behind the older woman's neck, the younger woman held a pair of wedding shoes. As Janice looked, the shoes went in and out of focus. She squinted and forced herself to concentrate on the delicate beading down the back of the heels. "So not you, but yes, you," Janice said, except it came out garbled.

Cynthia's face swam into view. She was grinning maniacally, and there were three of her. Janice opened her mouth again, but it felt like it was stuffed with cotton wool. She reached out to push Cynthia away. And then, everything went black.

"Janice here?" Graham said, looking around reception.

"No, sir. She went out."

"Huh, I was expecting her to interview Granby with me. Never mind; you'll do, Constable. Roach can man the desk."

"Righto, sir. Give me a moment if you will. My brother's coming down to take Carmen out for a walk. He should be here any minute."

CHAPTER FORTY-SIX

ER CHEEKS JUDDERED. Darkness enveloped her. Her neck cracked with every shake. A sharp pain pierced her skull, immediately followed by a dull ache. Janice shivered. She blacked out again.

Slowly, she realised she was in the boot of a car. Her nostrils stung. Musty carpet overlaid with the smell of petrol. The car's engine revved and came to a stop.

The small amount of light that seeped through her blindfold brightened. Restraints around her ankles snapped and loosened. Those around her wrists remained. "Get up!" Janice recognised Cynthia's voice.

Feeling around, Janice stuck her feet out of the car. She made a noise through the cloth between her teeth. A breath of warm air hit her cheek, then a hand grabbed her armpit and roughly pulled her from the car. She stood, wobbling. Distracting herself from the nausea that rose from her feet and the weakness that threatened to drop her to the ground, she strained to hear seagulls . . . and waves.

Another surge of nausea rolled over her. A shove in the

back forced her onward. Stumbling, she nearly fell. Uneven ground gave way to the crunchy, spongy texture of wet sand, the tiny, weathered particles of rocks and minerals slipping away beneath her with every step. She staggered again. The woman beside her silently took her weight.

The air was cool. Was it morning? Evening? Nighttime? Janice had no idea. She peered through her blindfold, but it was hopeless. After a few more feet, the ground rose.

The air temperature dropped further. Her skin tingled. Staccato plops of water seeped through her hair to her scalp, a cold creep. A sharp, sudden pressure on her shoulder and she tumbled to the ground. Once again, a wave of panic washed over her as her ankles were tied again. Whimpering, Janice lashed out, her boot connecting with nothing but air.

A curse and the tie around Janice's ankles tightened, her bones rubbing together painfully. She sagged and brought up her knees, curling into a foetal position. Her shoulders ached.

"What's your boyfriend's name, hmm?" Cynthia's voice was hard, cruel. Janice remained silent. A pain shot through her leg.

"Ah-eh-or."

"What?" The gag in Janice's mouth loosened. She spat it out.

"What the hell?" she cried. "What are you doing with me?"

Cynthia laughed. "I'm putting you somewhere you can't cause any trouble. By the time they find you, I'll be long gone. You too, probably. Tide'll rise tomorrow morning."

"What? Where am I? You're leaving me here to drown?" Janice wriggled like a maggot, and just as helpless. Cynthia laughed.

"Now, tell me your boyfriend's name."

"I don't have a boyfriend."

"Course you do. You've got wedding to-do lists in your Notes app. Are you going for the gluten-free almond flour cake or the one with the pâte à bombe icing? Name."

"No." Janice squealed with pain as Cynthia pressed down on her ankle.

"Want to rethink that?"

"What have you done?"

Cynthia squatted and reached behind Janice's head. She pulled off the scarf that covered her eyes. Light from Cynthia's phone assaulted Janice despite the gloom, and it took a moment before she placed herself. She was in . . . a cave? Janice glanced over Cynthia's shoulder. Nazi markings defaced the rock walls. An old war tunnel!

Cynthia wrapped the blindfold around her fingers. She pondered the scarf's striped pattern, brooding. "My niece died because of Silas. He effectively killed her. And he as good as killed my sister, inflicting unbearable cruelty on her." Cynthia looked up at the Nazi emblems. "My niece was ill, very ill. She had been for two years. She'd fought and fought but had exhausted her options except for this one drug. Her mum, my sister, found out about it, but Holly's doctors wouldn't prescribe it. In Holly's case, it was an off-label use for a disease that the drug wasn't intended to treat, but in a few cases had been found to be helpful.

"The doctors said it was experimental, unproven. It was also wildly expensive. Thousands of pounds for one vial, and Holly needed lots of them. Frances thought that if the company that manufactured it would give it to her for free, or just a small amount as a compassionate gesture, Holly's doctors would agree to administer it. Of course, there was no guarantee it would help, but Franny would have done anything, *anything* to save her daughter, her only child. Franny personally appealed to Silas to donate the drug. And he . . ." Cynthia pulled the scarf tight in her hands. "Refused."

Cynthia sighed, closing her eyes momentarily. "Holly died the day before her wedding. Franny was heartbroken and took the company to court. When her civil case failed, it was like Holly had died all over again. The next day, she simply walked into the sea."

"But what has that to do with anything?"

"It has everything to do with your case."

"What? How? Are you saying *you* killed Jamie Reeves? What did he have to do with what happened?"

"Nothing. He was merely a stick to beat Silas with. I wanted Silas to pay for what he did to my niece and sister, but I bided my time. Silas's reputation in pharma was mostly destroyed by the case, and he moved into wealth management. He has no idea the woman who took him to court was my sister. I quietly networked my way into his circles and persuaded him to take me on. I got to know the ins and outs of his business while I plotted my revenge for him hurting my sister so. I thought about bringing his company down. I could have done it easily. A well-timed rumour would have been enough, but I wanted more. I wanted recompense for my pain and, more than anything, justice for Holly and Franny.

"But he didn't recognise you? You look just like your sister."

"Oh no. Posh blokes like him don't notice the little people. I dyed my hair, changed my name. I'm older. It's been twenty years. That was more than enough to hide my real identity. The Silases of the world don't see people like you and me."

"So, what was your plan?"

"I went to the exhibition at the council offices and saw that Katya had been fooling around with the landscaper. There had been rumours. I realised this was my chance. I thought an affair the perfect cover for a double murder, framing Silas in the process and causing him emotional pain. Despite everything, he really loved Katya. He had to, to put up with that stupid dog memorial idea of hers . . ." Cynthia trailed off for a moment before snapping to attention. "So, I took a lump of concrete from a pile when I was at their house the day after the exhibition and killed the guy when he returned home the next evening."

"Cold."

"Icy. Frigid. When I left him, I thought he'd bleed out, but he hung on for a while. The damage was done though."

"Granby said he was in the air on the way back from Turin."

"He was, but there are no records, see? I could say anything I liked. I changed his calendar to show that he was at home to make you think he was lying. He wasn't. And you bought it."

"And you killed Katya too?"

"Yes. I didn't want to, but Silas had to go away for a long time, the rest of his life. I was worried that the Reeves murder wouldn't be enough for that. Shame, really. Katya wasn't too bad, but her death served my purposes perfectly. Not only would being found guilty of two murders put Silas away for good, just as importantly, the pain of losing someone he loved would floor him. I wanted him to suffer like I and my sister had."

"So how did you do it?"

"I went over to the house, spiked Katya's drink, like I did with your tea, then injected her with Ellipsis. Like with

Reeves, I planned to make it look like Silas had done it. I had arranged his calendar to make it seem like he was at home, but in reality he should have been on another of his business trips. Unfortunately for me, it seems border force were doing their jobs for once. They stopped him from leaving without the proper paperwork. I didn't know your boss had arrested him. I thought he was in New York."

"And the Ellipsis?"

"The drug that could have saved Holly. Silas had boxes of the stuff lying around. Talk about adding insult to injury. He said he had it in case anyone in his circles needed a favour or there was a chance of a bit of cash in it. I knew a colossal overdose would bring on a heart attack, and so it did. Katya never came around from the Rohypnol. I thought the urn a nice touch. I put her in a bikini too. My little joke. Now, tell me again, what's your boyfriend's name?"

Janice glared at her. "What are you going to do?"

"Wouldn't you like to know? Maybe I'm going to tell him where to find you."

Janice considered this. "Jack."

"Jack," Cynthia repeated as she scrolled.

"Right, sweetheart. I need to go. Dubai calls. Maybe Panama. A private jet and riches await me. Being Silas's assistant affords me certain benefits, don't you know? My just desserts." Cynthia looked at her watch. She unwound the scarf from her hands and reached to tie it around Janice's eyes. Janice pounced, biting Cynthia's hand hard. In response, a sharp sting and the clap of a slap stunned her.

"Tomorrow morning, this tunnel will be full of water. You'll be whisked out to sea. And I'll be whisked away on a private jet to live the life of Riley. Or maybe Jack will find you. Either way, sorry not sorry." Cynthia turned and headed to the beach.

In for four, hold for four, out for four, hold for four. Janice focused on her breathing. The sound of Cynthia's footsteps cracking and shooshing across the sand receded. Drops kept on plopping.

"Hellooo!"

Ten miles away, Jack opened the door to the house he shared with Janice. It was in darkness. His greeting was met with silence. He'd been working late and had popped into the supermarket on his way home. His phone pinged and he put the bags on the kitchen counter to check it.

"Hi,   sweetheart.   It's   an   all-hands tonight on the case. Don't wait up. Going to be a long one. See you tomorrow. XXX"

Huh. Janice didn't normally call him sweetheart, but he quite liked it. Jack put his phone away and unpacked the bags. He'd been planning to cook salmon, but it looked like he'd be eating a frozen microwave curry on his own instead.

In Laura's kitchen, Graham stared at the picture of him and Katie on the windowsill. He cradled a mug of camomile tea in his hand. Outside, the night was quiet except for an owl's mating call, persistent in the darkness. Graham's mind wandered to the case. Granby was still denying murdering Jamie Reeves. Tomorrow, without further evidence, the inspector would have to let him go.

Thoughtfully, Graham took a sip of his tea. He'd racked his brain to create new angles with which to break Granby's story. He simply couldn't fathom who else Reeves's murderer might be. Nor did they have any leads as to Katya's killer. He'd even had Tomlinson revisit the idea that she killed herself.

Above him, floorboards creaked. Laura was finished in the bathroom. Graham emptied his mug, and running it under the tap, he left it on the draining board. With one last hoot ringing in his ears, he turned off the kitchen light and went upstairs.

CHAPTER FORTY-SEVEN

"**H**EY, JIM!" JACK bundled through the front doors of the police station.

Roach looked up from his computer and quickly ran over to help Jack before he dropped the tray of coffees he was balancing onto the floor. "For us?"

"Yeah, you must be exhausted. Thought I'd bring you some breakfast." Jack dropped a brown paper bag onto the counter. "Four bacon butties and four coffees. Where's Jan?"

"I don't know. Don't you?"

"She sent me a text last night saying she was working late. I assumed you were pulling an all-nighter to wrap up this case."

"Not that I know of, mate. I'm the only one here. Got in half an hour ago." The double doors banged and in walked Barnwell, Carmen trotting at his heels. "Mornin', Bazz. Do you know where Janice is? She told Jack here she was working late last night, but there's no sign of her."

Barnwell stopped in the middle of the lobby. He threw his arms wide. "She went out after lunch yesterday, and that was the last I saw of her. She was going to spell me on reception when she said she had to go out. She was in quite the tizzy. Didn't hear from her again. I assumed she'd clocked off at the end of her shift and gone home."

Another bang. Graham walked through the doors. Three pale faces brought him up short. "What is it?"

"Janice is missing."

Janice arched her spine. Cold burned her nostrils and cheeks. Sleep had eluded her, and overnight, she'd dozed only fitfully in between shuffles designed to propel her inch by inch further into the tunnel. But she existed inside a black hole lacking any sense of time or distance. She shuddered. Her body seemed to weigh four times more than normal, her thoughts slow and dull like a particularly heavy blanket she lacked the strength to throw off. She had, she thought, slowly pushed herself further up the tunnel away from the rising tide, but she couldn't be sure.

Reaching deep into the dark cavern of her despair, Janice once again lifted her knees and pushed off with her feet, the hard rock under her shoulder grazing her skin despite her uniform jacket. Ahead of her, tiny shafts of light penetrated her blindfold. Was there a way out from this hellhole? Or did the tide and certain death await her?

"What were her last movements?" There had been no time for tea. Graham and the three men were at the whiteboard.

"She left here just after two p.m. She was going to cover me on reception so I could take Carmen out for a walk, but then she said she had to go out. I've no idea where she was going or why," Barnwell said.

"And what was she doing just before that?"

"She was in the break room having her lunch. She said she was looking for shoes on the internet." Barnwell was answering Graham's questions as he asked, but he couldn't shake the feeling that he'd failed in some way. Nothing he said appeared to be of any help whatsoever.

A picture swarmed Graham's memory. He was in the Fo'c'sle and Ferret. An undercover officer had told him her cover was blown. He hadn't reacted swiftly enough that time. He wasn't going to make the same mistake again.

"Alright, listen to me. Barnwell, raise the coastguard. I want the helicopter out and all boats patrolling the coastline. Alert the airport and ferry terminal."

"Sir."

Graham took two steps forward. He pointed his pen at his sergeant. "Roach, contact St. Helier. Tell them we've got an officer missing. They need to activate all units. I'll call the chief officer."

"Yes, sir!"

Graham reached for Jack and put a hand on his shoulder. "Trace her phone," he said, quietly.

"Where can she be? Where *can* she be?" Roach drove. In the passenger seat, Barnwell combed the crowds of tourists and schoolchildren enjoying the good weather. They had been driving for twenty minutes. An air/sea/land operation had been launched involving every coastguard and police patrol available. In an hour, resources from other islands would be mobilised. The ports were shut down. Jack was frantically working to determine the location from which the previous evening's text had come.

"Stop!" Roach slammed on his brakes. Barnwell opened the car door and sprinted down a causeway to a gaggle of lads in tracksuits hanging out at the water's edge. "Have you seen a policewoman, probably in uniform, about this high, mousey hair, sergeant's stripes?"

Neil Lightfoot smirked. "Lost 'er, 'have yer? Careless."

Barnwell grabbed him by the collar of his tracksuit. "None of your lip. This is serious," he fumed.

"Okay, okay. When?" Duncan Rayner asked, forcing an arm between them and pushing Barnwell off his friend.

"Anytime after two p.m. yesterday." Rayner turned down the corners of his mouth and shook his head. Barnwell huffed and made to run back up the causeway. Kevin Croft placed a hand on his arm.

"I think I saw her," he said quietly. "Marett Lane. We were going to the beach. She was getting out of her car. That was just after two yesterday. Yeah, I'm sure of it. I remember thinking she was pretty fit for a fuzz."

Barnwell ignored the reference. His heart leapt. "Good lad." He patted Kevin on the shoulder, and as he ran back to the car, he radioed the news to Graham, who was coordinating the search from the station. "Sighting: Marett Lane yesterday afternoon."

"Confirmed, Constable. I've just had a second sighting. Copper from the mainland heard about the search and phoned it in. Saw her park her car and cross to a cottage." Surging with optimism, Barnwell gave Roach a thumbs-up as he streaked up the causeway.

"Marett Lane, Roachie. Fast!"

Barnwell's radio crackled. Graham's voice floated through the air. "One forty-five Marett Lane, business address of Granby Investments. Also, home of Silas Granby's assistant, Cynthia Moorcroft. Janice interviewed her about Granby's alibi for the Jamie Reeves murder."

Roach spun the car like he was in a TV cop drama. Barnwell turned on the blue lights and sirens. It was only the third time he'd used both at the same time in his entire Gorey police career.

Janice's car sat forlornly across the road from Cynthia's cottage. Leaves from the tree above scattered across its roof like autumnal confetti. Roach shielded his eyes and peered through the front windows of the cottage. It was empty. Around the back, Barnwell was less restrained. He shouldered the rear door open and walked through the house to let Roach in. "There's no one here."

In the kitchen, mugs of tea still sat on the kitchen table. A fluffy, brown cat eyed the visitors curiously before deciding they were of no consequence and padding off up the narrow stone stairs.

Barnwell bent to pick up a piece of paper. "This looks like a printout from our printer." He showed it to Roach.

"That's Granby," Roach said.

"Who are the women? Frances Macintyre. Holly Macintyre."

From the table, Roach picked up the framed photo of the two women that Cynthia had showed Janice. "No idea, but these are the same people. Relative? Sister perhaps?"

"Says here Holly died because she didn't get the drug she needed from Granby's company. Frances, her mother, took him to court. She lost."

"Uh-oh. That can't be a coincidence. Maybe Janice worked out the connection."

"And came to confront her."

"And now she's been missing for hours."

"Why didn't she ask me to come with her?" Barnwell said, exasperated.

"You know what this means, don't you, Bazz?"

"Yeah." Barnwell looked around. "We need a photo, Jim. We can circulate it. Granby can identify this Moorcroft woman when we get back to the station."

"You do downstairs, I'll go up." Roach ran for the stairs the cat had just climbed.

Barnwell looked about. He heard a shout. "Found one!" Roach scrambled back down the steps. "At least I think this is her." He showed Barnwell a picture of three women as he picked up the framed photo from the kitchen table and compared them. "Look, these women are Frances and Holly Macintyre. I bet this one is Cynthia."

"Good enough for me! I'll circulate it on the way back. We need to find her."

The lapping water had got louder. It slapped against rock with every push of the tide. Janice rubbed the back of her head against a hard surface. The blindfold loosened, then slipped. Trapping it, she tilted her chin upward. The scarf fell away. A thrill passed through her like an easy, flowing stream.

Relief quickly gave way to despair, however. Sight was infinitely preferable to blindness but only confirmed her peril. The tide was most definitely rising.

With all units and ports alerted for signs of Cynthia Moorcroft, Barnwell quietly spoke to Graham. "How're you getting on, sir?" It had been fifty-five minutes since Jack had arrived with breakfast. It felt like fifty-five years.

Graham had given his office over to Jack and sat in reception, alert to notifications coming in from search patrols. He blew out his cheeks. "Jack's not had any luck locating the phone. She could be out at sea or in a dead zone, anywhere really. Besides, we'll only find out her last location. She could be long gone from that spot by n—"

"I know!" Jack shouted from Graham's office. The other three rushed in. Jack banged Graham's desktop with his hands. The slap must have hurt, but Janice's fiancé paid no mind to his stinging palms. "Her Fitbit. She's always wearing it. She goes a bit mad if she doesn't get her ten thousand steps in. For the wedding. She wanted—wants—to be in good sh-shape." Jack's voice cracked. He spent a second or two wrestling his emotions. "I might be able to get a signal from it if it's still charged."

"What do you need, Jack? Anything we can get you?" Graham asked.

"No, just peace. It's a long shot. I need to download an app . . . yes, here we are. Come on, come on. Okay, here we go." Jack stared at his phone's screen. "It's my Fitbit, really. If she's close by, it will sync to my phone." They all waited. After nearly a minute, Jack's shoulders dropped. "It's not syncing."

"What does that mean?" Barnwell whispered to Roach.

"She's not nearby, I think," Roach replied.

They looked at Jack. He was surrounded by screens, phones, cables, and headphones.

"Can we drive around trying to find her? If we are close to X marks the spot, won't the Fitbit tell us?" Roach asked him.

"Yes, but we need to narrow things down first."

A message flashed up on one of the phones strewn across Graham's desk. Jack pounced on it. "Wait . . . The text! It was sent from . . ." He reached over to punch some coordinates into his computer. A map flashed up on the screen. It showed a remote part of the island to the north. "What's there? Just woodland, right?"

"And a lot of rocks. I know where it is," Roach said. "I used to go crabbing there as a kid."

"Well, what are we waiting for?" Barnwell said, grabbing a backpack and Carmen's lead.

"Follow me. I'll take my bike!" Roach was already running to the break room and his leathers.

"I'll drive!" Graham cried, grabbing his jacket, for once prepared to break the speed limit.

"What about Granby?" Barnwell said. The wealth manager was still in the cells.

"Leave him. I'll get someone here from HQ." Barnwell winced. Leaving a prisoner locked in the cells while alone in the building was totally against the rules. But this was an emergency, and Graham didn't think twice. "We've got more important things to worry about! He won't even know we've gone if we don't tell him!"

CHAPTER FORTY-EIGHT

"JANICE!" THE FOUR men shouted themselves hoarse. They had spread out, working their way across woodland. Officers from all over the island were en route to join the search.

"She could have been moved by now. I mean, we don't even know if she was with the person who sent it," Jack said doubtfully. Initially elated at locating where the text had been sent from, he was struggling to remain calm and optimistic. "And it doesn't mean she's still here. That text was sent hours ago now."

"I'm confident we'll find her, Jack. It's the best lead we've got. Let's each take a lane. Stay in touch, everyone," Graham said.

For the next fifteen minutes, the four men crossed the wood, widening their search when they turned up nothing. Carmen pulled at her lead, sniffing her way through the undergrowth and once attempting to chase a squirrel. "Hold on, girl," Barnwell muttered, as he pulled her on. "Perhaps I should have left you with someone."

Yards to his left, Roach swished a pole through the

undergrowth. To Barnwell's right, Jack nervously stepped forward, his eyes on the ground, desperately hoping to find something but, at the same time, worried about what that might be. They were quiet now, alert to any sound. Up ahead, Graham led the charge. Every so often, he stopped and shouted, "Janice!"

They stopped and listened but could hear nothing but the cries of seagulls and the rustling of bushes as a forest animal ferreted around. They resumed their march through the brush, silently repressing their fears and focusing on the job at hand.

"Arrgghhh!" Barnwell and Roach turned to Jack in panic. He screamed at the woodland canopy, his face contorted, his fists clenched. In different circumstances, Barnwell might have expected him to turn green and explode out of his shirt. "This is hopeless! We're never going to find her!"

Barnwell walked over. He hesitated, but then wrapped Jack in a hug. "It's alright, mate. Jan's a tough cookie. Keep the faith, hmm? Why don't you go back to the car?"

Jack leant into Barnwell, taking comfort from the bulk of the big man. After a few moments, his equilibrium mostly restored, he pulled away. "No, no. I'll carry on." He looked across the woodland. There was a shout.

"Where's the boss?" Roach called out. Up ahead of them, Graham had disappeared. Jack, Barnwell, and Roach stood still, turning their heads in arcs over a hundred and eighty degrees.

"Bloody hell," Barnwell said. "Is this day going to get any better?"

Graham had gone ahead primarily to lead his men but also to clear his head. With each passing minute, his anxiety built. Ice filled the marrow of his bones. His muscles wound as tight as a boa constrictor; his mind fizzed. He did not want to convey his worries to his officers, and especially not to Jack.

Janice had been missing for hours. Jack was right; she could be anywhere by now, in any condition. He stamped the ground as he marched along, casting his eyes in a wide semicircle. They could be miles off target or right on top of her.

That last thought struck him as he fell. Darkness engulfed him, and his stomach churned as he flew through the air. Sharp pain assailed him as he banged his head, his limbs scraping rocks. He shut his eyes tight as he braced for impact. In those moments, he thought of Katie. Then Laura.

"Radio him, text him," Barnwell shouted across to Roach. He pulled out his own phone. "Where are the backup units from St Helier?" He blew out his cheeks. "Time to call reinforcements," he muttered as he began tapping his phone.

"Perhaps he's just out of sight, gone further ahead," Jack said.

"He's not replying," Roach shouted.

Jack's phone pinged. He punched the air, his worries about Graham forgotten. "The Fitbit's synced. She's close!"

Graham's eyelids fluttered. His skin tickled with damp and cold. Pain sliced through his shoulder. Another stab of pain carved down his leg. He moaned as it—first sharp, then dull — receded. Where was he? And why was he there? Then he remembered. There was a shuffling noise, a grunt. Someone or something—he wasn't sure it was human—was alongside him.

Janice! Her eyes, huge in her deathly pale face, bore into him. She made a small noise. Her lips were blue. Painfully, Graham lifted his hands to untie her gag.

As the scarf fell away, Janice sighed. "Thank you." She closed her eyes. "I managed to get my blindfold off, but the gag defeated me."

"Where are we?"

"You fell down a chute. We're in a war tunnel." Above them, a smidgen of daylight peeked between undergrowth that covered the entrance to the hole Graham had fallen into.

"And I hate to tell you this, but the tide is coming in. I've been shuffling away from it for ages, but I'm tired and very"—Janice let out another sigh, summoning some of the last reserves of her energy to finish her sentence—"very cold." She lifted her eyes to Graham's face. He noticed her long, wet eyelashes stuck together. "Sir, I'm frightened." Her voice was husky.

"The boys are up top. They'll find us. Don't worry. We'll be out in a jiffy." Graham made to sit up. Another shot of pain ran up his leg to his neck. "Arghhhh. My leg."

Janice wriggled around. "Looks broken, sir. Well, we're a right pair, aren't we? Not a full set of working limbs between us.

"What about I untie you?"

"Zip-tied, so unless you . . ." Janice couldn't finish her sentence. She pressed her lips together so tightly they went from blue to white.

"Perhaps my phone . . ."

"Smashed. Over there. Nothing doing. I already checked." Janice nodded in a direction Graham couldn't see. He'd have to take her word for it. Feet away, a trickle of seawater crept around a rock.

"Hey! Down here!" A pulse of adrenaline stabbed him. His voice wasn't carrying up the chute. Graham tried again. "Barnwell! Roach!" He turned to Janice. "Let's try together. Just make some noise. On three. One, two, three!"

Janice did her best. Her throat and lips were parched. She'd had no water since the day before. The irony of being surrounded by it, in great peril, wasn't lost on her. She yelled in time with Graham, but her voice was tremulous and weak. "It's just echoing around this chamber. They aren't going to hear us, are they?" Graham silently agreed with her. Janice shuddered.

"Here, squish up against me." Janice wriggled closer, and Graham lifted his good arm to pull her into him. They lay side by side like a pair of lovers, Janice's head on Graham's shoulder. He wrapped his arms around her. Hypothermia might take her before the tide.

"She can't be far. This thing doesn't have a long range. We're close!" Jack's energy had returned, making him hyper. His voice shook. "Janice!" Barnwell and Roach joined him.

"Graham!"

"Alright, let's keep doing what we're doing but keep in this local area. She has to be here somewhere," Roach said.

Carmen pulled hard on her lead, and Barnwell staggered, nearly falling into a bush. "Hold on, girl." The three men redoubled their efforts, searching the same ground from a different angle. Nothing. They congregated in a huddle.

"Any news from the boss?" Barnwell said.

Roach checked his phone. "Nope, he's well and truly gone."

Barnwell thought back to what Graham had told him over a week ago. "Is there a war tunnel running under here? Jack, can you see? Some of the tunnels reached to the coast so the Nazis could move supplies, men, and contraband in and out of the island without anyone knowing." Carmen pulled on her lead, and this time Barnwell let go, unwilling to spend more of his energy restraining her. She'd come back.

Jack interrogated his phone, swiping, tapping, scrolling, and finally, expanding. "Yes! Yes, there is one." Staring at his phone, he started to walk. "This way." Roach and Barnwell fell in behind him. After ten yards, he stopped. "It runs here." He waved his hand right to left. "The tunnel runs from the beach and heads toward St. Lawrence."

"That's where the war tunnel centre is. Is the Fitbit still syncing?"

"Yup. She's here, beneath us!"

"Then let's go!" Roach started running to the edge of the wood and the beach. Jack followed. Barnwell heard Carmen barking. He hesitated.

CHAPTER FORTY-NINE

WATER RUSHED INTO the tunnel. The strength of the tide was building. It soaked Graham's back, freezing-cold water filled his ears. "Janice, there's a ledge. It will lift us another two feet if we can get onto it. Do you think you can make it?"

Janice murmured. Graham, unsure if she really understood what was happening, took his arms from around her and forced himself into a seated position. He grabbed Janice around her waist and as he helped her, she roused herself into a sitting position. "Use your legs to push yourself to the ledge," Graham told her. "Like this . . ." White-hot pain shot up his broken leg. "Arghhhh." Graham closed his eyes and forced the stars he saw there to stop spinning. "You go. I'll think of something else."

"Wait, in my hands," Janice said. Behind her back, she held onto the scarf that had acted as her blindfold. "Strap your bad leg to your good one. It'll stabilise it. Use your arms to pull yourself along." Graham did as she suggested, and then, like crustaceans, they used their limbs to push and pull themselves across the rocks to the ledge.

"You go first," Graham said when they reached it. "Put your back against it and push yourself up with your legs until you can roll onto it."

Janice wriggled around and positioned her feet to manoeuvre herself onto the ledge. She paused. "I'm not sure I can. I don't have the energy."

"Yes, you do. Think of your wedding, Jack, your future, whatever you want it to hold. Go on."

Janice gritted her teeth and, her face twisted with effort, she shakily forced her body up onto the step that lay two feet above water level. She rolled away to give Graham the space to do the same.

With a broken leg, Graham's task was even harder. Grimacing, he pushed himself upright using his good leg, the broken one tied to it, having no choice but to follow. His thigh muscles trembled with exertion, the pain almost making him pass out. He thought of his past, Katie, of his future, Laura, and the colourful possibilities that might follow. When his chest cleared the ledge, he twisted to face it. Leaning on his hands, he stood up.

His last manoeuvre would be the toughest. He sat on the ledge, galvanising his resolve. Gritting his teeth and roaring in pain, he raised his legs and swung them around. Janice shifted over more, and he rolled in beside her. "We made it, Janice. We're good here," he whispered in her ear, panting, tears stinging.

Janice shook uncontrollably. Graham held her tight against his chest, although the warmth they were now able to share was negligible. Time was running out. "Stay with me, Janice. You've got to hang on. Jack is waiting up there for you."

She murmured. She was so sleepy. Her mind drifted.

Somewhere, though, in the swirling fog that was left, she understood she should talk, say something.

"Sir, have you ever regretted joining the force?"

Graham's mouth twitched. "Well, I'm not loving it right at this moment, I can tell you that." He couldn't see, but Janice, her eyelids closed, gave a small smile at his answer. "But no, not really. I've been in some tricky spots, but I wanted to be a policeman ever since our local village bobby returned my toy dump truck that someone else had taken when I was a little boy. After that, I got a uniform, and my mum said I would wear it to bed sometimes. I even had one of the old-style helmets, the ones with the chin straps. I would wear it to the shops, anywhere."

He reached for Janice's frozen hands and rubbed them. "Justice has always appealed to me. I want everything to be squared away, balanced, just so. Of course, it's a pie-in-the-sky endeavour, but I enjoy the challenge. It drives me on."

"Did you like cop shows? That's what enticed me. *Prime Suspect*, *Juliet Bravo* . . . Way before my time, but I loved watching them. I got given box sets for my birthday. Now, there are more female detectives on the telly."

"I was into *Morse*, although the plots got ridiculous towards the end."

"It's funny, isn't it, how we end up in the force . . . When I was younger, I was a free spirit. Travelled the world a bit . . . somehow got into cooking for rich people on yachts for cash . . . and I ended up here. Didn't want to leave. I went to bail out an idiot boyfriend who'd got done for being drunk on a night out in St. Helier . . . and ended up answering an ad I saw on their noticeboard. The job looked kind of interesting." Janice exhaled. That had taken a lot of effort.

"My route was less colourful. University, police recruitment scheme, Met, then I applied to come here." There was a long pause. Graham jiggled her. "Janice?"

"I've always wondered about that, sir. Why such a change? Fast, hard-charging career and then you swerve to this idyllic backwater." Janice's words were slurred. She was speaking slower with each breath. Each sentence cost her more of her rapidly depleting energy.

Graham cast a glance across the tunnel. The water was continuing to rise. Like Janice, he was starting to shake uncontrollably. His fingers had gone numb long ago.

"I was married. We broke up. I needed a change, a complete change. I thought Jersey sounded appealing, away from it all, about as different from working in London as could be."

"Do you think you'll get married again?" Janice mumbled.

"I hope so. I liked being married. Life is a bit grey without someone to enjoy it with."

"I worry about it sometimes . . . I love Jack to pieces, but the thought of being with the same person for the rest of my life is . . ." Graham jiggled her again. ". . . Daunting."

"Lots of people think of marriage the wrong way. They see it as limiting. But it isn't; it's freeing. If you've chosen the right one, and you have, you can be confident your person will be there for you. They provide you with a solid base from which to kick off. You can take risks and have adventures the likes of which we rarely experience on our own."

"When are you going to ask Laura to marry you then?"

Graham smiled. "I don't know. Do you think she'll have me?"

"Definitely. I think she's just waiting for you to ask. You

make a good couple. Not many women . . . um, never mind . . ."

There was a long pause. Graham tried rocking Janice. Her eyes stayed closed. "Janice," he said sharply. He attempted to pat her face, but his numb fingers refused to cooperate, and he had to settle for rubbing her cheek. The water level was still rising. It would cover the ledge soon.

Janice stirred. She wriggled around and turned to face him. Her eyes still closed, she lifted her head like a sleeping baby before laying it down on Graham's chest. "Last thing, sir. Who's the little girl in the photo on your windowsill? I saw it the other night."

"Ah, that's my daughter Katie."

"You've never mentioned her. Is she with her mother? Do you see her?"

Graham closed his eyes briefly. Behind his eyelids, he saw Katie laughing, squealing as he chased her around the garden with a spray hose. "She died in a car accident a few years ago. She was five."

"I'm sorry. Tell me about her." Janice snuggled in closer to Graham, and he squeezed her waist.

"Well, she was funny and happy and giggly. She loved platypuses and dogs. She'd have loved Carmen. When she was a toddler, if she ever had a tantrum, I'd plop her in the bath, and she'd calm right down."

"When I was little, I loved dressing up in my Disney princess dresses. Did she do that?"

"She loved her Disney princesses, but we did a lot of Legos too. Just before she died, her favourite thing was bedtime. I'd read her a story, then roll her back and forth on the bed super-fast. When she was out of breath, I'd give her Eskimo kisses and she'd give me butterfly kisses, then it would be lights out." Graham smiled in the dark. "I miss that bedtime routine."

Janice sighed. "Do you think you'll have children with Jack?" Graham asked her. There was no answer. He looked down. "Janice? Janice!"

Searching for a way into the tunnel, Roach and Jack streaked to the edge of the woodland. It ended in a cliff across the top of which was a hiking trail worn into the grass. A small fence four feet away from the edge warned hikers not to get close. Jack ignored it. He peeked over the edge. His face, flushed with excitement and exertion, paled. "The tide's in." Roach joined him. "Look down there. The entrance to the tunnel is flooded." Jack's stricken face turned to Roach. "Oh my God. If she's in there, she's dead, Jim, dead!"

Feeling almost as panic-stricken as Jack, Roach gripped his arms. "Let's not give up now, lad. She might be making her way to St. Lawrence for all we know. She's a smart girl." A shout went up. "Come on, that was Bazza. Maybe he's got something."

They found Barnwell standing in a clearing with Carmen by his side. She was still barking. Roach and Jack rushed up. "I've found them. Or Carmen did. Shush, girl." Barnwell bent down and she licked his hands. "They're down there." Jack and Roach peered as Barnwell parted the bushes. Graham's white face looked up at them, his eyes a bright blue in the gloom. He held Janice in his arms, her eyes closed like she was a sleeping child. The tide was rising. Deep water surrounded them. Graham was submerged up to his shoulders as he fought to keep Janice's head above the surface.

A shout. Barnwell turned. "About *bloody* time." Running toward them were twelve men, headed up by their leader, former SAS major, Bash Bingham. Members of Fortytude, the early morning running group Barnwell ran with, had arrived in response to Barnwell's SOS. Bash carried survival gear. Behind them, marching at a slower pace, were paramedics Sue Armitage and Alan Pritchard, Melanie Howes, the Gorey fire crew manager, and half a dozen firefighters. Marcus Tomlinson brought up the rear. All of them carried equipment that Barnwell, confronted with the rescue operation that faced them, felt quite sure would be essential.

"Step back! Cavalry's here!" Bash cried out. He walked up to the hole in the ground and looked over. The members of Fortytude stood back, as did the paramedics. The firefighter captain joined Bash at the opening.

"I hope they get a move on. They don't have much time," Barnwell murmured to Roach. Roach bit his nails, a habit he'd broken with effort as a teenager. Catching himself, he grabbed hold of Jack and held him in a tight embrace.

"Harness! Rope!" the firefighter captain shouted. Bash took the equipment and threw it down to Graham. He knelt on the ground. "Put the harness around her!" the fire captain instructed as Bash and another firefighter fitted a contraption that looked like an instrument of torture across the top of the chute.

Graham had his hand under Janice's chin, lifting her face

out of the water so she could breathe. She was unconscious. He lifted the harness over her head and brought her arms through it. Feeling around in the water, he was able to bring the lower strap under her body and lock it to her front. It had to hold her in place. Barnwell, Roach, and Jack joined eight other men around the chute to hold the winch in place while two others readied to operate a mechanism that would pull Janice to safety. Two more stood by to bring her to ground when she emerged.

It was a job of brute force. Straining, the eleven men exerted all their strength to pin the winch down as Janice was slowly lifted to safety. "Unconventional, but effective," Bash muttered as an unconscious Janice cleared the chute and was gently levered onto a stretcher.

Paramedics Sue and Alan immediately got to work. Sue cut off Janice's wet clothes and wrapped her in blankets, tucking hot packs in between the layers while Alan took her vitals and fed her oxygen. Tomlinson hooked up an IV through which he delivered warmed salt water into her veins. His voice shaking uncharacteristically, the pathologist kept up a constant stream of chatter, and after a few minutes, Janice's eyelids trembled before opening. She blinked rapidly as her eyes adjusted to the sunlight. After wrapping her in another layer of thermal blankets, they moved her away from the rescue theatre as Jack hovered.

Down in the tunnel, matters had become even more urgent. Cold, exhaustion, and pain had rendered Graham barely conscious. "We're just over sixty seconds away from submersion," Bash said. "He's exhausted, in shock, hypothermic, and injured. A lamb to the water."

"We need to get him out! He'll be swept away, or he'll drown in place!" Barnwell cried. "We need to get someone down there to help him."

"Out of the way!"

"Hey!" Bash yelled.

Roach curled into a ball, tucking his arms in as he dropped into the chute. The water broke his fall. There was a splash, and he bobbed up beside Graham in the tunnel.

"Throw me the harness!" he shouted, spluttering.

Twenty minutes later, Graham and Janice loaded into the ambulance, Barnwell turned to Roach, who clutched a thermal pack. He was pale and shivering. Barnwell wrapped him in a shiny emergency blanket.

"Tomlinson told me you couldn't swim."

"Yeah, no, I can't. But I wasn't letting you get *another* medal."

CHAPTER FIFTY

OF COURSE, THE rain that had been promised stayed away now that Barnwell had remembered his jacket. He'd walked from the station to the Foc's'le and Ferret up on the hill. Its reassuring presence gave him confidence, somehow, that despite the day's torrid events, the world would continue to rotate on its axis as it should.

"And they found her!" he heard a voice at the bar cry. "Took eleven men to bring her up." His brother leant into the ear of a pretty young woman next to him. Barnwell stood for a second, admiring his brother's unerring ability to make new friends. He caught his eye. "The man of the hour! Lewis! Lewis, lad, it's an emergency." Steve waved an empty pint glass at the barman. The woman sidled off. "Lewis, I demand that you pour this man a double of your finest scotch."

"They're *all* fine," the barman insisted. "Wouldn't pour them otherwise."

"Then it's dealer's choice," Barnwell said. "And it's just a tonic water for me, thanks."

"Wha—?" his brother cried in mock astonishment. "Well, not for me. I'll have a single."

"You've just got yourself a new pint," his brother pointed out.

"And I shall have a whisky chaser. Don't worry. That'll be my limit."

Lewis hauled a box from the shelf, wiped dust off the top, and brought out a slender bottle with a simple, white label. "Ever tried a twenty-one-year-old Bruichladdich?"

"Since you've gone to the effort of pronouncing it, it'd be rude not to," Steve said.

Once served, the men found their usual table and settled in. Barnwell spotted Matthew Walker at the end of the bar, talking amicably with a couple of lads his age. He gave Barnwell the tiniest hint of a salute.

"There I was," Steve said, "hoping that the highlight of my visit this week would be the sight of you hauling that big old barrel down to the station in handcuffs."

Barnwell sipped his tonic, finding it refreshing. "Actually, I did, but we released him after an hour or so."

"You don't say!" Steve exclaimed.

"He ended up being just another poor fella who found himself caught up in something." He took a sip of Steve's whisky. It tasted peaty and medicinal. He found it lowered his stress levels. Just focusing on the flavour profile—a robust earthy eruption tempered by meltwater from a woodland glen—gave him valuable moments of calm and quiet, but he wouldn't have any more. He wanted to take Carmen out for a run later.

"Well?" Steve said. "You going to leave me hanging or what? What happened with your case? Everyone's talking about the rescue."

"The age-old tale," Barnwell replied. "Girl meets boy,

but girl is already married to a fabulously wealthy banker-type. Then someone paints a portrait of boy and girl swimming together and everything falls apart. Someone with a historical beef settles some scores, necessitating some heroics from people other than yours truly, and the mystery is solved. Straightforward, really. Just humans being exactly as they are. Flawed. Extremely so in some cases. We haven't actually caught the perp yet—she's on her way to Honduras —but she'll have a surprise when she arrives."

Steve wrinkled his nose, puzzled. "I guess I'll follow when it comes to trial. Well done, by the way," he said. "Must feel pretty good."

"It's a relief more than anything. Started to do my head in not knowing what had happened, or why."

"Speaking of not knowing, did you have any success getting the you-know-what from the you-know-where?"

The envelope was in Barnwell's jacket pocket. "I printed the whole thing. Fairly standard file for the time. I had to get some help it was so old, but it'll be fine." Barnwell hadn't fully explained to Jack what he wanted or why, but there'd been an unspoken understanding between them that they'd never speak of it.

"Did you read it?" asked Steve, his pint held in midair.

"Yes."

Steve set down his glass. "Am I in for a shock?"

"I suspect not, Steve. Seems to me that you always knew."

"Maybe. Not for certain. Just little bits and pieces down the years." Steve looked down at the envelope Barnwell held in his hand. "Can I read it?"

"Yes, but then I'm going to eat it. I could get sacked for this, and Dad never wanted us to know. After you've read it, we're going to forget all about it, okay?"

Steve nodded. Barnwell gave him the envelope. His younger brother tore open the flap and took a deep breath. "Wow, you've got a photo too."

"From his arrest," Barnwell explained.

Steve read, and as he did, he was almost overcome. How many times had he guessed what this report would say? Now everything was clear. "He hit someone with a pint glass?" Steve wondered quietly. "Our dad? He glassed someone?"

"Look at the details," Barnwell said. "It was 'last orders.' You know how things got before the laws changed."

"People pouring drink down their necks at top speed before the barman chucked them out," Steve said.

"And the guy he attacked, I looked him up." Barnwell leafed to one of the final pages in the report, a simple biographical data sheet for one Anthony Hood, later Councillor Hood, Anthony Hood MP, and then Baron Hood, member of the House of Lords. The man was their father's age. "They were at school together. He nearly lost an eye in the attack."

"So, what happened?" Steve wanted to know. "I mean, Dad didn't just go around *hitting* people. He never raised a hand to us."

Barnwell explained the quiet effort he'd put in to get to the bottom of his father's eighteen-month absence. "I called the old barman at the Queen's Arms, where it all happened."

"Hellfire, Bazz. How old's he?"

"Eighty-nine. His hips were a bit rickety, but his mind was as clear as a bell. He remembered the incident."

"What did he say?"

"That Hood wound Dad up. Started talking about their school days, how he'd been more popular than Dad, had more girlfriends, all the usual childish stuff. Barman said Hood was upright but pretty drunk."

"Dad hit him because of *that*?"

"He made a comment," Barnwell explained carefully, "about Mum. Something about her, umm, *behaviour*."

"He didn't!" Steve said.

"Yeah, in front of the whole pub. Dad got two years, ended up serving eighteen months."

"Eighteen months. Otherwise known as a stint on the oil rigs." They were both quiet as they digested this revision of their family history.

"Makes more sense now, doesn't it?" Steve said. "How he'd not want to see his son a copper. They were the enemy to him."

"Mebbe, or maybe he just didn't want his secret getting out. I'm amazed it hasn't before now to be fair."

The news was a shock, but also it wasn't. There had been signs—whispered conversations, adult tears quickly wiped away, their father's moodiness. That there had only been one incident and with mitigating factors was an enormous relief. To Barnwell, that he might discover that his father was a repeat offender, a violent thief, or something worse had been terrifying.

"Anyone," Steve said, "*anyone* can get themselves into something. Don't care who you are. When there's booze and emotions, it doesn't take much."

"No, but he shouldn't have done it. No wonder he never drunk a drop again." Barnwell fingered the report. "I hadn't the first *clue* he'd been through this," he said. "Me applying to the force must have been shocking, him thinking his secret was going to get out. What I can't understand is how I got here."

"What do you mean?"

"I'm a police officer. A background check on me, standard procedure during the recruitment process, would have turned up this information. I would have been questioned about it. They would have to make sure I wasn't open to bribery or blackmail because of it."

"Wow, they must have thought you were worth taking a chance on. Perhaps they saw you were no threat—it had been a one-off—and decided to let things slide."

"I can't remember really, it was too long ago, but I would have answered negatively when they'd asked about convictions in the family. They must have concluded that I genuinely didn't know about Dad's record, decided it didn't affect my application, and let me through to the next round. Amazing really when you think about it."

"Dad must have been in ribbons, though, thinking his secret was about to be exposed. He was a proud man. Reputation stood for something back then. He wanted to be our dad. He would never have wanted us to see him as a criminal. The shame of it."

"But he kept it in all those years! I just didn't know. Me prancing around in my uniform must have been excruciating for him. No wonder he tried to persuade me to do something else. I thought it was because it was embarrassing. The police weren't the most popular round our way, were they?"

"I don't think he saw it like that," said Steve. "Actually, I can prove it." He pulled a frame from a plastic bag he'd been carrying.

It was an image Barnwell recognised immediately. Taken from above, the green-black night vision image showed a man suspended under a helicopter, gesturing to someone. Beneath him was a tiny, storm-tossed boat, and beyond that, the blackness of the English Channel at night.

Tucked into the frame was a wallet-sized photo of Barn-well's visit to Buckingham Palace to collect his Queen's Gallantry medal, his mother standing next to him, smiling proudly.

"Dad had this on the mantel above the fireplace in the living room. Said he couldn't believe you'd ever do anything so stupid." Steve laughed.

"He didn't know me that well then."

"But you know what else?" Steve said. "He mentioned it every time I saw him. Every *single* time, he told me how much he admired you."

"Ah well, guess I made him proud in the end. Better late than never." Barnwell picked up Steve's scotch glass. "To Dad," he said.

"To Dad," replied his brother.

CHAPTER FIFTY-ONE

"SLOWLY, JACK. SLOWLY!" Jack manoeuvred Janice's wheelchair down the corridor. She still looked pale, and there were purple half-moons under her eyes, but a sparkle had returned to them when her nurse said she could visit her boss. They were making their way to Graham's room now. A bunch of yellow roses lay across her lap.

As Jack wheeled her through the door to Graham's room, Janice's eyes widened. Laura, Barnwell, Roach, and Tomlinson turned to look at her.

"Here she is!" someone cried.

In their midst lay Graham, his arm in a sling, a blanket hiding the metal frame that pinned the bones of his leg together.

"Good to see you looking so well, Sergeant," Graham said.

"You too, sir," Janice replied. Awkwardly, she put the flowers on his bed. "I, um, brought you these."

"They're beautiful, Janice," Laura said. "I'll put them in

water." She wandered off, her eyes beckoning Jack to accompany her.

"So how are you both doing?" Marcus Tomlinson said. "That's a fearsome Ilizarov frame you've got there, David. Your leg was badly broken. I took the liberty of looking at your X-rays."

"Yeah, there was a long surgery to straighten everything out and fix them into place. Just got to wait for the bones to knit back together now."

"How long before you're back on your feet, sir?" Janice asked.

"Hmm, some months to fully recover they tell me. I'll go stark staring mad before that, so I'll be back in the office way before then, even if Barnwell has to carry me around. How about you?"

"Oh, I'll be fine. Nothing a few days rest and some decent food won't fix."

"It's good to see you looking so well, Janice," Tomlinson said, putting his hand on her shoulder. "I was so glad to be able to help when you were pulled out. You had me very worried."

Tears welled at his kindness. Janice's throat tightened and her chin wobbled. Graham noticed, and he smiled at her. That just made it worse, and Janice looked down at her hands in her lap.

"Hey, I have an announcement," Roach said. He'd also noticed Janice's distress.

"Oh? What's that?" Graham responded.

"I'm not sure. I haven't opened the letter yet. It's from the Met. About a . . . a job application I put in a few weeks ago." He pulled a white envelope from his inside jacket pocket. It had the Metropolitan Police insignia stamped in the corner.

"You bugger, you did put in for a transfer," Barnwell said. "We wondered if you would. But you didn't breathe a word."

"No, I wasn't sure if I'd get it, or if I'd take it if I did. I'm still not sure if I'm honest." Roach took in a deep breath and dropped his shoulders on the exhale.

"Well, go on then, Roachie, don't keep us in suspenders," Barnwell said. "Open it."

Roach turned over the envelope and tore at the flap. Pulling out the letter, he unfolded it and began to read. His eyes gleamed. A smile fluttered across his lips.

Unable to wait, Barnwell looked over his shoulder. "Congratulations, mate!" Barnwell wrapped his arm around Roach as the younger man continued to stare at the letter that told him his application to join Homicide and Major Crime Command based at Scotland Yard had been accepted.

Tomlinson reached over to shake his protégée's hand. "Well done, young man. I'll be sorry to see you go, but our loss is the Met's gain. Don't forget the little people." Roach laughed.

While the three men huddled over Roach's letter, Janice wheeled herself over to Graham. "Good for Roachie. About time."

"It is. Time for him to fly. He'll do well." Graham settled his gaze on Janice, searching her face. "And how are you? Really, I mean."

"I'm okay. Still shocked if I'm honest. Might take some time off."

"Take as much time as you need, Sergeant. And avail yourself of the force's counselling services. That was a scary situation you found yourself in."

"It was my own fault, sir. I should never have gone to

Cynthia Moorcroft's alone. When I realised she'd been lying to me, I was livid. I let my personal feelings get the better of me. It was unprofessional."

"Well, I got it wrong about Granby, and perhaps if I'd paid more attention to your contributions, you might not have had such a visceral reaction. I think that means we're quits. And thankfully everything turned out alright."

"Thanks to you, sir. If you hadn't found me, I'd have drowned."

"I'm glad I was able to help, Sergeant."

"And thank you for entrusting me with your story about your daughter. It can't have been easy. You must miss her a lot."

"Yes, I do, but I'm glad it's finally out in the open. I don't want people to feel awkward or like they have to say anything. It is what it is. Katie's part of the story of my life that makes me who I am, just like this incident will mould you."

"You know, I was thinking about the people in this case. No one was really the person they claimed to be. They all lived behind some kind of front."

"Don't we all, Sergeant? One way or another to a greater or lesser extent? None of us present a completely authentic picture of who we are. We're all painting a portrait of a person we'd like others to see."

"Yes!" Barnwell's fist shot into the air like a firework. Graham, Janice, Tomlinson, and Roach turned to look. Barnwell was staring at a text on his phone. "She failed!" He looked at them, his eyes shining much like Roach's had a moment ago. "Carmen's new handler took her for a physical. She failed!" Barnwell looked around at his stunned, silent audience. "Don't you see? Carmen can't move forward to sniffer dog training! She can stay with me. She has a stigmatism. Might make her squirrel hunts a bit pointless, but hey, I'll take it."

Everyone relaxed, smiles on their faces at the thought of Carmen staying with them. Graham quietly spoke again to Janice. "Of course, dogs are the exception to that rule. They are the very definition of authenticity."

"Even Pomeranians, sir?"

"*Especially* Pomeranians, Sergeant.

EPILOGUE

Cynthia Moorcroft was met on her arrival in Honduras by government secret police who committed to returning her to Jersey despite there not existing an extradition treaty between the country and the United Kingdom. Rumours abound of a swap with a Honduran drug lord living in Kent, but this has been neither confirmed nor denied by the British government. On her return, Cynthia can expect to be charged with double murder and sentenced to a whole life tariff—life imprisonment without any possibility of parole or conditional release.

After it was revealed that his assistant had killed his wife and her lover, **Silas Granby** returned to the Granby house, where he lives alone quietly. The house was recently listed for sale, and both the Ferrari and Maserati have disappeared. Granby Investments is no longer registered at Companies House, and it is assumed that Silas Granby is between enterprises or retired. Willow was given to Katya's friend, **Magda Padalka-Lyons**. Willow and Pom-Pom live in mutual conflict.

Molly Duckworth gave her notice at Sanderson Landscaping and travelled Australia and New Zealand, supporting herself as a cattle drover and camp cook. She spends her days on horseback and her mornings and evenings preparing food for hungry cattlemen and women.

Adrian Sanderson was deeply affected by Jamie Reeves's death. In a frank and moving interview with Freddie Solomon, he spoke of the plans he'd quietly made for he and Jamie to run the business together as an equal partnership. Sanderson Landscaping continues to operate on Jersey, and Adrian hopes that one of his sons will eventually take over the business.

Paula Lascelles broke up with **Matthew Walker** immediately on her return to London. Shortly thereafter, she made a splashy engagement announcement in *The Times*, sharing that she was to marry the deputy assistant head of corporate accounts at the company she works for, only to rescind and cancel everything four days later. She's currently dating her ex-fiancé's boss, described by his own sister as "nice, but dim." Matthew half completed an application to join the police force, but he soon forgot the idea and returned to his life in London.

Sir Peregrine Wordsworth FRSA MPhil (Oxon) recently announced on his website that his twice-annual "Wordsworth of Seascapes" workshops were fully booked for the foreseeable future. He recently appeared in a web-

TV show entitled *To Catch a Murderer*, where he joined experts to discuss "the intersection of art and justice." He claims to have made his "first and final" attempt to make a lake vibrate using only a paintbrush.

Three weeks after the rescue, **Detective Inspector Graham** was discharged from hospital and embarked on a rigorous program of rest and rehabilitation. He was occasionally seen in a wheelchair around Gorey, accompanied by one of the members of his police team. After a further month, he progressed to crutches and began appearing at the station, professing a need to return to work. To the relief of many, he has no plans to return to refereeing.

Following a period of panic over leaving Jersey for his new posting and ultimately an intervention led by Dr. Tomlinson and his mum, **Sergeant Jim Roach** set off for the Met. A tankard bearing the words "Shipshape and Bristol Fashion" was a gift from his fellow Gorey officers. Over seventy people attended his leaving do in the Foc's'le. The latest word is that he is settling into London ways nicely but is a "little Jersey homesick." He has joined a gym with a pool.

Janice and Jack cancelled their wedding plans in favour of a rethink. They are now organising something smaller and more spontaneous, possibly a surprise. They have been coy about their thoughts and will only say that "time will tell," although they plan on keeping the cake with the Swiss chocolate French buttercream pâte à bombe icing. Janice's mother took the opportunity to accept a great deal on a package holiday to Greece and had a wonderful time.

Barry Barnwell couldn't be happier with **Carmen's** failure to pass through to the next stage of police dog training, and they continue to be seen running around Gorey together. His "Dog and Doughnut" stories have proved to be extremely popular with the Year Ones, and to avoid further tears, he now has a monthly standing order with Ethel's for an entire box of iced doughnuts, all of them with sprinkles.

Thank you for reading *The Case of the Uncommon Witness*! I will have a new case for Inspector Graham and his gang soon. To find out about new books, sign up for my newsletter: https://www.alisongolden.com

If you love the Inspector Graham mysteries, you'll also love the sweet, funny *USA Today* bestselling Reverend Annabelle Dixon series featuring a madcap, lovable lady vicar whose passion for cake is matched only by her desire for justice. The first in the series, *Death at the Cafe* is available for

purchase from Amazon. You can sample the series by turning the page and reading the first chapter. Like all my books, *Death at the Cafe* is FREE in Kindle Unlimited.

And don't miss the Roxy Reinhardt mysteries. Will Roxy triumph after her life falls apart? She's sacked from her job, her boyfriend dumps her, she's out of money. So, on a whim, she goes on the trip of a lifetime to New Orleans, There, she gets mixed up in a

Mardi Gras murder. *Things were going to be fine. They were, weren't they?* Get the first in the series, Mardi Gras Madness from Amazon. Also FREE in Kindle Unlimited!

If you're looking for something edgy and dangerous, root for Diana Hunter as she seeks justice after a devastating crime destroys her family. Start following her journey in this non-stop series of suspense and action by purchasing Hunted—the prequel to the series—from Amazon. Hunted is FREE in Kindle Unlimited.

I hugely appreciate your help in spreading the word about *The Case of the Uncommon Witness*, including telling a friend. Reviews help readers find books! Please leave a review on your favourite book site.

Turn the page to read an excerpt from the first book in the Reverend Annabelle Dixon series, *Death at the Cafe...*

A Reverend Annabelle Dixon Mystery

death
at the
café

ALISON GOLDEN
JAMIE VOUGEOT

DEATH AT THE CAFE
CHAPTER ONE

NOTHING BROUGHT REVEREND Annabelle closer to blasphemy than using the London public transport system during rush hour. Since being ordained and sent to St. Clement's church, an impressive, centuries-old building among the tower blocks and new builds of London's East End, Annabelle had been tested many times. She had come across virtually every sin known to man, counselled wayward youths, presided over family disputes, heard astonishingly sad tales from the homeless, and still retained her solid, optimistic dependability through it all. None of these challenges made her blood boil, and her round, soft face curl up into a mixture of disgust, frustration, and exasperation. Yet sitting on the number forty-three bus to Islington, as it moved along at a snail's pace, was almost enough to make her take her beloved Lord's name in vain.

On this occasion, she had nabbed her favourite seat: top deck, front left. It gave her a perfect view of the unique streets London offered and the even more varied types of people. Today, however, her viewpoint afforded her only a teeth-clenchingly irritating perspective of a traffic jam that extended as far as the eye could see down Upper Street.

"I know I shouldn't," she muttered on the relatively empty bus, "but if this doesn't deserve a cherry-topped cupcake, then I don't know what does."

The thought of rewarding her patience with what she loved almost as much as her vocation—cake—settled Annabelle's nerves for a full twenty minutes, during which the bus trundled in fits and starts along another half-mile stretch.

Assigning Annabelle, fresh from her days studying theology at Cambridge University, to the tough, inner-city borough of Hackney had presented her with what had been an almost literal baptism of fire. She had arrived in the summer, during a few weeks when the British sun combined with the squelching heat of a city constantly bustling and moving. It was a time of drinking and frivolity for some, heightened tension for others. A spell during which bored youths found their idle hands easily occupied with the devil's work. An interval when the good relax and the bad run riot.

Annabelle had grown up in East London, but for her first appointment as a vicar, her preference had been for a peaceful, rural village somewhere. A place in which she could indulge her love of nature, and conduct her Holy business in the gentle, caring manner she preferred. "Gentle" and "caring," however, were two words rarely used to describe London. Annabelle had mildly protested her city assignment. But after a long talk to the archbishop who explained the extreme shortage of candidates both capable and willing to take on the challenge of an inner-city church, she agreed to take up the position and set about her task with enthusiasm.

Father John Wilkins of neighbouring St. Leonard's church had been charged with easing Annabelle into the complex role. He had been a priest for over thirty years, and for the vast majority of that time had worked in London's poorest, toughest neighbourhoods. The Anglican Church was far less popular in London than it was in rural England, largely due to the city's disparate mix of peoples and creeds. Father John's congregation was mostly made up of especially devout immigrants from Africa and South America, many of whom were not even Anglican but simply lived nearby. The only time St. Leonard's had ever been full was on a particularly mild Christmas Eve.

But despite low attendance at services, London's churches played pivotal roles in their local communities. With plenty of people in need, they were hubs of charity and community support. Fundraising events, providing food and shelter for London's large homeless population, caring for the elderly, and engaging troubled youths were the churches' stock in trade, not to mention they provided both spiritual and emotional support for the many deaths and family tragedies that occurred.

The stress of it all had turned Father John's wiry beard a speckled grey, and though he knew his work was important and worthwhile, he had been pushed to breaking point on more than one occasion. Upon her arrival, he had taken one look at Annabelle's breezy manner and fresh-faced, open smile and assumed that her appointment was a case of negligence, desperation, or a sick prank.

"She's utterly delightful," Father John sighed on the phone to the archbishop, "and extremely nice. But 'delightful' and 'nice' are not what's required in a London church. This is a part of the world where faith is stretched to its very limits, where strong leadership goes further than gentle guidance. We struggle to capture people's attention, Archbishop, let alone their hearts. Our drug rehabilitation programs have more members than our congregations."

"Give her a chance, Father," the archbishop replied softly. "Don't underestimate her. She grew up in East London, you know."

"Well, I grew up in Westminster, but that doesn't mean I've had tea with the Queen!"

Merely a week into Annabelle's assignment, however, Father John's misgivings proved unfounded. Annabelle's bumbling, naïve manner was just that—a manner. Father John observed closely as Annabelle's strength, faith, and intelligence were consistently tested by the urban issues of her flock. He noted that she passed with flying colours.

Whether she was dealing with a hardened criminal fresh out of prison and already succumbing to old temptations, or a single mother of three struggling to find some composure and faith in the face of her daily troubles, Annabelle was always there to help. With good humour and optimism, she never turned down a request for assistance, no matter how large or small it was.

When Father John visited Annabelle a month after the start of her placement to check on a highly successful gardening project she had started for troubled youth, he shook his head in amazement "Is that Denton? By the rose bushes? I've been trying to get him to visit me for a year now, and all he does is ignore me. You should hear what he says when his parole officer suggests it," he said.

"Oh, Denton is wonderful!" Annabelle cried. "Fantastic with his hands. He has a devilish sense of humour—when it's properly directed. Did you know that he plays drums?"

"No, I didn't know that. He never told me," Father John said, giving Annabelle an appreciative smile. "I must say,

Reverend, I seem to have misjudged you dreadfully. And I apologise."

"Oh, Father," Annabelle chuckled, "it's perfectly understandable. You have only the best interests of the community at heart. Let's leave judgement for Him and Him alone. The only thing we're meant to judge is cake contests, in my opinion. Mind those thorns, Denton! Roses tend to fight back if you treat them roughly!"

To get your copy of *Death at the Cafe* visit the link below:
https://www.alisongolden.com/death-at-the-cafe

"Your emails seem to come on days when I need to read them because they are so upbeat."
- Linda W -

For a limited time, you can get the first books in each of my series - *Chaos in Cambridge* (exclusively for subscribers - not available anywhere else), *The Case of the Screaming Beauty, Hunted, and Mardi Gras Madness* - plus updates about new releases, promotions, and other Insider exclusives, by signing up for my mailing list at:

https://www.alisongolden.com/graham

TAKE MY QUIZ

What kind of mystery reader are you? Take my thirty second quiz to find out!

https://www.alisongolden.com/quiz

BOOKS BY ALISON GOLDEN

FEATURING REVEREND ANNABELLE DIXON

Death at the Café

Murder at the Mansion

Body in the Woods

Grave in the Garage

Horror in the Highlands

Killer at the Cult

Fireworks in France

Witches at the Wedding

FEATURING ROXY REINHARDT

Mardi Gras Madness

New Orleans Nightmare

Louisiana Lies

As A. J. Golden

FEATURING DIANA HUNTER

Hunted (Prequel)

Snatched

Stolen

Chopped

Exposed

ABOUT THE AUTHOR

Alison Golden is the *USA Today* bestselling author of the Inspector David Graham mysteries, a traditional British detective series, and two cozy mystery series featuring main characters Reverend Annabelle Dixon and Roxy Reinhardt. As A. J. Golden, she writes the Diana Hunter thriller series.

Alison was raised in Bedfordshire, England. Her aim is to write stories that are designed to entertain, amuse, and calm. Her approach is to combine creative ideas with excellent writing and edit, edit, edit. Alison's mission is simple: To write excellent books that have readers clamouring for more.

Alison is based in the San Francisco Bay Area with her husband and twin sons. She splits her time between London and San Francisco.

For up-to-date promotions and release dates of upcoming books, sign up for the latest news here: https://www.alisongolden.com/graham.

For more information:
www.alisongolden.com
alison@alisongolden.com

facebook.com/alisongolden.books

twitter.com/alisonjgolden

instagram.com/alisonjgolden

THANK YOU

Thank you for taking the time to read *The Case of the Uncommon Witness*. If you enjoyed it, please consider telling your friends or posting a short review. Word of mouth is an author's best friend and very much appreciated.
Thank you,

Printed in Great Britain
by Amazon